MY FINEST GIFT FOR HUMANITY

Evincepub Publishing

Parijat Extension, Bilaspur, Chhattisgarh 495001

First Published by Evincepub Publishing 2018

ISBN: 978-93-87063-17-4

Price: Rs.430/-

MY FINEST GIFT FOR HUMANITY

(STORIES THAT ONE SHOULD READ)

By

Dr. S.R.BOSELIN PRABHU

ACKNOWLEDGEMENTS

I would like to express my gratitude to the many people who are going to see me through this book, to all those who provided support, talked things over, read, wrote, offered comments, allowed me to quote their remarks and assisted in the editing, proofreading and design. This book entitled My Finest Gift for Humanity (Stories That One Should Read)is a repository of stories that touched my heart personally when I was reading.

I had the good fortune to have Dr. S. Sophia as my research supervisor. Her thoughtful guidance shaped me as a researcher and writer. I am grateful to my friend Dr. Eng. Hamid Ali Abed AL-Asadi, Professor inComputer and Communication Network Engineering, Computer Science Department, Basra University, Iraq who was an inspirational motivator for writing articles.I am grateful to my beloved friend Dr.E.Gajendran, Associate Professor, Sree Dattha Group of Institutions, Hyderabad because of whom I was enriched with the skill of writing articles.

I remember my beloved family members who supported and encouraged me in spite of all the time it took me away from them. It was a long and difficult journey for them. Above all, I thank the Lord Almighty Jesus Christ for His everlasting showers of grace and blessings.I beg forgiveness of all those who have been with me over the course of the years and whose names I have failed to mention.

More Importantly, I express my sole credits of this book and complete acknowledgement to the authors who have originally written these stories, as the compilation work is the only work done by me. I express my complete acknowledgement to them.

ABOUT THE BOOK

This book entitled My Finest Gift for Humanity (Stories That One Should Read) is a repository of stories that touched my heart personally when I was reading. On completion of reading this book, I am sure that these stories will take you to different parts of the world and teach you varied cultures.

ABOUT THE AUTHOR

 **Dr. Boselin Prabhu S.R.** obtained his doctorate **(Ph.D)** from **Anna University Chennai, India**. He is currently working as an **Associate Professor** with **8 years of experience in teaching and research**. He has **published 154 research articles** in International Journals and Conference Proceedings. He is an **editorial board member, advisory board member and reviewer of 272 International Journals** both Scopus and ISI Indexed. He is an elected fellow member **FUAMAE, FISECE, FISRD, FUAAMP, FISQEM, FUACEE and FISEEE**. He has attained **Google scholar citations-963 and h-index-16.** He is the recipient of awards like Excellent Professional Achievement Award Winner from Society of Professional Engineers, Biography Included in Marquis Who's who in the World (Academic Year 2015 and 2016), Dedicated Professional Engineer Award Winner from Society of Engineers & Technicians, Albert Nelson Marquis Lifetime Achievement Award Winner (2017), Best Young Scientist from Association of Scientists, Developers and Faculties (2017) and Best Young Researcher from Association of Scientists, Developers and Faculties (2017). He has written three books and two monographs for students.

BALD BOY AND THE MAGICAL SEAL

Credit: Meltem Basel

One day, Bald Boy was walking back from the marketplace after selling his crops to the people of the neighbouring village. He had made three gold coins that day and was very pleased with himself because now his mother would be able to buy food and clothing to last through the long winter.

Suddenly Bald Boy came across a group of men who were teasing a cat with a long stick. The cat looked very scared and was unable to escape. Bald Boy walked up to the men and said in a kindly voice: 'Please stop teasing that poor cat. If you stop, I will give you a gold coin.'

The men agreed to put down the stick and Bald Boy handed over a shiny gold coin. The cat was very grateful to the boy and walked by his side. He promised that if ever he was able to repay the boy's kindness, he would surely jump at the chance. Bald Boy could not imagine how a cat might help him in his life, but he agreed that the cat could join him, and so the two friends continued on their journey back to the boy's home in the neighbouring village.

The boy and the cat walked for a few miles until they came across an old man and an old woman who were beating a dog because it had been barking too loudly. Bald Boy approached the old couple and said in a kindly voice, "Please stop beating that poor dog. If you stop, I will give you a gold coin."

The old couple stopped beating the dog and took the gold coin from the boy. The dog was very grateful to the boy for saving him from the old couple, and he asked to join the boy and promised that he would always be faithful and help whenever he could. The young boy could not imagine how a dog might help him in his life, but he agreed that the dog could join him, and so the three friends continued on their journey home.

Not long after this, Bald Boy and his new companions stumbled upon two woodcutters in the forest who were trying to kill a snake with their sharp axe. Bald Boy walked up to the angry woodcutters and said in a kindly voice, "Please do not kill that snake with your axe. If you leave the snake in peace, I will give you a gold coin."|

The woodcutters thought about Bald Boy's proposition for a moment and then agreed to put down the axe. The boy handed over his last gold coin without thinking because he was happy to have saved the snake from certain death.

The snake was very grateful and slithered up to whisper in the boy's ear.

'Thank you, Son of Adam, for saving my life. I am the son of the Snake Emperor and you must come home with me so that my father might thank you in person for your kindness.'

Even though Bald Boy had no more gold coins to buy food, he was happy to have saved his three friends and agreed to go and see the Snake Emperor before returning home to his mother.

When they arrived in the forest, the Snake Emperor was very grateful to Bald Boy for saving his son's life.

"I will give you anything that you ask of me", said the Snake Emperor to the boy.

It was then that the young snake whispered in the boy's ear once more.

'Ask my father for his magic seal which he keeps under his tongue. With this seal all of your wishes will come true. All you have to do is ask and it will be given.'

And so the boy asked the Snake Emperor for his magic seal, and the Snake Emperor replied, "You ask me for my most precious possession, but you saved my son's life and I will grant you what you ask."

The Snake Emperor relinquished his magic seal and Bald Boy stuffed the seal into his pocket and returned home with his faithful cat and faithful dog by his side.

When Bald Boy's mother learned that her son had given away all of their gold coins she was very angry, but the boy promised that he would make up for this loss by marrying the Emperor's daughter and making a new life for his mother.

'And how will you do that, my son? This cat and this dog will not help you do such a thing.'

It was then that Bald Boy told his mother all about the magic seal that would grant his every wish.

The very next day, Bald Boy set off with his faithful cat and dog to the palace to ask for the hand of the Emperor's daughter.

"I cannot allow my daughter to marry such a poor boy", said the Emperor when Bald Boy asked to marry the beautiful princess. 'If you wish to marry my daughter you must first build a palace next to mine so that I know she will be well looked after. But I know that you will not build such a palace with the help of a cat and a dog.'

That night, Bald Boy held the seal under his tongue and wished that he had a palace of his own. Suddenly there was a blinding light in the night sky. And when the light faded, there at the edge of the forest stood a magnificent palace gleaming beneath the light of the full moon! The most magnificent palace the boy had ever seen. And it was his!

When the Emperor saw that the young boy had indeed built a beautiful palace, he agreed to the marriage at once. And so it was that Bald Boy and the Princess were wed that very same day.

The mother moved in with her son and daughter and lived like a queen in her new home. And the cat and the dog were also very happy in their new life.

The months passed and Bald Boy wished for nothing else as he was so happy with his new wife whom he loved very much. And so he placed the magic seal in a room all of its own and never told the Princess of its magical powers.

But one day, when Bald Boy was out at the marketplace, a crafty old bead seller knocked on the door of the palace and enticed the beautiful Princess to buy some of his beads.

'They are very fine beads, my Princess, and you would do well to buy them from me.'

'But I have no coins with which to buy them', the Princess replied.

The crafty old bead seller said that he would be willing to trade his wares for something within the palace. 'I hear that you have a dusty old seal which you keep in a room in the palace; surely that is no use to you. I will take the seal in exchange for all of my beads.'

Because she did not know any better, the Princess handed over the magic seal to the crafty old bead seller who quickly disappeared across the lake towards his home in the dark forest somewhere on the other side.

As soon as the seal was gone, the palace disappeared into thin air and the Princess and the mother were left standing in the cold.

When the Emperor saw that the palace had disappeared, he reclaimed his daughter and promised that she would not be with her new husband if he could not look after her.

When Bald Boy returned home that day he was very sad to find his mother alone, his palace vanished, and his beautiful wife returned to her father. He did not know how to find the magic seal and was sure that his new life was over forever.

The cat stepped up to the boy and said to him, "I can find the seal but I cannot swim across the lake."

Then the dog stepped forward and said to the cat, "I can swim across the lake with you on my back and together we will find the magic seal."

And so the faithful cat and the faithful dog set off on their journey to recapture the magic seal from the crafty bead seller.

When they reached the river, the cat climbed up onto the dog's back and the dog swam across to the opposite bank. Once they were across, the cat began sniffing at the air and followed the scent of the bead seller through the forest with the dog close behind.

It did not take long to find the cottage where the bead seller lived, and they could see through the window that the old man was fast asleep in his chair before the fire.

"I will catch us a mouse", said the cat, 'while you find us some peppercorns to grind up with your strong paws.'

And so the cat caught a little mouse and told it to sneak into the cottage and take the seal from under the tongue of the crafty bead seller. The dog sprinkled the ground peppercorns onto the mouse's tail and the little mouse scurried into the cottage and climbed up the bead seller's leg as he slept soundly by the fire.

When the mouse wiggled his tail, the peppercorn dust went straight up the old man's nose and caused him to sneeze. It was then that the magic seal flew out into the air and the mouse caught it in his tiny paws!

The little mouse ran from the cottage and returned the magic seal to the cat and the dog who quickly made their way back through the forest towards the river.

Once again the cat climbed up onto the dog's back and the brave dog swam across the great river.

And so the faithful cat and the faithful dog returned the seal to their master and the palace reappeared in a blinding flash of light.

Upon seeing the palace returned, the Emperor agreed that his daughter might once more live with Bald Boy. After all, the Emperor could tell that his daughter was very much in love.

Bald Boy decided to throw a huge party to celebrate the return of his beautiful wife. The whole village was invited and so began a feast that lasted for forty days and forty nights.

The mother and the Emperor agreed that there was indeed much that a cat and a dog could do if they were faithful to their master.

Bald Boy smiled because he had learned that friends always help each other when they can, and there is magic in such friendship. Perhaps even more so than in the magic seal.

———◆———

DICK WHITTINGTON AND HIS PRETTY CAT

Credit: Niz Smith and Avril Lethbridge

A long time ago there was once a poor boy called Dick Whittington who had no Mummy and Daddy to look after him so he was often very hungry. He lived in a little village in the country. He'd often heard stories about a far away place called London where everybody was rich and the streets were paved with gold.

Dick Whittington was determined that he would go there and dig up enough gold from the streets to make his fortune. One day he met a friendly waggoner who was going to London who said he would give him a lift there, so off they went. When they reached the big city Dick couldn't believe his eyes, he could see horses, carriages, hundreds of people, great tall buildings, lots of mud, but nowhere could he see any gold. What a disappointment, how was he going to make his fortune? How was he even going to buy food?

After a few days he was so hungry that he collapsed in a ragged heap on the doorstep of a rich merchant's house. Out of the house came a cook:

"Be off with you", she shouted "you dirty ragamuffin", and she tried to sweep him off the step with a broom.

At that moment the merchant arrived back at his house and, being a kindly man, took pity on poor Dick.

"Carry him into the house", he ordered his groom.

When he was fed and rested, Dick was given a job working in the kitchen. He was very grateful to the Merchant but, alas, the cook was always very bad tempered and, when no one was looking, used to beat and pinch him. The other thing that made Dick sad was that he had to sleep in a tiny room at the very top of the house and it was full of rats and mice that crawled all over his face and tried to bite his nose.

He was so desperate that he saved up all his pennies and bought a cat. The cat was a very special cat, she was the best cat in all of London at catching mice and rats. After a few weeks Dick's life was much easier because of his clever cat who had eaten all the rats and mice and he was able to sleep in peace.

Not long after, Dick heard the merchant asking everyone in the house if they wanted to send anything on board his ship they thought they could sell. The ship was going on a long voyage to the other side of the world and the captain would sell everything on the ship so they could all make some money. Poor Dick, what could he sell?

Suddenly, a thought came to him

"Please sir, will you take my cat?"

Everyone burst out laughing, but the merchant smiled and said:

"Yes Dick, I will, and all the money from her sale will go to you".

After the merchant had left from the city Dick was on his own again with the mice and rats crawling over him by night and the cook being even nastier in the day because there was no-one to stop her. Dick decided to run away.

As he walked away the bells of all the churches rang out and seemed to say:

"Turn again Dick Whittington

Three times Lord Mayor of London"

"Goodness, gracious, gosh" thought Dick astonished. "If I'm going to be Lord Mayor I'd better stay. I'll put up with cook and the scurrying mice and rats, and when I'm mayor I'll show her!"

So back he went.

Across the other side of the world, the merchant and his ship had arrived at their destination. The people were so pleased to see them and were so welcoming that the merchant decided to send some presents to their king and queen. The king and queen were so delighted that they invited them all to a feast. But, believe it or not, as soon as the food was brought in hundreds of rats appeared as if by magic and gobbled it all up before they had a chance to eat.

"Oh, dear", said the king "this is always happening – I never get a chance to eat my apple pie. What can I do?"

"I have an idea", said the merchant "I have a very special cat which has travelled with me all the way from London, and she will gobble up your rats faster than they gobbled up your feast."

Sure enough, to the king and queen's joy, the next time a feast was prepared and the rats appeared, the cat pounced and killed all the rats as quick as lightning.

The king and queen danced for joy and gave the merchant a ship full of gold in return for the very special cat.

When the ship returned to London Dick was overwhelmed with the amount of gold the merchant gave him for his cat. Over the years he used his money so wisely, and did so much good for all the people around him and who worked for him, that he was elected Lord Mayor of the City of London three times. But he never forgot his kind friend the merchant, who had been so honest in giving him all the money that the cat had earned and kept nothing for himself. When Dick grew up he fell in love with Alice, the merchant's beautiful daughter, and married her. They lived happily ever after as people do in stories.

"Turn again Dick Whittington

Three times Lord Mayor of London"

They were right you see.

————•◆•————

FINEST GIFT OF THE FOREST

Credit: Bindu Chander

Venu had spent the day with his mother at the busy bazaar in Kodaikanal town selling their crops of fresh cauliflower, cabbage, garlic and onions. As they wearily made their way back to their village, Venu played his flute. He carried this flute everywhere and played exquisite music which always made his mother happy.

On entering their farmhouse in Vilpatti, Venu sat on a stool next to the bed where his father was resting. 'Tantai', said the boy, 'please eat some more rice. It does not look like you have eaten at all today and the doctor said you need to try and keep eating regularly so that you might keep up your strength.'

The old man looked lovingly at his son. 'Venu, my sweet boy, the doctor says all sorts of things, but the truth is my health is getting no better. If only I had not worked in that mining factory for all those years I am sure my health would not be so bad. Poor Adhir's wife has received no compensation from the company after losing her husband and he worked so hard. What does the company do? They just brush it aside under the carpet as if nothing happened. They are getting away with murder!'

Venu was always upset whenever his father spoke of his illness. 'Tantai, please don't talk like that, it makes me sad. I love you, Tantai!'

'I love you too, my boy, but there is no future for you here.' It was then that the old man's face took on a very serious expression. 'That is why you must leave this place. I do not want you ever working in the mining factory. Not ever!'

'But I don't want to leave, Tantai. I love the forest and have many friends here. I don't want to leave.'

The boy was very upset at his father's words and he began to cry, but the old man, despite his sickness and his frailty, remained stern. He said:

'How many times have we discussed this, Venu? There is no cure that can rid my body of the damage done by the mercury pollution. No cure for me or for my fellow workers. These companies have no shame: coming to our beautiful land and taking over, destroying nature just for money. They do not care about the beautiful trees or the animals who make their home deep within the forest.'

'But I care!' said Venu as he jumped to his feet and stormed out of the house. His father knew where the boy was going to his favourite place, his beloved forest.

Venu had always loved the forest, ever since he could remember. It enchanted him, made him feel alive, safe and loved. He felt a freedom within the forest that he did not feel in any other place in the whole wide world. And he loved to play his flute there, alone with the wildlife and the music.

Deep within the forest, the blue and purple flowers of the Kurinji were in bloom. 'How majestic', thought Venu as he admired the colourful plants spread here and there between the big cypress, eucalyptus and acacia trees.

Venu's favourite gifts of the forest were the wonderful fruits which he could pick off of the trees and eat. He spotted a tree with peaches on it and picked himself a plump, juicy specimen that he knew instinctively would be ripe. He bit into the red and orange flesh and the rich juice oozed out and ran down his cheeks.

How he delighted in this simple pleasure, sitting in his forest eating his peach while watching the nilgiri monkeys up above chasing each other from branch to branch. Vinu also admired a beautiful flock of Red-Whiskered BulBul birds that flew towards him out of the blue sky above. Then he saw Laila the baby elephant approaching. He had been witness to her birth the previous year and they had been close friends ever since.

Venu walked up to Laila and offered her the remaining half of his luscious peach which she accepted in one mouthful. The boy looked at his friend, his heart full of sorrow. 'My father has plans for me to leave Kodaikanal, to leave my forest, but I don't want to go! This is my home.'

Once these words had left Venu's lips, the young boy began to cry. Laila looked up at the boy and said:

'Venu, my mother and father are both dead after drinking from the lake where the factory dumps its mercury waste. It is not safe here anymore. They have spoiled our paradise and they are not stopping. You must leave, Venu. I do not want you to fall ill! When you arrive in your new home, tell them what is happening to our forest. Tell them that the forest needs help. Tell them that the factory and the mines must go!'

Venu wiped the tears from his eyes. 'You are right, Laila. That is exactly what I am going to do. I will let people know what is happening here.'

As the sun slowly fell from the sky, the two friends sat side by side in silence and took in the variety of sounds, textures and colours of their beloved forest. Eventually, Venu got to his feet and brushed himself down. He felt much better for being in the forest but it was time to get home.

'Laila, I must leave now. Dusk is falling and I ran out of the home in a real huff. Tāy and Tantai are probably worried sick.'

The little elephant smiled at the young boy. 'Ok, Venu', she said, 'you go home. And thank you for caring.'

'Thank you for being my friend', said the boy. And with these words they parted company.

Venu got back to his house and saw a star in the night sky. It was all alone, but it was so bright and it twinkled silver and white in the night sky. Venu stopped to admire this sight until his thoughts were interrupted by his father's voice.

'Venu, come here, my son.'

The boy approached his father and gave him a big hug. The old man was very grateful to have such a loving son. He said:

'Your mother and I are not angry with you. We do not want you to leave. We just want what is best for you. A very generous friend in London has offered you a place in his home and he will support your schooling there. You will be leaving next week. I am sorry, my son. I cannot work anymore so we cannot afford to keep you with us.'

Venu put on his bravest face but was unable to stop the tears. 'Yes, Tantai', he said in a quiet voice, 'I understand that you love me and want what is best for me so I will go to London.'

Venu held his father as tightly as he could because he did not know when he would see him again. The young boy was also very nervous because he knew nothing of London or of Britain. But he carried a glimmer of hope in his heart; He hoped that one day he would return to the forest, that he would come back and see the tall trees and the monkeys. He would see Laila and together they would watch the kunjiri flower bloom once again.

Venu was deeply unhappy about leaving his parents, but the forest needed him to stop the factory so he braved the shock of landing in a foreign land with the most courageous face he could muster.

He was met at the airport by his father's friend who was known to him simply as Balu. Balu was a large man with a jolly disposition. His favourite pastime was singing along to Tamil songs whilst he prepared his meals. Balu wanted to make the boy feel at home so he had prepared a large array of dishes for Venu's first meal in London.

Tamil songs played on the radio in the background as the two of them ate together that first evening. Venu shared with Balu what was happening in the forest back home, how the gifts of the forests were being destroyed, polluted by the mercury from the mining factory. 'I am saddened to hear of what is happening to our beloved forest', said Balu.

'I need to tell people about what is happening back home so that they might help us', said Venu, 'but all I can do is play my flute. I do not know what else I can do.'

The man and boy sat in silence over their dinner. They enjoyed the music on the radio but neither of them had a very good appetite. Then, quite suddenly, Balu shot up out of his seat with a look of excitement etched on his face.

'That's it!' he exclaimed.

'What is it?' asked Venu

'We will make a song about the forest and we will put it on the internet. We will get people to sign a petition to stop the factories and the pollution!'

'How will we put a song on the internet? I have never done that.'

'It's easy', said Balu. 'You have the talent. Your father has told me many times about your beautiful flute playing. And me... well, I have the technology. Ha, ha! I love doing stuff like this, making up Tanglish songs. This is going to be fun, I can feel it.'

'What is Tanglish?' asked Venu.

'It is when the words of a song are a mixture of Tamil and English... Pretty cool hey?' said Balu, chuckling to himself as though he had just found a secret key. 'Come on, let's do it now. We've had a lovely meal and I feel good. I've got all my equipment set up in the living room already. You have got your flute haven't you, Venu?'

The young boy was very excited by Balu's idea, but he was also a little bit nervous as he had never recorded his music before. He said:

'I take my flute everywhere, but I am not sure about playing and recording. So many people might listen if we put it on the internet.'

'That is the whole point, my boy! And you are not just going to play', said Balu with a big, mischievous smile. We are both going to sing too, you and I. We shall sing about the beautiful forest and how the factories are destroying our lands. Come on, let's get started.'

And so Balu and Venu spent the whole night recording music and thinking up lyrics that would capture what Venu wanted to say about the forest and all of its natural beauty and wonder. And most importantly of all, Venu wanted to tell people how the factories were causing damage to his beloved forest and how they should be made to stop.

All night long the duo worked on their song about the forest. They wrote and recorded the lyrics that would fit nicely alongside Venu's flute playing and some very strange and wonderful sounds that Balu created on his computer. All night long they worked, right up until the young boy was so tired that he dragged himself to bed and fell asleep instantly.

'Good Morning, Venu', said a cheery Balu as the young boy walked into the kitchen the following day. 'Did you sleep well? Was the duvet warm enough for you? Britain can be very cold at times.'

Venu took a seat at the table as Balu prepared a breakfast of paratha and sweet chai.

'I've got a surprise for you', he said.

'What is it?' asked Venu, still half asleep.

'Well, after we finished creating our song last night, I uploaded it onto the internet. I was just too excited and wanted to share it with everybody as soon as possible. You're not angry with me are you, Venu?'

'Not at all. It *was* finished and it is *our* song. It belongs to us both.'

'Good, good', said Balu, now barely able to contain his excitement, 'because guess what? We've already had over three million people listen to it so far! Three million!'

'What!' said Venu, his mouth full of paratha.

'It's gone viral! Unbelievable! And there are emails from people who are asking about the petition. An environmental charity wants to talk to you as soon as possible. They want to stop the mercury pollution from further damaging the forest, and they say they have the power to do this. Can you believe it?'

'Venu could barely believe his ears. 'Let's call them!' he said, as excited as Balu. 'I'm ready to talk to them right now!' He jumped out of his chair and hugged his friend. 'Without your help none of this would have been possible. Thank you Balu.'

'I just want you and all children to experience the gifts of our forest. No company has the right to destroy such a beautiful place. Come on; let's call the environmental charity who are going to help us.'

Balu dialled the number and Venu spoke to the serious-sounding gentleman who answered the phone. The man explained how many of the people who worked for the charity had listened to the song on the internet and how they were all very impressed. Venu told the man about the factories and how his father was sick, and how Laila's mother and father had died after drinking from the contaminated lake.

The man from the environmental charity promised Venu that the factories would be made to stop. 'It will not be easy', he said. 'It will be a long fight. But we will make sure they leave the forest in the end. And we shall make them pay compensation to the workers.'

When Venu put down the phone he was as happy as he had ever been. He and Balu had begun the process of saving the forest. Venu realised that one person could make a difference if they really cared, and he promised himself that he would never forget this lesson. 'And one day soon', he thought, 'I will return home to my family and to Laila and the kurinji flowers, and all of the beautiful gifts of the forest.'

SMART TURTLE AND THE MONKEY

Credit: David Heathfield

Monkey stood at the edge of the river and watched Turtle swimming against the torrent with a tree that he had caught in the flood: a young tree.

'Oh, Monkey, I have caught a banana tree. Monkey, will you help me to drag it to the clearing and plant it? It will grow and there will be sweet bananas.'

Turtle pulled the tree by its heavy end – the roots and the trunk – across the ground. Monkey carried just a couple of green fronds from the top end of the tree.

Lazy Monkey.

When Turtle wasn't looking, Monkey jumped onto the fronds.

Monkey nimble, Monkey quick, Monkey play a monkey trick – and was pulled along by Turtle to the clearing.

Turtle made a hole. He pulled the tree down into the hole and pressed the earth down around it. 'Soon it will grow, Monkey. We will tend the tree together. We will water it. We will weed around it. We will share the bananas.'

'Share the tree', said Monkey. 'Very well.' And Monkey climbed half way up the tree, just below where the green fronds grew, and with his strong hands he broke off the top of the tree and ran away with it, laughing.

He pressed his half, the top half, into the damp earth. Soon he would have bananas, he thought.

Turtle tended the bottom half of the tree. There was no green.

Turtle wisdom, Turtle slow, Turtle knows what turtles know.

Time passed, and the bottom half of the tree began to green up. Fronds appeared and green bananas began to grow.

Monkey, with the top half of the tree, had green fronds that wilted and died. There was nothing.

Turtle worked hard around his tree, weeding it and watering it, and now big, long, yellow bananas were hanging down in bunches.

'Oh, Monkey, won't you help me? Climb the tree and pick the bananas. I cannot climb the tree.'

Monkey nimble, Monkey quick, Monkey play a monkey trick – up the tree he went to the top, and there he picked one banana and peeled it and ate the delicious fruit. He tossed down the skin so it struck Turtle upon his shell.

Monkey took another banana and ate it, tossing the skin down upon the shell of Turtle. Banana after banana…

Monkey nimble, Monkey quick, Monkey play a monkey trick.

But Turtle, without Monkey noticing, went and fetched thorns and placed them around the trunk of the banana tree…

Turtle wisdom, Turtle slow, Turtle knows what turtles know.

When Monkey had finished and was fat, had eaten all of the yellow bananas, he jumped down from the tree… 'Ow, ow, ow, ow, ow!'

The thorns stuck in the bottom of his feet as he ran. He sat down and he pulled the thorns from his feet and he was full of anger. He ran and quickly, quickly caught Turtle.

'I am going to carry you to the cliffs and dash you down upon the rocks so your shell breaks! I'm going to take you to the top of the mountain of fire and throw you into the flames!'

'Yes, yes, said Turtle, throw me into the flames! Yes, dash me from the cliff onto the rocks! But whatever you do, Monkey, don't throw me into the torrent of the river.'

'Ah, that's what you're afraid of', said Monkey.

Monkey ran, carrying Turtle to the edge of the river, and tossed him high into the air. Turtle landed with a splash in the deep waters and sank down… and then rose to the surface.

'Oh, Monkey, don't you know that Turtles love to swim in the river.'

Turtle wisdom, Turtle slow, Turtle knows what turtles know.

But what of the banana tree?

The Turtle and the Monkey did not work together, and the tree was grown over with weeds.

No more bananas.

———◆———

THE FOOL AND THE DONKEY

Credit: David Heathfield

One morning, the fool woke up and he thought, 'There is one thing I need, I need a donkey.'

So he left his home and walked until he came to the town. He came to the donkey stall. There were many donkeys. Some were big and some were small. Some had long ears and some very short. But among them, there was one donkey that had long, floppy, silky ears.

'This is the donkey for me.'

The fool paid the donkey stall holder and he led that donkey tied by a rope away from the stall and through the streets of the town, and *there* were two boys.

'We can trick that donkey from that fool.'

One boy went up and he took the rope from around the donkey's neck and he put it around his own neck and followed the fool, who didn't even notice.

The other boy led the donkey back to the stall to sell it.

On through the streets and on away from the town to his home went the fool. And when he got to his home he turned and... uhhh: 'When I bought you, you were a donkey. But now you've turned into a boy.'

'It's true, I was a donkey when you bought me, but, you see, before that, I was a boy. I was rude to my mother, and my mother said, 'If you are ever rude to me again may you be turned by the devil into a donkey.'

And so it was. But now that you have bought me, I am a boy once more and I belong to you.'

'You belong to me?' said the fool. 'I cannot own a boy. Go, go, but promise me this: when you go to your mother, do not be rude to her again.'

The fool slept that night, and when he woke in the morning he realised there was something he still needed... He still needed a donkey. He went away from his home, taking his last few coins, and walked until he came to the town; through the streets he came until he came to the donkey stall. And there were all those donkeys large and small, some with larger ears than others. And among the donkeys he noticed there was one donkey with long, floppy, silky ears. He knew that donkey. He went over to it and he lifted its ear and said: 'You foolish boy, I said never be rude to your mother again!'

———————◆———————

HOW THE TORTOISE GOT HIS CROOKED SHELL

Credit: Abimbola Alao

A long time ago, a terrible famine hit an ancient animal kingdom. It had not rained for two whole years and all of the crops were dying. The animals hoped and prayed for an end to the terrible drought, but the sky was no longer able to gather enough clouds, and the rains did not come.

Ijapa, the cunning tortoise, lived on the outskirts of the village with his wife and two sons.

The famine was very bad and was already having a devastating effect on all the animals, so Ijapa could no longer trick them into parting with what little rations of food they possessed.

One morning, very tired and hungry, Ijapa left his house with the intention of searching the marketplace for scraps of food, but there was no food in the market, and so the tortoise remained as hungry as ever.

However, just as the tortoise was about to return home he saw Ehoro, the rabbit, hopping towards the marketplace. There was something strange about Ehoro. He looked radiant, well fed, and full of exuberance. Ijapa was curious. 'Why is Ehoro looking so well and I am so hungry?' he thought. So he approached the rabbit with his head bowed as if he were in mourning. Then he began to cry.

When Ehoro saw Ijapa, he rushed to meet him. 'What is it, my friend?' asked the kindly rabbit.

Ijapa answered, 'My father is ill in hospital. My wife is expecting our third child but she is so hungry that I fear for her health. And only last night I heard that my mother-in-law is dying of starvation because she does not have enough food to eat! I feel terrible because there is nothing I can do!'

Ehoro was suspicious because it was well known that the tortoise was very sly and could not always be trusted. But Ijapa was an excellent performer and soon won the rabbit's sympathy.

'Meet me at Ore Brook after dark', said Ehoro. 'I will help you in spite of my doubts. I just hope that I do not regret this.'

Soon it was night, and Ijapa set out into the darkness to find Ehoro waiting at the brook. Once they had said their hellos, both animals made their way into the deep forest: the rabbit leading the way while the tortoise followed closely behind.

Before long, they came to a narrow path that led to an open clearing among the trees in the middle of the forest.

The rabbit stopped and pulled the tortoise to his side. 'What you are about to see must be kept a secret, do you understand?' The tortoise nodded in agreement and the rabbit cupped his hands around his mouth and began to sing...

'Iya, iya ta'kun wale o

CHORUS: Alu jan jan ki jan

'Iya, iya ta'kun wale o

CHORUS: Alu jan jan ki jan

Suddenly, a long, white rope descended from the sky. Ehoro grabbed the rope and began to climb. After hesitating for just a moment, Ijapa also took a hold of the rope and followed the rabbit up into the night sky.

————◆————

THE PRINCESS AND THE GOLDEN BALL

Credit: Ali Hassan

Once there was a beautiful princess who lived with her father in a huge palace. Although the princess was very beautiful she was also very selfish and conceited. The princess always got her own way and the king was often disappointed with his daughter. He was worried that she would grow into a selfish woman and that she would not be a good example to his people.

One day the princess was playing in the gardens of the palace. She was playing with her favourite possession in the whole world, a golden ball. The princess loved the golden ball because it was so shiny and she could see her reflection upon its surface. She also loved the ball because it was so valuable.

The princess threw the ball high into the air where the sun made it sparkle against the blue sky. Higher and higher she threw the golden ball. So high that she imagined the golden ball was a second sun; a sun belonging to her and her alone.

The golden ball went so high up into the air that it really did begin to look like a sun, and the reflections dazzled the princess who had to close her eyes. The ball landed some way away and began to roll towards the lake in the shadows of the giant Nakla trees.

The princess let out a cry and ran towards the golden ball with her arms outstretched. But she was too late. The ball rolled into the lake and sank beneath the surface out of sight. The princess collapsed onto the ground and began to cry. She cried to hard that her tears fell into the lake making a sound like raindrops. Little ripples stretched across the surface of the lake and still the princess cried and cried.

Then a small voice came out of nowhere. 'Why are you crying, princess?' The princess looked all around but she could not see a single person near the lake. Again the small voice asked, 'why are you crying, my princess?'

When she looked down she saw a small frog sitting on the edge of the lake with wide eyes and little webbed feet.

'I have lost my golden ball and now I will never get it back.'

'Where have you lost it, princess?' said the little frog. 'I can help you find it if it will stop your tears.'

The princess wiped her tears away. Perhaps this little frog can help me, she thought.

'It is at the bottom of the lake where I cannot reach.'

The little frog looked at the princess and smiled. 'I can fetch it for you, princess. I will dive to the bottom of the lake and I will bring back your golden ball for you.'

The princess was delighted by the news and also smiled, but before the frog jumped into the water her wanted the princess to make him a promise.

'I will promise you anything if you will bring me back my golden ball', said the princess.

'I want you to take me with you back to the palace and be my friend. If you promise to do this then I will dive to the bottom of the lake and find your golden ball.'

The princess agreed right away and so the little frog jumped into the lake and swam all the way to the bottom where he took the golden ball in his mouth. The ball was very heavy and the little frog struggled to get back to the surface. Eventually he appeared on the edge of the lake and dropped the ball onto the grass at the princesses' feet.

The princess took the ball and held it to her chest and laughed with glee. Then she ran towards the palace, leaving the frog behind.

'Wait for me', cried the little frog. 'You promised to take me with you!'

But the princess ignored the frog, forgetting all about her promise. All she could think about was how happy she was that she had her golden ball. And she knew it would be dinner time at the palace and she was hungry. The princess only ever thought about herself and the poor frog was left alone on the edge of the lake.

Later that evening the princess and the king were sitting down to dinner in the palace. The princess did not spare a thought for the frog, or for the promise she had made him.

Then there was a knock at the palace door. A moment later the frog hopped into the dining hall and jumped up on to the table next to the princess. The princess was horrified and cried out, 'go away you disgusting frog!' But the king silenced his daughter and asked the frog what he was doing inside the palace. The frog told the kind all about the promise the princess had made to him. The king was very angry with his daughter and commanded her to keep her promise to the frog.

'We must always do as we promise, daughter.'

'But he is just a frog and I am a princess', she said, almost in tears once again.

'That does not matter. You must do as you said you would do.'

The king made the princess serve the frog a small plate of food which the little frog hungrily gobbled down.

The princess was angry at her father and even angrier at the frog. She thought it wrong that a frog should be inside the palace, eating at her table with the king. But the king paid no attention to his daughter's foul mood.

Eventually the princess had had enough of the little frog and stood to go to bed. She bid her father goodnight and made to leave, but the frog reminded the princess of her promise to stay with him and be his friend. The king agreed that the princess must take the little frog to bed with her so that he might sleep on her pillow.

'I will not do it!' exclaimed the princess. But the king insisted his daughter keep her promise.

Although she did not want to, the princess knew that she must do as her father instructed. She placed her hand on the table and the little frog jumped into her palm. Then she went up to her bedroom. Once away from the king, the princess was very mean to the little frog. She threw him onto her bed and told him that he was an ugly creature, and that he was very impudent to assume he could sleep on the pillow of a princess. She got ready for bed and pulled the covers up close around her, ignoring the little frog who was sitting on the edge of her pillow.

'Why do you hate me so?' asked the frog. I did as you asked and rescued your golden ball from the bottom of the lake. All I asked in return was for you to keep your promise to be my friend.'

The frog lowered his head and tears escaped from his sad, wide eyes as he began to cry. 'I have been living by the lake for many years and all I wanted was to have your company. It is not a good life to be all alone with nobody to talk to.'

The princess was very moved by the frog's tears and her heart began to soften. Although she was a princess, and she had everything a young woman might want, she was an only child with no brothers or sisters to play with. The princess had grown up alone in the palace and she often wished that she was able to share her time with others. Often she would hear the young children playing on the other side of the palace walls and she was envious of their laughter and games.

The princess and the frog talked into the night and soon the princess forgot altogether that he was a frog and thought of him in a kind way. She shared stories her father had told her as a baby, and the frog enjoyed listening very much.Towards dawn both the frog and the princess were very tired. The princess realised that she was happy to have a friend to talk to, and she regretted being so mean to the little frog. Just as they were both about to fall asleep, the princess leaned forwards and kissed the frog on the lips.

Instantly there was a blinding flash of silver light. The princess closed her eyes in shock. When she opened them a handsome prince stood before her and the little frog had vanished altogether.

'You have set me free with your kindness, princess', said the handsome prince. 'You kept your promise and you befriended me even though I was just a frog.'

The very next morning the prince asked the king for his daughter's hand in marriage. The king agreed at once and the young couples were wed in the palace grounds next to the lake, beneath the shadows of the Nakla trees.From that day forwards the princess was a changed person. She knew how important it was to keep a promise, and she treated her people with kindness and respect no matter how rich or how poor they were.

———————◆———————

A COUPLE OF SILK STOCKINGS

Credit: Kate Chopin

Little Missus Sommers one day found herself the unexpected owner of fifteen dollars. It seemed to her a very large amount of money. The way it filled up her worn money holder gave her a feeling of importance that she had not enjoyed for years.

The question of investment was one she considered carefully. For a day or two she walked around in a dreamy state as she thought about her choices. She did not wish to act quickly and do anything she might regret. During the quiet hours of the night she lay awake considering ideas.

A dollar or two could be added to the price she usually paid for her daughter Janie's shoes. This would guarantee they would last a great deal longer than usual. She would buy cloth for new shirts for the boys. Her daughter Mag should have another dress. And still there would be enough left for new stockings — two pairs per child. What time that would save her in always repairing old stockings! The idea of her little family looking fresh and new for once in their lives made her restless with excitement.

The neighbors sometimes talked of the "better days" that little Missus Sommers had known before she had ever thought of being Missus Sommers. She herself never looked back to her younger days. She had no time to think about the past. The needs of the present took all her energy.

Missus Sommers knew the value of finding things for sale at reduced prices. She could stand for hours making her way little by little toward the desired object that was selling below cost. She could push her way if need be.

But that day she was tired and a little bit weak. She had eaten a light meal—no! She thought about her day. Between getting the children fed and the house cleaned, and preparing herself to go shopping, she had forgotten to eat at all!

When she arrived at the large department store, she sat in front of an empty counter. She was trying to gather strength and courage to push through a mass of busy shoppers. She rested her hand upon the counter.

She wore no gloves. She slowly grew aware that her hand had felt something very pleasant to touch. She looked down to see that her hand lay upon a pile of silk stockings. A sign nearby announced that they had been reduced in price. A young girl who stood behind the counter asked her if she wished to examine the silky leg coverings.

She smiled as if she had been asked to inspect diamond jewelry with the aim of purchasing it. But she went on feeling the soft, costly items. Now she used both hands, holding the stockings up to see the light shine through them.

Two red marks suddenly showed on her pale face. She looked up at the shop girl.

"Do you think there are any size eights-and-a-half among these?"

There were a great number of stockings in her size. Missus Sommers chose a black pair and looked at them closely.

"A dollar and ninety-eight cents" she said aloud. "Well, I will buy this pair."

She handed the girl a five dollar bill and waited for her change and the wrapped box with the stockings. What a very small box it was! It seemed lost in her worn old shopping bag.

Missus Sommers then took the elevator which carried her to an upper floor into the ladies' rest area. In an empty corner, she replaced her cotton stockings for the new silk ones.

For the first time she seemed to be taking a rest from the tiring act of thought. She had let herself be controlled by some machine-like force that directed her actions and freed her of responsibility.

How good was the touch of the silk on her skin! She felt like lying back in the soft chair and enjoying the richness of it. She did for a little while. Then she put her shoes back on and put her old stockings into her bag. Next, she went to the shoe department, sat down and waited to be fitted.

The young shoe salesman was unable to guess about her background. He could not resolve her worn, old shoes with her beautiful, new stockings. She tried on a pair of new boots.

She held back her skirts and turned her feet one way and her head another way as she looked down at the shiny, pointed boots. Her foot and ankle looked very lovely. She could not believe that they were a part of herself. She told the young salesman that she wanted an excellent and stylish fit. She said she did not mind paying extra as long as she got what she desired.

After buying the new boots, she went to the glove department. It was a long time since Missus Sommers had been fitted with gloves. When she had bought a pair they were always "bargains," so cheap that it would have been unreasonable to have expected them to be fitted to her hand.

Now she rested her arm on the counter where gloves were for sale. A young shop girl drew a soft, leather glove over Missus Sommers's hand. She smoothed it down over the wrist and buttoned it neatly. Both women lost themselves for a second or two as they quietly praised the little gloved hand.

There were other places where money might be spent. A store down the street sold books and magazines. Missus Sommers bought two costly magazines that she used to read back when she had been able to enjoy other pleasant things.

She lifted her skirts as she crossed the street. Her new stockings and boots and gloves had worked wonders for her appearance. They had given her a feeling of satisfaction, a sense of belonging to the well-dressed crowds.

She was very hungry. Another time she would have ignored the desire for food until reaching her own home.

But the force that was guiding her would not permit her to act on such a thought.

There was a restaurant at the corner. She had never entered its doors. She had sometimes looked through the windows. She had noted the white table cloths, shining glasses and waiters serving wealthy people.

When she entered, her appearance created no surprise or concern, as she had half feared it might.

She seated herself at a small table. A waiter came at once to take her order. She ordered six oysters, a chop, something sweet, a glass of wine and a cup of coffee. While waiting to be served she removed her gloves very slowly and set them beside her. Then she picked up her magazine and looked through it.

It was all very agreeable. The table cloths were even more clean and white than they had seemed through the window. And the crystal drinking glasses shined even more brightly. There were ladies and gentlemen, who did not notice her, lunching at the small tables like her own.

A pleasing piece of music could be heard, and a gentle wind was blowing through the window. She tasted a bite, and she read a word or two and she slowly drank the wine. She moved her toes around in the silk stockings. The price of it all made no difference.

When she was finished, she counted the money out to the waiter and left an extra coin on his tray. He bowed to her as if she were a princess of royal blood.

There was still money in her purse, and her next gift to herself presented itself as a theater advertisement. When she entered the theater, the play had already begun. She sat between richly dressed women who were there to spend the day eating sweets and showing off their costly clothing. There were many others who were there only to watch the play.

It is safe to say there was no one there who had the same respect that Missus Sommers did for her surroundings. She gathered in everything —stage and players and people -- in one wide sensation. She laughed and cried at the play. She even talked a little with the women. One woman wiped her eyes with a small square of lace and passed Missus Sommers her box of candy.

The play was over, the music stopped, the crowd flowed outside. It was like a dream ended. Missus Sommers went to wait for the cable car.

A man with sharp eyes sat opposite her. It was hard for him to fully understand what he saw in her expression. In truth, he saw nothing -- unless he was a magician. Then he would sense her heartbreaking wish that the cable car would never stop anywhere, but go on and on with her forever.

———————◆———————

THE PITILESS GUEST

Credit: Nathaniel Hawthorne

One December night, a long, long time ago, a family sat around the fireplace in their home. A golden light from the fire filled the room. The mother and father laughed at something their oldest daughter had just said.

The girl was seventeen, much older than her little brother and sister, who were only five and six years old. A very old woman, the family's grandmother, sat knitting in the warmest corner of the room. And a baby, the youngest child, smiled at the fires light from its tiny bed.

This family had found happiness in the worst place in all of New England. They had built their home high up in the White Mountains, where the wind blows violently all year long. The family lived in an especially cold and dangerous spot. Stones from the top of the mountain above their house would often roll down the mountainside and wake them in the middle of the night.

No other family lived near them on the mountain. But this family was never lonely. They enjoyed each others company, and often had visitors.

Their house was built near an important road that connected the White Mountains to the Saint Lawrence River. People traveling through the mountains in wagons always stopped at the family's door for a drink of water and a friendly word.

Lonely travelers, crossing the mountains on foot, would step into the house to share a hot meal.

Sometimes, the wind became so wild and cold that these strangers would spend the night with the family. The family offered every traveler who stopped at their home a kindness that money could not buy.

On that December evening, the wind came rushing down the mountain. It seemed to stop at their house to knock at the door before it roared down into the valley.

The family fell silent for a moment. But then they realized that someone really was knocking at their door. The oldest girl opened the door and found a young man standing in the dark.

The old grandmother put a chair near the fireplace for him. The oldest daughter gave him a warm, shy smile. And the baby held up its little arms to him.

"This fire is just what I needed," the young man said. "The wind has been blowing in my face for the last two hours."

The father took the young man's travel bag. "Are you going to Vermont?" the older man asked.

"Yes, to Burlington," the traveler replied. "I wanted to reach the valley tonight. But when I saw the light in your window, I decided to stop. I would like to sit and enjoy your fire and your company for a while."

As the young man took his place by the fire, something like heavy footsteps was heard outside. It sounded as if someone was running down the side of the mountain, taking enormous steps.

The father looked out one of the windows.

"That old mountain has thrown another stone at us again. He must have been afraid we would forget him. He sometimes shakes his head and makes us think he will come down on top of us," the father explained to the young man.

"But we are old neighbors," he smiled. "And we manage to get along together pretty well. Besides, I have made a safe hiding place outside to protect us in case a slide brings the mountain down on our heads."

As the father spoke, the mother prepared a hot meal for their guest. While he ate, he talked freely to the family, as if it were his own.

This young man did not trust people easily. Yet on this evening, something made him share his deepest secret with these simple mountain people.

The young man's secret was that he was ambitious. He did not know what he wanted to do with his life, yet. But he did know that he did not want to be forgotten after he had died. He believed that sometime during his life, he would become famous and be admired by thousands of people.

"So far," the young man said, "I have done nothing. If I disappeared tomorrow from the face of the earth, no one would know anything about me. No one would ask Who was he. Where did he go? But I cannot die until I have reached my destiny. Then let death come! I will have built my monument!"

The young man's powerful emotions touched the family. They smiled.

"You laugh at me," the young man said, taking the oldest daughters hand. "You think my ambition is silly."

She was very shy, and her face became pink with embarrassment. "It is better to sit here by the fire," she whispered, "and be happy, even if nobody thinks of us."

Her father stared into the fire.

"I think there is something natural in what the young man says. And his words have made me think about our own lives here.

"It would have been nice if we had had a little farm down in the valley. Some place where we could see our mountains without being afraid they would fall on our heads. I would have been respected by all our neighbors. And, when I had grown old, I would die happy in my bed. You would put a stone over my grave so everyone would know I lived an honest life."

"You see!" the young man cried out. "It is in our nature to want a monument. Some want only a stone on their grave. Others want to be a part of everyone's memory. But we all want to be remembered after we die!"

The young man threw some more wood on the fire to chase away the darkness. The firelight fell on the little group around the fireplace: the father's strong arms and the mothers gentle smile. It touched the young man's proud face, and the daughters shy one. It warmed the old grandmother, still knitting in the corner. She looked up from her knitting and, with her fingers still moving the needles, she said, "Old people have their secrets, just as young people do."

The old woman said she had made her funeral clothes some years earlier. They were the finest clothes she had made since her wedding dress. She said her secret was a fear that she would not be buried in her best clothes.

The young man stared into the fire.

"Old and young," he said. "We dream of graves and monuments. I wonder how sailors feel when their ship is sinking, and they know they will be buried in the wide and nameless grave that is the ocean?"

A sound, rising like the roar of the ocean, shook the house. Young and old exchanged one wild look. Then the same words burst from all their lips.

"The slide! The slide!"

They rushed away from the house, into the darkness, to the secret spot the father had built to protect them from the mountain slide.

The whole side of the mountain came rushing toward the house like a waterfall of destruction. But just before it reached the little house, the wave of earth divided in two and went around the family's home. Everyone and everything in the path of the terrible slide was destroyed, except the little house.

The next morning, smoke was seen coming from the chimney of the house on the mountain.

Inside, the fire was still burning. The chairs were still drawn up in a half circle around the fireplace. It looked as if the family had just gone out for a walk.

Some people thought that a stranger had been with the family on that terrible night. But no one ever discovered who the stranger was. His name and way of life remain a mystery. His body was never found.

———•———

THE GOD OF HIS FATHERS

Credit: Jack London

Silently the wolves circled the herd of caribou deer. Gray bellies close to the ground, the wolves in the pack surrounded a pregnant deer. They pulled her down and tore out her throat. The rest of the caribou herd raced off in a hundred directions. The wolves began to feed.

Once again the Alaska territory was the scene of silent death. Here, in its ancient forests, the strong had killed the weak for thousands and thousands of years.

Small groups of Indians also lived on this land at the end of the rainbow. But their Stone Age life was ending. Strange men with blond hair and blue eyes had discovered the lands of the North. The Indian chiefs ordered their warriors to fight them. Stone arrow met steel bullet. The Indians could not stop the strangers. The White men conquered the icy rivers in light canoes. They broke through the dark forests and climbed the rocky mountains.

One of these men sat in front of a tent, near a river. His name was Hay Stockard. Over the smoke and flames of his fire, he watched an Indian village not far from his own camp.

From inside his tent came the cry of a sick child, and the gentle answering song of its mother. But the man was not concerned now with them. He was thinking of Baptiste the Red, the chief of the Indian village, who had just left him.

"We do not want you here," Baptiste had told him. "If we permit you to sit by our fires, after you will come to your church, your priests and your God." Baptiste the Red hated the White man's God. His father had been an Englishman; his mother, the daughter of an Indian chief. Baptiste had been raised among White men.

When Baptiste was a young man he fell in love with a Frenchman's daughter, but her father opposed the marriage. A Christian priest refused to marry them. So Baptiste took the girl into the forests. They went to live among his mother's people. A year later, the girl died while giving birth to her first child.

Baptiste took the baby back to live among the White people. For many years he lived in peace with them, as his daughter grew up -- tall and beautiful. One night, while Baptiste was away, a White man broke into their home and killed the girl. When Baptiste asked for justice, he was told the White man's God forgives all sins. So Baptiste killed his daughter's murderer with his own hands, and returned forever to his mother's people.

"I have sworn to make any White man who comes to my village deny his God if he wants to live," he told Hay Stockard. "But since you are the first, I will not do this if you go and go quickly."

"And if I stay?" Hay Stockard had asked quietly as he filled his pipe. "Then soon you will meet your God, your bad God, the God of the White man!" The Indian chief rose to his feet and left Hay Stockards camp to return to his village.

The next morning Hay Stockard watched with angry eyes as three men in a long canoe came to the river bank. Two of the men were Indian. The third, a White man, wore a bright red cloth around his head. Hay Stockard reached for his gun, and then changed his mind. As soon as the canoe landed, the White man jumped out and ran up to Stockard.

"So we meet again, Hay Stockard! Peace be with you. I know you are a sinner, but I, Sturges Owen, am Gods own servant. I will bring you back to our church.

"Listen to me," Stockard warned, "if you stay here you will bring trouble to yourself and your men. You will all be killed and so will my wife, my child, and myself!"

Owen looked up to the sky. "The man who carries God in his heart and the Bible in his hand is protected."

Later that morning, the Indian chief Baptiste came back to Stockards camp. "Give me the priest," Baptiste demanded, "and I will let you go in peace. If you do not, you die."

Sturges Owen grabbed his Bible. "I am not afraid," he said. "God will protect me and hold me in his right hand. I am ready to go with Baptiste to his village. I will save his soul for God."

Hay Stockard shook his head. "Listen to me, Baptiste. I did not bring this priest here, but now that he is here, I can't let you kill him. Many of your people will die if we fight each other."

Baptiste looked into Stockard's eyes. "But those who live," he said, "will not have the words of a strange God in their ears."

After a moment of silence, Baptiste the Red turned and went back to his own camp. Sturges Owen called his two men to him and the three of them kneeled to pray. Stockard and his wife began to prepare the camp for battle.

As they worked they heard the sound of war-drums in the village.

As Sturges Owen waited and prayed, he began to feel his religious fever cooling. Fear replaced hope in his heart. The love of life took the place of the love of God in his mind. The love of life! He could not stop himself from feeling it. Owen knew that Stockard also loved his life. But Stockard would choose death rather than shame.

The war-drums boomed loudly. Suddenly they stopped.

A flood of dark feet raced toward Stockard's camp. Arrows whistled through the air. A spear went through the body of Stockard's wife. Stockard's bullets answered back. Wave after wave of Indians warriors broke over the barrier. Sturges Owen ran into his tent. His two men died quickly. Hay Stockard alone remained on his feet, knocking the attacking Indians aside.

Stockard held an ax in one hand and his gun in the other. Behind him, a hand grabbed Stockard's baby by its tiny leg and pulled it from under his mother's body. The Indian whipped the child through the air, smashing its head against a log. Stockard turned, and cut off the Indians head with his ax.

The circle of angry faces closed on Stockard. Two times they pushed up to him, but each time he beat them back. They fell under his feet as the ground became wet with blood. Finally, Baptiste called his men to him.

"Stockard," he shouted. "You are a brave man. Deny your God and I will let you live!"

Two Indians dragged Sturges Owen out of the tent. He was not hurt, but his eyes were wild with fear.

He felt anger at God for making him so weak. Why had God given him faith without strength?

Owen stood shaking before Baptiste the Red. "Where is your God now? " demanded the Indian chief.

"I do not know," Owen whispered.

"Do you have a God?"

"I had."

"And now?"

"No."

"Very good," Baptiste said. "See that this man goes free. Let nothing happen to him. And send him back to his own people so he can tell his priests about Baptiste the Reds land where there is no God."

Baptiste turned to Hay Stockard. "There is no God," Baptiste said. Stockard laughed. One of the young Indian warriors lifted the war spear.

"Do you have a God?" Baptiste shouted.

Stockard took a deep breath. "Yes, he said, "the God of my fathers."

The spear flew through the air and went deep into Stockard's chest. Sturges Owen saw Stockard fall slowly to the ground. Then the Indians put Owen in a canoe. Sturges Owen went down the river to carry the message of Baptiste the Red, in whose country there was no God.

————◆————

CURIOUS VISITOR TO THE STAR

Credit: Chris Rose

Anna Winter pulled on her Gucci sunglasses and sprayed herself with the extra-strength mosquito repellent she had bought in the airport. That was the biggest problem about her work, she thought. Mosquitoes and things like that. Bad hotels, and bad food. How could she be a front-line, award-winning, adventurous journalist if she had to stay in bad hotels and eat bad food?

Anna Winter thought her job was very difficult, and she told everybody about this.

As she landed in Lagos airport, she worried about the hotel where she was staying, and how she would be able to eat for the week she was staying in Nigeria. Perhaps that would make a good article, she thought. Lots of local colour.

Joseph Adoga collected a printed copy of the article he was working and put it in his bag as he left the small office of the Star. The Star was a local paper in Lagos. It came out every evening and had a mixture of stories – politics, current affairs, local news, human interest stories and sport. It was only a small newspaper, but Joseph enjoyed his job. He liked finding things out, and informing people about what was going on in the city, in Nigeria as a whole, in Africa generally, and in all the world. When he heard that the famous international journalist Anna Winter was coming to Lagos to do a story he was interested, and was even more pleased when her agency got in touch with Joseph. "You should be able to help her" the agency said, and Joseph hoped he could help her.

Instead of driving out to the usual part of the city where he lived, tonight Joseph drove into one of the rich areas of the city. He stopped outside one of the big hotels and went in to meet Anna Winter. Anna Winter was disappointed by the hotel. It was one of a big international chain, so she expected more. The air-conditioning in her room wasn't working properly, and there were mosquitoes inside. She hoped that the local journalist she was going to meet would be able to help her.

"Let's go to somewhere really characteristic to eat" said Anna to Joseph when they met in the hotel foyer. "I want a really typical little place…the kind of place where I'm sure you go to eat…somewhere full of local colour…"

Joseph thought hard about a place where they could go and eat. Eventually, he thought of somewhere and took Anna in his car to a restaurant he knew where they served traditional Nigerian food. Joseph really liked the place, but Anna wasn't happy.

"Hmmmm…it's very clean," she said. "Very clean and very quiet…"

"What did you expect?" asked Joseph.

"Well, erm, something more African" said Anna.

"How do you mean?" asked Joseph.

"More noise, more colour…lots and lots of people…"

"Well" said Joseph. "Lagos is quite a noisy and a colourful city, and there are a lot of people who live here...but we like to eat good food in good surroundings...like anyone else!"

Anna looked disappointed. "But I'm not getting a real feel of Africa here" she said. "Anna" Joseph tried to explain. "Africa is a continent. There are 54 countries in Africa, and 900 million people. Nobody even really knows how many languages are spoken in Africa...hundreds!"

Joseph wanted to explain to Anna that it was impossible to talk about "Africa" as if it was just one place, but Anna wasn't listening. Joseph changed the subject of the conversation.

"So, what are you going to write about Nigeria?" he asked her.

"I'm not sure yet" said Anna. "I want to look around and get a feel for the place first. Something about guns and crime, perhaps, and I need some pictures of starving people...starving people with guns if possible..."

Joseph thought for a minute. "Well, like any big city, there is a crime in Lagos...sure. But I'm not sure how interesting that is. You won't find many starving people here though.." He pointed to the plates of food on their table. "Here we eat pretty well!"

"Tell me what things you write about in your paper." said Anna.

"All sorts of things" said Joseph. "It's only a small paper, so I have to write lots of the stories. Sometimes there are crime stories, yes. I can show you those if you like…."

"That could be interesting…I think I can use my influence to change things…"

"I've got a good idea" said Joseph. "Why don't you write an article about everyday life here in Lagos…you know, so many articles about Africa are just about famine or war or corruption…but that's not the reality of many of our lives."

Anna look confused. Joseph continued.

"Why don't you write about some ordinary scenes, a restaurant like this, happy children at school…"

"People don't want to hear that" said Anna. "It doesn't sell. I need big sunsets over the Serengeti, and I need to contrast with the darkness of Africa…I've already got my title, yes, 'Darkness at noon' I 'm going to call the article…"

Joseph sighed and wondered why people always talked about "darkness" in Africa. Joseph had been to London in December – now that was darkness! It was dark at three o'clock in the afternoon. Nigeria was the brightest, lightest place he'd ever visited. Anna ignored him and continued.

"And I need to contrast that with the nobility of the people…"

"I see," said Joseph, "but be clear… there are some noble people here, but there are also some very bad ones. We are not noble just because we are African.

Why not write about some of our Nigerian writers and intellectuals...there are many – Chinua Achebe, Ben Okri, Wole Soyinka...they have some fascinating things to say..."

Joseph could see that Anna wasn't interested. Anna thought she was the only intellectual and writer who mattered.

A few days later Anna was on the plane back to London. "I have to file some copy...what can I write...?" She took out her laptop and began to type...

"As soon as I got off the plane I was in love with Africa. Like a noble man, disappearing into the huge sunset, Africa is impossible to know, but it will always haunt you..." Yes, this is good thought Anna to herself..."Jospeh Adoga is one such man, a face of Africa, a noble journalist, fighting for the cause of free speech in the Dark Continent...and without our help, he is in trouble..."

At the same time as Anna was typing, Joseph was sitting down to read the latest edition of The Star. He began to read his own article in it. "European journalists are strange people..." it began.

———•———

THE DREADFUL AND SERIOUS CASE

Credit: Chris Rose

I have a friend who is afraid of spiders. This isn't very unusual; a lot of people are afraid of spiders. I don't really like spiders much myself. I don't mind them if you see them outside, in the garden, as long as they're not too big. But if one comes in the house, especially if it's one of those really big spiders with furry legs and little red eyes, then I go "yeeucch" and I try to get rid of it. Usually, I'll use a brush to get rid of the spider, but if I feel brave then I'll put a glass over the top of it, slide a piece of paper under the glass and then take it outside.

This is quite normal, I think. But my friend isn't afraid of spiders in any normal way. She isn't just afraid of spiders, she is totally, completely and utterly terrified of them. When my friend sees a spider she doesn't just go "uurgghh!" or run away, or ask someone else to get rid of the horrible creepy crawly. No: she screams as loud as she possibly can. She screams so loud that her neighbours worry about her, and think about calling the police. When she sees a spider, she shivers all over, and sometimes she freezes completely – she can't move at all because she is so terrified. Sometimes she even faints.

But my friend had a surprise for me when we met for coffee last week.

"Guess what?" she asked me.

"What?" I said.

"I've got a new pet!"

"Great," I said. "What is it? A dog? A cat?"

"No"

"A budgie?"

"No"

"A rabbit?"

"No"

"What then?"

"I've got a pet spider."

"I don't believe you!"

"It's true! I decided that it was the time I did something about my phobia so I went to visit a doctor, a special doctor. A psychiatrist. This psychiatrist specialised in phobias – helping people who had irrational fears to get better, and live normally. He told me I suffered from 'arachnophobia'."

"It's an irrational fear of spiders," he said. "About one in fifty people suffer from a severe form of arachnophobia. It's not very uncommon."

"Thanks" said my friend. "But that doesn't help me much..."

"There are lots of different ways we can try to cure your phobia," said the psychiatrist. "First, there is traditional analysis."

"What does that mean?" asked my friend.

"This means lots of talking. We try to find out exactly why you have such a terrible fear of spiders.

Perhaps it's linked to something that happened to you when you were a child."

"Oh dear," said my friend. "That sounds quite worrying."

"It can take a long time," said the psychiatrist. "Years, sometimes, and you can never be certain that it will be successful."

"Are there any other methods?"

"Yes – some psychiatrists use hypnosis along with traditional analysis." My friend didn't like the idea of being hypnotised. "I'm worried about what things will come out of my subconscious mind!" she said.

"Are there any other methods?" asked my friend,

"Well", said the psychiatrist, "There is what we call the 'behavioural' approach."

"What's the behavioural approach?" asked my friend.

"Well," said the psychiatrist, "It's like this..."

The psychiatrist got out a small spider from his desk. It wasn't a real spider. It was made of plastic. Even though it was only a plastic spider, my friend screamed when she saw it.

"Don't worry," said the psychiatrist. "It's not a real spider."

"I know," said my friend. "But I'm afraid of it just the same."

"Hmmmm," said the psychiatrist. "A serious case..." He put the rubber spider on the desk. When my friend stopped screaming, the psychiatrist told her to touch it. When she stopped screaming again – the idea of touching the plastic spider was enough to make her scream – she touched it. At first she touched it for just one second. She shivered all over, but at least she managed to touch it.

"OK," said the psychiatrist. "That's all for today. Thanks. You can go home now."

"That's it?" asked my friend.

"Yes."

"That's all?"

"Yes, for today. This is the behavioural approach. Come back tomorrow."

My friend went back the next day, and this time the plastic spider was already on the doctor's desk. This time she touched it and held it for five minutes. Then the doctor told her to go home and come back the next day. The next day she went back and the plastic spider was on her chair. She had to move the spider so she could sit down. The next day she held the spider in her hand while she sat in her chair. The next day, the doctor gave her the plastic spider and told her to take it home with her.

"Where do spiders appear in your house?" asked the psychiatrist.

"In the bath, usually," said my friend.

"Put the spider in the bath," he told her.

My friend was terrified of the spider in the bath, but she managed not to scream when she saw it there. "It's only a plastic spider," she told herself.

The next day the psychiatrist told her to put the spider in her living room. My friend put it on top of the television. At first, she thought the spider was watching her, and she felt afraid. Then she told herself that it was only a plastic spider.

The next day the psychiatrist told her to put the spider in her bed.

"No way!" she said. "Absolutely not!"

"Why not?" asked the psychiatrist.

"It's a spider!" replied my friend.

"No it's not," said the psychiatrist, "It's a plastic spider. It's not a real one." My friend realized that her doctor was right. She put the plastic spider in her bed, and she slept there all night with it in her bed. She only felt a little bit afraid.

The next day, she went back to the psychiatrist. This time, she had a shock, a big shock. Sitting in the middle of the doctor's desk there was a spider. And this time it was a real spider.

My friend was about to scream and run away, but she didn't. She sat on the other side of the room, as far away as possible from the spider, for about five minutes, then she got up and left the room.

"See you tomorrow!" shouted the psychiatrist to her as she left.

The next day she went back and this time the psychiatrist let the spider run around on his desk. Again, my friend stayed about five minutes, then left. The next day she stayed for ten minutes, and the day after that, fifteen. Eventually, the psychiatrist held the spider, the real spider with long furry legs and little eyes, in his hand. He asked my friend to come and touch it. At first, she refused, but the doctor insisted. Eventually, she touched the spider, just for a second. The next day she touched it for a few seconds, then for a few minutes, and after that, she held the spider in her own hand.

Then she took the spider home, and let it run around in her house. She didn't feel afraid. Well, OK, she did feel afraid, but only a tiny bit.

"So now I've got a pet spider!" she told me again.

"Well done!" I said.

"There's only one problem," she said, and as she spoke I noticed that she was shivering all over. Then she screamed and climbed up on the chair. She was pointing to something on the floor.

"Over there!" she screamed. "Look! It's a beetle...!!"

———◆———

THE WOODSMAN AND THE CRANE

Credit: Jin Lou

A crane was standing in a stream, hoping to catch some fish. A huntsman was crawling through the bushes on the riverbank, and spotted the crane. He'd not caught anything that day, and carefully readied his bow and arrow. He took aim and sent an arrow flying towards the crane. The crane heard the movement of the arrow through the air, and raised her wings. Just as she was airborn, the arrow hit her in the thigh. She squealed, but was able to stay in the air and fly away. She didn't get very far before the pain forced her down. She landed awkwardly in a clearing in the woods. A woodsman who'd been working there, gathering branches, found the poor crane. He took pity on her, and dropped his wood, and carried the crane to his hut. There he removed the arrow, and applied some herbs to help heal the wound. The woodsman took good care of the crane, he fed her and changed her dressing every day. As her wound healed, the crane fell in love with this kind woodsman.

Unbeknown to the woodsman, the crane happened to possess magic powers, and she was able to turn herself into a young woman. When the woodsman came home from his work that evening, he found the woman there, who had prepared a meal for him.

The next day she went into the village and procured a weaving loam that she placed in one of the rooms. That night the woman explained to her husband that she'll be weaving cloth for him to sell in the market. That way they can earn much more money than he can possibly make from selling wood. But she warned him that he must never come into the room when she is working, or something really bad will happen.

Weeks and months passed. Every day the man went to the market to sell the cloth and every evening when he arrived back home, there was a large quantity of newly woven cloth. They were now very well off, and they had a very good life.

One day the man became curious, and he determined to see how his wife managed to produce all this very fine cloth day in day out. He set off for the market as usual with the cloth, but once out of sight of the house, he hid the cloth behind some trees, and went back to the house. Keeping very quiet, he crept up to the room where she worked. He could hear her working inside. He slowly opened the door, and peeked inside.

To his great shock, there working at the loam was the crane he rescued! Immediately the magic spell was broken, and the crane returned to her natural state.

Because he could not control his curiosity, the man lost his wife, and his income from selling the cloth she used to weave.

THE WOLF AND THE SEVEN BILLY GOATS

Credit: Grimm Brothers

Once upon a time there lived an old mother goat in a pretty little cottage on the edge of the forest. She had seven little billy goats, and she loved them all dearly. On occasion she would have to leave the cottage to get food for herself and her kids, and today was one of those occasions. She called all her kids together to give them a little lecture on safety. "Listen carefully, my dear children", she began. "I need to go out to get some food, and I want you all to be very careful because I heard there is a wolf about. If he comes here and sees you out and about he will surely gobble you all up, all of you, your skin, your ears, your teeth, your guts, everything. He is a very crafty wolf, and he may well try to deceive you by disguising himself, so stay inside the house, and don't open the door to anybody!"

"Don't worry, mother, the little goats replied, "we will be really, really, careful, and do everything you say. We won't let anybody in, don't you worry about us!" And so she shooed her seven little billy goats into the cottage, and made sure they locked the front door before she went on her way, into the forest.

I think that wily old wolf must have been hiding behind a tree and watching the old mother goat because only a few minutes later there was a loud knock on the door. "Who's there?" shouted the oldest of the kids. "Open the door!" the wolf replied, "It is your mother and

I've got some nice things for all of you!" But the little goats heard the rough voice and knew that this was not their mother, so they said: "You're not our mother, she has a really nice sweet voice, and you sound all rough and rotten. You must be the wolf, so go away, because we won't open the door!"

So the wolf went away and thought about how he could disguise his voice. He went to see the bees and bought a pint of honey, which he downed in one go, to make his voice nice and sweet. Then he went back to the goats' cottage and knocked on the door again. "Open the door, my children", he called out. "It is I, your dear mother, and I've brought some wonderful things for all of you to feast o!" But without thinking, in order to make sure his voice was gentle, the wolf had placed his great big black paws on the window, and the billy goats saw them, and they knew something was wrong. "No, no, no", shouted the oldest billy goat, "our mother does not have great big black paws like that! Hers are dainty. You must be the wolf! We won't open the door for you, ever!"

The wolf went away again and thought how he could disguise his paws. He had a brilliant idea. He rushed round the corner, where the baker lived and asked him to put some dough on his paws, saying he's hurt his foot running away from a hunter. From there, he ran to the miller and asked him for some white flour to put on the dough that covered his paws. But the miller was reluctant to do so because he assumed that the wolf was up to one of his tricks. But the wolf growled at the miller fiercely, and said: "Come on, give me some flour or I'll bite your nose off!" So the miller put some flour in a bag, which he gave to the wolf, and immediately locked his door as soon as the wolf had gone on his way. Wolf now rushed back to the cottage, and when he got there, he opened the bag with the flour and sprinkled it all over the dough that covered his paws. "Now we'll see if those miserable billy goats won't open the door", he muttered to himself.

He knocked on the door for the third tie, calling out: "Open the door, my dear little children, It is your mother, and I've brought something very tasty for you all to eat." The oldest little goat went up to the window and shouted: "Show us your feet, so we can see if you really are our mother". The wolf put his feet, covered in dough and flour, up against the window. "You see?" he asked. "it really is me, your mother, this time". That's how the billy goats were tricked into believing it really was their mother outside the door, and the oldest billy goat carefully opened the door. Immediately the wolf burst in, with a great howl in that rough voice of his, and the little goats started screaming and scrambling for places to hide in the little cottage. One tried to hide under the table, but the wolf found him and gobbled him up. A second tried to hide behind the cooker, but the wolf found him and gobbled him up. The third hid in the pantry, but the wolf found him and gobbled him up. The fourth hid behind his mother's easy chair, but the wolf found him and gobbled him up. The fifth hid under the bed covers, but the wolf found him and gobbled him up. The sixth tried to hide in the wash tub, but the wolf found him too, and gobbled him up. Only the seventh, the youngest and smallest one, who managed to hide behind the old grandfather clock, escaped. When he couldn't find anybody else, the wolf grumbled, "I really can't remember how many of them there were in here, was it six or seven? I can't remember how many of them I've already gobbled up!" He laughed, and rubbed his stomach. "I'm pretty full, anyway, he said, I'll go and have a little lie down, if there are any left, I will catch them later, that's for sure!"

So he sauntered outside, found a nice cosy place under an apple tree, and went to sleep. It did not take long before he was snoring loudly.

Eventually old mother goat returned with her shopping, and to her consternation, she saw that the front door to the cottage was wide open. She ran inside and started crying; what a mess, all the furniture was upside down, the wash tub had rolled over, and the bed covers were on top of the cooker. She knew that this could only mean one thing: the wolf had been in here and had taken all her children. She groaned and she wailed. But then she heard a little voice coming from a corner of the room: "Mummy is that you?" She stopped crying, and replied: "it's me, where are you? What happened here?" Then the littlest of her children came out from his hiding place behind the grandfather clock, and told her everything that had happened. "oh dear, oh dear", the old mother goat cried, "what a calamity!!" She decided to have a look outside to see if any of the others might have got away, and there, under the apple tree, she saw the bulky figure of the old wolf, fast asleep and snoring like he had swallowed a few pints of schnapps. She went up close to him, and she saw that there was some movement inside the wolf's stomach. That made her think that her children might still be alive, inside that horrible creature. She rushed into the kitchen, and got a big pair of scissors. She proceeded to cut open the wolf's stomach, and as the hole she was cutting got bigger, she could see one head, that came sticking out, then a tail, and then a leg. She cut as fast and as far as she could, and before long, her six children jumped out of the wolf's stomach, one after the other. The old mother was filled with joy. That nasty wolf had been so greedy that he had just gulped them all down, without chewing, so that not only were they still alive, but they were all in one piece!

She rushed inside again, and came back with a great big needle and some thread. She told her children to go and fetch some large stones. "We'll fill up his stomach with stones, she explained, and then we'll stitch him up again. That will teach him a lesson!" each of the little billy goats soon came back with a big stone, as big as they could carry, and old mother goat deposited them all inside the wolf's stomach. Once that was done, she proceeded to stitch him up again, and when that was finished, they all went inside the cottage, where they all sat by the window and watched and waited for the wolf to wake up.

Eventually the wolf did wake up. He felt rather tired and heavy, especially heavy. And thirsty, boy, was he thirsty! With great difficulty he managed to raise himself, and started tottering towards the brook, moaning and groaning all the while. "Oh boy, oh boy, I am so thirsty, I could drink a whole river!" Eventually he came to the brook, and lowered his head to take a drink. But he was so heavy, what with all these stones in his stomach, that he just slid down the bank and straight into the water, where he disappeared below the surface, and drowned.

The old mother goat and her seven little billy goats had followed the wolf at a safe distance, and when they saw the nasty creature disappear beneath the waves of the rook, they all started singing and dancing: "The wolf is dead! The wolf is dead, our dear mother tricked the wolf and now he is dead! Hurrah, hurrah!" old mother goat called all her children together. "Now listen to me, she began, first we'll go and clean up the house, then we'll have a big party with some of the wonderful things I brought back from the forest to celebrate that we all survived this adventure!" And the seven little billy goats had the best ever party of their lives!

———◆———

THE LOVERS WHO TURNED INTO BUTTERFLIES

Credit: Jin Lou

A long time ago in a certain part of China, only boys were allowed to go to school. It was thought that girls should not be educated, but should remain ignorant.

In fact they were rarely allowed out of the house, and if they did go out they should be accompanied by a male.

Zhu Ying Tai was the daughter of a wealthy merchant, and she was possessed of a boundless thirst for knowledge. She was always questioning her father, her mother, her brothers, the servants.

She was envious of her brothers when they started school, and she was determined that she herself should go to school as well and get an education.

She pestered her parents day in day out. They kept telling her, No, it just is not done for a girl to go to school, but she would not give up.

They tried to take her mind of school by buying her nice clothes, dolls and other toys. Nothing could dissuade her. School became an obsession.

Her parents loved her very much, and after some time they started to think what they could do to satisfy Zhu's lust for learning.

The only thing they could think of was that Zhu should pretend to be a boy. She could go to school if she dressed up in boys' clothing!

That's how Zhu finally entered school. She didn't find it too difficult to live like a boy. She was only interested in learning and hardly ever got involved with any of her schoolmates after lessons.

In any case, they thought this new boy was a bit strange, and were quite happy to leave him alone. There was only one boy she became friendly with.

His name was Liang Shan Bo, and he was a studious young man with very gentle manners. They often studied together, and gradually they became good friends.

Years passed, and Zhu did very well. By this time Zhu had become aware that her feelings for Liang had grown strong, beyond the way two fellow students would normally feel, even if they were the best of friends.

Liang too, felt something similar, he couldn't quite understand why he felt so strongly attracted to this other boy.

Then one day, Zhu's parents send one of their servants with a message that she is to return home immediately. The servant doesn't tell her very much, other than to insist that it is her father's wish that they return without delay.

Zhu fears the worst, maybe her mother is on her deathbed! So she travels home with the servant, and she is mightily relieved to find both her parents in good health.

But she is shocked when her father tells her the reason why she has been summoned home. One of her father's business associates has a son, just a little older than Zhu, and they have arranged for the two to get married.

Zhu is in despair; now she realises that she is in love with Liang, and it is him she wants to marry. Zhu then arranges for the servant to go back to the school, and to ask Liang to come to the town, and to take a room at a local inn.

The next day the servant returns and informs Zhu that her friends are lodging in the inn. She dresses up as a boy once more and goes to see Liang.

She tells Liang that because of a family problem, she won't be able to come back to school, but that she has a cousin who is staying at their house.

Liang should make her acquaintance, Zhu says she feels sure that when the two of them meet, they will fall in love, and Liang should then ask her parents for the cousin's hand in marriage.

Zhu tells Liang to present himself at the house later that afternoon.

She goes back home to change back into her girl's clothes. She is going to play the part of her cousin, she feels sure that when Liang sees her as she really is, he too will realise that what he has been feeling for his friend all this time is nothing but love!

Eventually, her servant comes to announce that Liang has arrived, and she goes to meet her friend. She introduces herself as Zhu's cousin, but Liang is struck by the likeness between this cousin and his friend.

Now that Zhu finally stands before him in without any disguise she cannot control herself, and she bursts out crying and tells Liang the whole story of who she really is, and how much in love she is with him.

At first Liang is angry that he has been deceived, but then he is relieved, because he too realises that he is deeply in love with Zhu.

Zhu then tells Liang about the arranged marriage her parents have planned for her, and they agree that he must ask Zhu's father for her hand in marriage.

That same afternoon, Liang asks to see the father. Of course, he doesn't have any idea who this young man is. When he hears that Liang wants to marry his daughter, he just laughs.

He questions Liang about his parents, where they come from, what they do, how much money do they have? Liang's parents don't have very much, his mother works as a weaver, and his father is a fisherman.

They can only pay for Liang's education by living a very frugal life. Zhu's father dismisses him, tells him to go back to school and to find a girl in his own social class.

He forbids Zhu to have any more contact with Liang, and tells his servants to make sure she doesn't leave the house unsupervised.

Liang stays in the inn, he cannot face going back to school alone, and he feels he has to stay close to Zhu. But he has lost his appetite and he can't eat anything.

He sits at his window every day, all day long, and looks out to see if he can catch a glimpse of Zhu.

He gets sick, and pines away. Zhu can't get out of the house, the servants are not prepared to disobey their master.

She spends her days crying for her lover. One of the servants has offered to take messages to the inn and back. That's how one sad day she learned that Liang had died.

Zhu cries more and more, but her parents carry on with the preparations for the wedding regardless. Her father is certain that eventually she will forget this poor student, and will accept her duties as a good daughter and wife.

But Zhu doesn't stop crying, she cries and cries until all the tears in her body are used up. Then she starts crying blood, instead of tears, small pearls of blood come out of her eyes. The day of the wedding arrives.

Zhu will be carried in a palanquin to her new husband's house. She instructs her bearers to take the route that oases the cemetery where Liang is buried.

When they get there, she orders them to stop, and she gets out to say a prayer over his grave. As she kneels down by the grave, a butterfly appears, it seems as if it came out of Liang's grave.

It circles around her head, and she watches it, spellbound. She is sure this butterfly looks just like her dead lover, Liang. She stretches her arms out towards the butterfly, which flies up a bit, over her head. She lifts her head and her arms towards it, and as the butterfly flies higher up, she realises that her arms have turned into butterfly wings, and she can join him now, at last, and together they fly away from this place full of dead people.Her servants come looking for her, but they don't see anybody. All they can see is a pair of butterflies cavorting over the graves, then disappearing into the blue distance.

———◆———

THE COWHERD AND THE HANDSOME WEAVER

Credit: Jin Lou

Deep in the Chinese country side a poor boy called Lai lived with his older brother and his wife. They just had a small piece of land where they managed to grow just about enough food for the three of them to live on, and they only had one cow.

Lai didn't get treated very well, but he never complained. It was Lai's responsibility to look after the cow. Every morning he took her to the foothills of the mountains, where the cow grazed on the long grass and leafy bushes. Every night the cow would give them a little milk.

Lai was quite lonely, his brother and sister-in-law only spoke to him when they wanted something, and he'd taken to talking to the cow. The cow never said anything back to him, of course. Lately, the main topic of conversation between Lai and the cow had been Lai's longing to find a wife.

He felt he was old enough now to start his own family, but they were so poor, he knew they would not have enough food to feed another person.

One fine day Lai was sitting on a rock under the hot sun, watching the cow and pondering his fate. The cow looked up from her grazing, and looked at the boy.

She came walking up to him. "Listen, boy" the cow said softly, "maybe I can help you." The boy jumped up,

85

and looked around, expecting to see somebody behind him. There's nobody there! Just he and the cow, and a few birds flying over the meadow.

"It's me!" the cow spoke again. Lai shook his head and took a step back, ready to run away. The cow lifted her head. "Don't worry, boy," she said, "only you can hear me speak."

"But how is this possible," asked the boy, quite astounded and still pretty scared. "You're a cow! You can't speak!" The cow let out a long mooo.

"I don't know exactly how it works, she started, but you're always very kind to me, and maybe there is a way I can help you fullfil your dreams."

Lai had to sit down again. He realized there was some kind of magic going on, he certainly didn't understand it, so he asked "How do you know what my dream is? And how could a cow help me? Are you going to turn into a beautiful young woman?"

The cow shook her head. "You know the lake where you take us to drink sometimes? The other side of the meadow there?" Lai nodded. He knew the place well.

The cow continued, "This afternoon some fairies will be there, bathing and swimming. You should go there. Make sure they don't see you, but look around for their dresses. You should take one of the dresses, one only, mind you, and hide it. Something good will happen."

The boy shook his head again. "You want me to sneak up to the fairies and steal their clothes? That's not a very nice thing to do! How could something good come from that?"

The cow mooed again. "Trust me", she said, "if you do as I suggest, something good will happen. You should go now, by the time you get to the lake, the fairies will be there." Having said that, the cow turned around and walked away. She started grazing again.

The boy scratched his head. "Cow!" he shouted, and ran after her. "How come you know all this? How come you can suddenly speak?" But the cow just carried on grazing. The magic had obviously worn off.

For a few moments the boy wondered what to do. The only thing he could think of was hat some friendly spirit had taken over the cow for a few minutes. Maybe there was somebody or something in the land of the spirits who wanted to help him.

It was true, as the cow had said, that he always tried to be kind and gentle. Not just to the cow, but to his brother and his wife and the other people in the village as well. It was just possible that somebody wanted to reward him , even though he himself thought it was just his duty to act like that.

But what did he have to lose? He reckoned he could reach the lake in less than half an hour; if there was nothing there, he could be back here in an hour at the most. He patted the cow.

"Very well, my good friend," he said softly, "let's go see if you really want to help me. I'll be back in an hour. Don't wander off!" With that, he turned around and started running across the meadow, in the direction of the lake. The cow just carried on grazing.

Lai ran and skipped and tumbled. His heart beating in his throat. His curiosity mounted by the minute, as did his anxiety. Eventually he reached the long grassy dunes that surrounded the lake. He slowed down and moved tentatively.

He thought he could hear something, singing? Someone singing? Or was it just the birds. No, now he could definitely hear voices, singing, he was sure now.

Gingerly, he climbed to the top of the dune, and peeked over it. There in the lake he could see several figures swimming and cavorting in the water.

What an amazing sight! There were about six or seven of them, he'd never seen anything so breathtakingly beautiful in his life! He remembered what the cow had said about the clothes.

He started searching for them, taking care to stay out of sight. Then he spotted them, seven neatly folded dresses, side by side. He crept closer and grabbed the nearest one, then ran and his behind the first tree.

A few minutes later the singing voices came nearer, and he peeked from behind the tree trunk. He could see the fairies picking up their dresses and putting them on, then flying up into the air, still laughing and singing.

But of course one of them stayed behind. The poor fairy looked everywhere for her dress. Lai could see she was getting more and more distressed and he felt sorry for her.

He came out from his hiding place, carrying her dress. When the fairy saw him, her first reaction was to run away. But then she saw that he was carrying her dress.

"What are you doing with my dress!" she shouted at him. The poor boy couldn't speak. He had never seen such a beautiful creature, and he'd fallen head over heels in love with her.

"Well?" the fairy spoke again, "what have you got to say for yourself?" "P-p-please don't b-b-be angry," Lai stuttered. "I-I-I-…," but he couldn't finish his sentence.

The fairy stood there looking at him, but of course, being a kind and gentle creature herself, she couldn't stay angry for very long. She began to feel a little sorry for this poor shy boy.

As well as being kind and gentle, fairies can see right through people, and she could see that this boy was so shy because he was falling in love with her.

Finally, Lai found enough courage to explain himself. "I didn't mean to upset you," he started, "but my cow told me that something good would happen if I took your clothes." At first the fairy wanted to laugh. "I see," she said the, "this must be a very special cow indeed. We'd better go and have a word with her."

She took her clothes from Lai and they set off together, to the meadow where he had left his animals grazing. On the way there she told him her name was Qi Xianv, which means the Seventh Princess, and he told her all about his life, about his brother and sister-in law and their existence, and the fact that they were so poor that he couldn't possibly afford to take a wife.

When they reached the meadow, the fairy could see immediately that a friendly spirit was living in the cow's body, who wanted to make the boy's life better.

She looked at Lai again, and realised that now she is beginning to fall in love with him. Ouch!! This was a big problem for her, because fairies are not allowed to fall in love with mere humans.

The long walk and the conversation they had seemed to have given Lai more courage. He asked Qi Xianv if she would consider marrying him. She knew she should say no, and that she should just fly away and join the other fairies.

But against her better judgement, she said "Yes!" They embraced there and then in the meadow. That's how the poor cowherd and the beautiful fairy came to live together as man and wife.

They set up home together and Qi Xianv started weaving cloth. She turned out to be quite good at it, and they were able to make enough money to live on. After a while Qi Xianv gave birth to a healthy baby boy, and the three of them lived a happy, peaceful, life.

One day the cow got very sick. Lai looked after her as well as he could, but the cow got sicker and sicker. Even the fairy couldn't do anything about it.

Since that one day in the meadow, the cow had never spoken again. One day, however, when Lai was bringing some fresh water into the shed, she spoke to him again. "My dear boy," she said. "this old cow's body is getting too fragile. Soon I'll be gone. But if you do as I tell you, I can leave you some protection."

Lai nodded, "I'll do whatever you say," he said. "After I'm dead, keep my skin in one piece. Keep it in a safe place, and you'll find it will be very useful in an emergency," spoke the cow. Lai promised to do so. A few days later, the cow passed away. Lai hid her skin in a secret place beneath their little house.

In the meantime, in Fairyland, where all the fairies lived, the goddess in charge of the fairies was very unhappy. She had been very upset when the fairies came back from their little excursion to the lake without their sister Qi Xianv.

She'd sent the fairies out again to look for her, time and again, week in week out, they had been searching for her all over China. They searched in the forests. They searched on the plains. They searched in the mountains. They searched in the rivers. They searched in the villages and the cities. They searched all along the coast. But they always came back empty handed.

They just couldn't find her anywhere, and the goddess got more and more miserable as time went by. But the fairy goddess was very determined, and she kept sending out new search parties.

Some of the other goddesses were poking fun at her that she kept losing fairies. She just could not afford to give up.

So one sad day, yet another search party of fairies was flying over the countryside, when one of them spotted a fair figure tending a vegetable patch.

She alerted her companions and they swept down to get a closer look. They recognised their missing sister, and without asking for explanations they took held of Qi Xianv and pulled her up into the sky with them.

Later that afternoon, Lai came back to the hut from the forest where he'd been gathering herbs, to find his son, sitting all by himself, crying for his mummy.

His wife was nowhere to be found. His son pointed up to the sky, and flapped his arms about. Lai realised that the fairies must have come for his wife. At first he was totally despondent, and broke out in tears.

Then he remembered the cowskin. He took it from its hiding place and wrapped it around himself, like a cloak. Immediately he felt a strange new power inside himself. He picked up his son, and started to run.

To his amazement he found himself flying! Up they went, higher and higher. He had no idea where they were going, but his cowskin cloak seemed to know the way. It took them over mountains, over valleys and over rivers. It took them way beyond the clouds.

Eventually, Lai saw a strange golden arch in the distance. It looked like some kind of a gate, and he thought it must be the entrance to Fairyland. He was right, and the guard fairies at the gate had spotted him approaching.

They alerted their boss, the fairy goddess, and she flew into a rage. How dare this little simple human peasant come all the way up here! She would stop him there and then!

Using all her considerable magic powers, she conjured up a torrential stream in the sky between Lai and the gate to Fairyland. Lai's cloak came to a halt. Lai could see there was no way he could get across or around this torrent.

He cried out in despair. On the other side of the gate, the fairies had gathered together to watch this amazing piece of magic, Qi Xianv among them.

She could just make out the figures of her husband and son on the other side of the water, and she also started screaming. Some of the other gods and goddesses who lived nearby came to see what the commotion was all about.

They saw the crying fairy at the gate, and the crying man with his crying son at the other side of the river that had just appeared there out of nothing. "What's going on," they demanded to know," why are you keeping these lovers apart?"

The fairy goddess explained the whole situation to her colleagues. "The law of the fairies is quiet clear," she concluded, "fairies are not allowed to associate with humans, and the law must be upheld!"

All the gods were agreed that the law is the law, but some of them looked at the poor separated pair and felt there should be some room for compromise.

"Show some mercy!" shouted one of the gods, "let her go back to him!" The fairy goddess shook her head. "No! No! No!"

"Let the boy live in Fairyland," suggested another. The fairy goddess shook her head. "No! No! No! That is quite impossible!" "I know," said yet another goddess, "Each year you could allow the fairy one day to be with her husband!"

All the other gods and the fairies who were watching thought this was a terrific suggestion, and they all started clapping and shouting their approval.

The fairy goddess looked at Qi Xianv, and she looked at Lai, and she said: "All right, this is what we'll do." She summoned all the fairies, and told them to round up all the birds they could find in the sky.

As they came back with thousands and thousands and thousands of birds of all shapes and sizes and colours, the fairy goddess arranged the birds in such a way that they formed a bridge over the torrential stream she had created.

She told Qi Xianv that she could cross the bridge of birds and stay with Lai for that day. Once she returned to Fairyland in the evening, the birds would be sent back to wherever they had come from.

And from that day onwards, on every anniversary of that day the fairy goddess summoned all her fairies to gather together all the birds in the sky to form the bridge which made it possible for Qi Xianv and Lai to meet.

MONKEY ON A MANGROVE TREE AND THE SHARK

Credit: Zarah Mohamed

Monkey lived on the branches of an old mangrove tree, right on the spot where the land ends and the sea begins. He liked living here. There were lots of other animals to talk to and play with, most of them much smaller than he was, which he particularly liked because it made him feel safe and comfortable at home. The big hunters like the lion hardly ever ventured here because the ground was so soggy that their heavy paws would sink into the mud and they wouldn't be able to move fast enough to catch their prey. There were birds of all shapes and sizes, some that flew and some that could only run along the ground, like the guinea fowl; and the fish! He loved talking to the fish, listening to their stories of life under water. In fact his best friend was Shamus the Shark.

Every evening when the sun was about to go down, Shamus would wind his way through the roots of the mangroves and look for Monkey. Monkey was always expecting his friend, and he'd find a nice cosy branch that hung close to the water's surface to sit on while he waited for his friend. The first thing he usually saw was the triangular tip of Shamus's fin sticking up above the water.

Monkey would jump up and down on his branch, and wave and shout. "Over here, Shamus, I'm over here, Uh Uh Ugh Ugh Un Ugh. Shamus would roll over a few times in the shallow water while he swam the last few yards, and lift his enormous jaws out of the water to greet Monkey: "Yo, Monkey my man, how's life in the trees?"

"Toil and toil and toil, my salty friend", Monkey would joke.

Then they would fill each other in on all the news from among the mangrove trees and under the deep blue sea. Monkey would talk about all the mischief he'd got up to that day, how he chased the birds, or caught a ride on Uncle Turtle's back, or hid from the preying eyes of a hovering hawk. Shamus would tell him about all the beautiful creatures at the bottom of the sea, the squids with their trailing tentacles catching glimpses of light from the surface, the sea anemones that were always waving at passers by.

But Shamus's favourite subject by far was food!

He loved to talk about delicate textures and flavours of the different species of fish he devoured on a daily basis. And he was always curious to know what Monkey's favourite dish was. To be honest, monkey didn't think that much about food. He was a strict vegetarian and usually dined on mangrove leaves. But he did remember once a long time ago he did eat something rather special. That was when his cousin from Zanzibar had paid him a visit. He'd brought along a large bag stuffed to the rim with palm hearts. And they'd been delicious! So Succulent! So chewy! So tangy and so sweet! So utterly Yummy!! They'd feasted for days on end. So whenever Shamus asked him about his favourite food, Monkey would lie back on his branch, rub his tummy and tell the tale of eating palm hearts for three whole days and nights.

Then one day, not so long ago, Shamus turned up at the usual time, the setting sun painting the whole mangrove a glorious bright palm oil red. He seemed a little excited, as if he couldn't wait for their usual banter to pass so he could get down to business.

"Hey Monkey my man", he burst out, "GUESS WHAT?!? You know those palm hearts you're always going on about, yea, well, guess what? I just mentioned it to my wife, you know, a while ago now, just casually, in passing you know, the way you do, you know what I mean, and she just, and she only, you know what, she's got this friend, who's a bit of a merchant in the fine food business, you know, he can get hold of anything you like, just like that, you just mention it and he'll get it for you…………"

Monkey was nodding away through this monologue of Shark's, to be honest he was getting a bit bored and he wished Shamus would get to the point whatever it was. So he just nodded and smiled and made a few polite noises every now and then when Shamus happened to look his way. "Um, Uhm. Ya Ya, Great, ya, triffic, Groovy, Ugh, Ugh, Uhn Uhm".

Finally Shark got to the point. "Well! She got some!!!"

"She got a whole bag of these palm heart thingy-me-bobs. And she's inviting you to dinner! She's preparing a feast right now, as we speak! Do you wanna come?"

Monkey was so surprised, he didn't know what to say at first, and believe me, that doesn't happen very often with monkeys! "D'you wanna come? D'you wanna?"

"Well, Shamus, my salty mate, how we gonna do that? Where do you live?" Shamus pointed his pointy nose out towards the sea.

"That's what I thought," said Monkey. "How'm I gonna get there? I can't swim that far! Y'know, here in the mangrove I can just about get by, I paddle around a bit in this shallow water, that's OK, 'cause I know it's not deep enough for me to drown. But out there…….."

But Shamus had obviously thought about this a great deal because he had a plan and he set out to explain it to Monkey. Monkey could sit on his, Shamus's back, and hold on to his fin, and he, Shamus, would stay right on top of the water, right on the surface, so Monkey wouldn't even hardly get wet at all. "What do you think? Shall we go? Let's go! My wife has done all this work, she's been in the kitchen all afternoon!"

Well, as you know, Monkeys are nothing if not adventurous and intrepid, not to mention foolhardy. So Monkey agreed to come and join the feast. He jumped from his branch and onto his salty friend's back, clinging on to the hard fin, and with a swoosh! of his strong tail and a "YIPPEE!" from his grinning mouth full of teeth, Shark set off.

This was really the strangest and weirdest and most wonderful and utterly frightening thing Monkey had ever done. He'd never been out to sea before and he was impressed by the huge waves that pushed them up and down, and the force behind them. Shark must be very strong indeed to swim through this lot! After they'd gone some way, Shark slowed down and lifted his head out of the water.

"You know, Monkey, my friend, there's something you should know. You see, even though my wife is preparing this wonderful feast for you, she herself is very sick."

Monkey sat up a bit from his position on Shark's back, so he could listen better. "Oh really", he managed to say, feeling very wet and very cold and really rather scared, "I'm sorry to hear that man. What's wrong with her? Anything I can do?"

"Actually", said Shark, looking rather sheepish, "there may be something you can do. You see, she went to see her doctor the other day, and he told her there was one thing that would improve her condition without fail and immeasurably enhance her chances of getting better, Surefire guarantee."

"So what's that?" asked Monkey.

Shark coughed and hesitated, then he said, softly, menacingly: "Well, the doc told her to get a hold of a monkey's heart and eat it raw!"

Monkey almost fell into the roaring sea. He looked around nervously. He didn't at all like what he was hearing! Not at all! Instinctively he tightened his grip on Shark's fin.

"So," Shark continued, making his voice sound eerily calm, "we were wondering, you know, if we give you the palm hearts, whether you'll give us your heart. Like an exchange", shark explained.

"Hey, Shark!" Monkey shouted, because there was a roaring in his ears, and he wasn't sure whether it was the sound of the sea or his heart pumping, "Sure! Of course, man, no problem at all! Whatsoever! Man! Are you my friend or what? I mean, what's a little bit of heart between friends!" Shark smiled. "Aaagh", he sighed, "Monkey, man I can't tell you how happy it makes me to hear you say those words. I tell you man, if you do this for me, I mean for my wife, anything, anytime, anywhere, anything at all you ever want at any time in the future, man, I'll get it for you or my name isn't Shark!"

"You know, Shark, my salty friend", Monkey said in a very small voice, "there's only one thing, though, you know, I wish you'd mentioned this before we set off, because you know, I left my heart at home! I left it in a very secret place in my tree where I always hide it!" Monkey almost stopped breathing while he waited for Shark to digest this information.

Shark Sputtered. He coughed. He gurgled. "You left it at home??" He grinned his crooked grin at its most crooked. Monkey knew he had to be very careful what he said right now. He knew he had to get this exactly right. He could feel his heart beating in his throat, and he was afraid it might just jump out right into Shark's open mouth. He hoped the thumping wouldn't make Shark suspicious.

"You see, my friend, it's like this. For a monkey like me, the heart is the most important thing, the most vital possession. If a monkey loses his heart, well, you might as well give up living right there and then! So you see, I'm always really, really, careful with it and make sure it's always in a safe place somewhere, so I can find it when I need it!"

"I see", grumbled Shark grimly, "I see, so what do we do now, Monkey, my man?"

"Well", said Monkey, hopefully, "we're not that far out yet, are we? We could race back, I'll jump up into my tree, get the heart, and we can be back here in what, ten, fifteen, minutes at the most! Let's hurry, let's not keep your wife waiting any longer than is strictly necessary."

Now Shark was in a real quandary. Was Monkey telling the truth or was he having him on? But of course, he didn't really have a choice. If he was not to arouse Monkey's suspicion he had to go along with him and pretend to believe him even if he wasn't at all sure that was the right thing to do. So he swooshed his tail, and turned his pointed nose back towards the land.

"OK, Monkey, my mate, let's hurry!" He swam as fast as he could, thinking that the quicker he got this done, the less time Monkey would have to change his mind.

They got back to the mangrove in less than five minutes, they'd hardly reached the first tree, and Shark had barely started to slow down, when Monkey got up and made an almighty leap from his friend's back towards the nearest branch, caught it, then swung up and over, and onto the next branch, and up and over again onto the next highest one, and higher and higher he swung and hurled himself until he was at the highest point in the highest tree in the middle of the mangrove. Then he stopped and looked down.

The sun had gone down completely now and the full moon shone a pale greyish yellow light over the mangrove. Below him Monkey could see the silver dorsal fin of Shark against the black water, his jaws snapping at the cool night air.

"Monkey, Monkey, where are you? You promised, your heart? Where is it, where have you hidden it? Where is it then? Monkey, your heart!"

Monkey couldn't help himself. Suddenly all the tension left him and he started jumping up and down. "Ugh Ugn Ugm Ugh Ugh Oh my friendly fiendish shark! I was almost done for, wasn't I? The only thing that saved me is that you are even more stupid than me!!"

———•◆•———

THE SMALL RED CAP

Credit: Anonymous

Once upon a time, in a small village in a land not that far away, there lived a very sweet little girl, with her mother and father. Her grandmother lived about half an hour's walk away, outside the village, in a clearing in the forest that covered the whole area. The grandmother as especially fond of the little girl, and she had made her a cute little red hat, out of velvet. The girl loved that hat so much that she wore it all hours of the day and night, and so people had started calling her Little Red Cap.

The grandmother was getting very old, and she had become bedridden and infirm. One day Little Re Cap's mother called her over, and gave her a parcel to take to her grandmother. There is some meat here, and a bottle of wine, which will no doubt cheer her up no end. Now be nice and polite when you get there, say, Good morning, Grandmother when you come in, and don't go snooping about the place, upsetting her. Go straight there, and don't linger on the path through the forest, make sure you don't run and skip, and don't drop the bottle. Have you got all that?" Little Red Cap assured her mother that she understood perfectly, and would do everything just as mother told her to.

So off she went, down the village lane, toward the track through the wood leading to her grandmother's house. After she had gone some distance, she heard a rustling in the undergrowth and there appeared before her the wolf. Now this wolf was not a very nice creature, but Little Red Cap, being young and naïve, always assumed everybody she met was just as nice, sweet and honest as she was, so she stopped and greeted the wolf in her usual friendly way.

"Good morning, Wolf", she said.

"Good morning, replied the wolf. You are looking very dainty today. Where would you be going so early in the morning?"

"I'm on my way to see my grandmother, replied Little Red Cap.

"your grandmother indeed, said the wolf. And what is that you are carrying I that little basket? Some nice presents for your grannie, I guess?"

That's right, said Little Red Cap. My mother roasted some nice beef yesterday, so that my grandmother might have something nourishing, and I have some wine to lift her spirits. She has not been very well, recently, she added.

And where does this grandmother of yours live? Asked wolf.

Little Red cap gave a detailed description of where grandmother's house was, down the track a while longer, near some oak trees, and behind some bushes, with a brightly painted front door. A little crooked chimney and a thatched straw roof. "you can't miss it!"

Now you may not know this, because in the times that we live we don't really encounter many wolves when we go for walks, but in those days, wolves were notorious for their ginormous appetites, and they were as likely to gobble up a few chickens as a small human being. So this wolf was eying up Little Red Cap, and thinking about her grannie at the same time, working out the best way to make sure he could have them both. He sauntered along the path a little, keeping up with Little Red Cap, and then he spoke again; "You see how beautiful this place is, with all the beautiful wild flowers growing amongst the tree trunks and the bushes. Why don't you have a little look around, and pick some of the flowers for your grannie, then she will not only have something nice to eat and drink, but she will have something nice to look at as well!" Little Red Cap forgot all her mother had told her about not lingering on the path, and she walked into the woods, amongst the trees, and started picking some of the delightful wild flowers that grew there in such abundance.

Our friend wolf, in the meantime had rushed as fast as he could to grannie's cottage which he found without any difficulty at all. He knocked on the door, and heard grannie's weak voice call out: "Who's there?"

"it is I, Little Red Cap, I've brought you some meat and wine from my mother. Please open the door for me, grannie", replied Wolf, making his voice sound as high pitched as he could to deceive the poor grandmother. "Just push up the latch, called grannie, I'm so weak I just can't get out of my bed!"

So the wolf lifted the latch, threw open the door, and rushed to the bedroom, where he jumped on the bed, and without any further ado, gobbled up the poor grandmother. He then put her cap on his head, and got into her bed, covering himself as much as he could with the bedsheets. There he waited.

He did not have to wait all that long before Little Red Cap appeared outside the cottage. She had collected a nice little bunch of wild flowers and was looking forward to see her grannie's eyes light up. She was a little surprised to see the front door wide open, she thought that perhaps grandmother had felt a bit better and had been up and about. She stepped into the room, and she thought there was a slightly odd smell about, but she shook off this feeling and called out to her grannie: "Good morning, grannie! Where are you?"

She heard some grumbling coming from the bedroom, so she walked inside there. It was quite dark in the room, as the curtains were still drawn, so she walked across, and opened the curtains and a window, to let in some fresh air. Then she turned toward the bed, where she saw what she thought was her grandmother lying down, her covers almost covering her whole face. She could see her ears and her eyes, both looked much larger than she remembered.

"Oh grandmother, said Little Red Cap, what great ears you have!"

That's so I can hear you better, answered wolf.

"And what great eyes you have, grannie!"

"That's so I can see you properly!" answered wolf, keeping his mouth covered.

"And what great hands you have, grannie!" exclaimed Little Red Cap.

"That's so I can lift you up!" said wolf.

"But grannie, what great teeth you have!"

"That's the better to eat you with", shouted wolf, and he immediately threw aside the bed covers, and jumped out of bed to gobble up poor Little Red Cap.

Having now feasted on both the grannie and her little gran daughter, wolf felt particularly satisfied, and he decided he might as well enjoy the home comforts of grannie's cottage a little longer, and spread himself on the bed. Before long he was fast asleep, emitting very loud snoring noises. Just then, a huntsman passed by the cottage, and he heard the strange noise coming from the bedroom window. His curiosity awakened, he decided to check out the source of this noise, and looked into the window. He immediately recognized the wolf he'd been hunting now for a number of weeks, and cocking his rifle, he stepped into the cottage and made his way to the bedroom. Taking careful aim, he shot the wolf dead.

———————◆———————

THE SADDEST STORY EVER

Credit: Stephen Elliott

I was heading home from my girlfriend's house and it was taking a while. She lived well south of San Francisco and it was a weekend so the trains weren't running. Instead you had to go to the station and a take a bus but the bus didn't stop at every station and I had been at the wrong depot so I had to take a bus just to get to the place where I caught the bus and that bus didn't come for half an hour so I sat on the long pews with the other passengers and waited for my ride home.

I only saw my girlfriend maybe once a week because she lived so far away and when I saw her I was stuck there for 24 or 16 hours. But maybe stuck isn't the right word. I was only happy when I was with her but she was so difficult, so intense, that once a week seemed like enough. It took me the rest of the time to recover. And often, after seeing her, I would lie in bed the whole next day, only getting up to eat, constantly hungry. It was like I had climbed a mountain or been beaten up.

I was in the middle of finishing my novel, *Happy Baby*, and I felt very emotional a lot of the time. She hated the book, at least the pieces of it I let her read, and she wasn't at all afraid to tell me so. After telling me how much she disliked what she had seen she asked me to read other parts to her which I did while she ignored me. I loved her so much it made me ill sometimes.

At the time I was worried that *Happy Baby* was not funny enough. My editor had mentioned that to me, that if the book had a little more light in it there would be a wider audience. In fact, the book is not funny at all. It's a very sad book about a man, Theo, who is molested as a boy in the detention center by a guard, Mr. Gracie. Mr. Gracie physically and verbally abuses him but also protects him from the other boys. In this way Theo learns to associate abuse with affection and searches out Mr. Gracie's replacement for the rest of his life. I was wondering if anyone would be interested in such a dark book. My publisher didn't think so.

It was during that long bus ride away from my girlfriend and with my sad novel coming due that I read "I Want To Live" by Thom Jones from his collection *The Pugilist At Rest*. In "I Want To Live" we meet Mrs. Wilson just as she is finding out she has cancer. It seems, on the face of it, a terrible idea for a story. Like it's almost too easy to be good, a story about a woman who gets cancer and dies. But somehow Thom Jones pulls it off with perfect, beautiful minimalism. We rise with her highs and lows, though the dilaudid and the pain. We get brief, unexplained glimpses of her estranged daughter, her good for nothing son-in-law who turns out to be the unexpected hero when given a chance. Jones holds nothing back, guiding us through all of Mrs. Wilson's small, terrible moments:

She began to nod. She was holding onto a carton of milk. It would spill. Like diarrhea-in-the-bed all over again. Another mess. The daughter tried to take the carton of milk away. She… held on defiantly. Forget the Shopenhauer–what a lot of crap that was! She did not want to cross over. She wanted to live! She wanted to live!

It's an incredibly sad story. Perhaps the saddest story I've ever read. I leaned against the window and felt the bumps of the road through my forehead. There were so many passengers on the bus. I didn't want them to see me crying. I thought my relationship had gone too far; I couldn't keep going like this. We'd only been together a few months and already I was crying on the bus. I never knew if she was going to let me sleep in the bed with her or if she was going to let me go in the morning. Sometimes she told me to sleep on the floor only to invite me into her bed later. She was always angry with me; I had always ruined whatever was planned. She said the most awful things about my writing, about my relationship with my family: "I'm not your father. I'm not your mother re-incarnate." I thought there was something really wrong with me. It was sunny south of San Francisco, the way it always is. Then I read the story again and cried some more.

Later I showed the story to others. Sometimes they liked it. More often they thought it was too sad. People don't like to be sad. More people disliked than liked it. But somehow throughout it all Thom Jones had come to explain the meaning of life, why it's important to enjoy what you have, what you mean and don't mean to the people around you, why life matters, that it's such a fleeting thing and you don't get to do it again. Simultaneously he described the meaningfulness and meaninglessness of it all. He had written a story that was so perfect that it exposed some of the most basic truths of human existence. I now knew what it felt like to learn you were going to die and the process of that long, painful slide into nothingness. When I was younger, starting when I was eight years old, I had watched my mother go through it over five years as she fought her swift, losing battle with Multiple Sclerosis. For most of that time she was laid up on the couch practically paralyzed, unable to even make it to the bathroom. I had grasped nothing at the time. I was too young and selfish. And yet here, in this short story, there it all was.

And I remember thinking, almost in San Francisco where the bus would leave us at 8th and Mission Street and I would walk the mile and a half back to my dirty studio, that happiness is bullshit. Not on a personal level; a person should strive to be happy. But in a story happiness was irrelevant. People work too hard to make their fiction funny. There's nothing wrong with funny but it's not what matters. The most important thing fiction can do is teach the truth, illuminate something that couldn't be discovered in any other way. I stopped thinking of ways to make *Happy Baby* funnier and more accessible. I cut every adjective, removed all traces of backstory. I wasn't going to explain the unnecessary. I was writing a book about a man who equated abuse with affection. I was exploring, through fiction, how that could happen and where that might come from. I wanted my reader to understand this condition and I wanted to understand it myself. I will never write anything as good as "I Want To Live" (which was in the *Best American Short Stories* that year as well as the *Best American*

Short Stories of the Century) but that doesn't mean I'm not going to strive toward its virtue.

I stayed with my girlfriend for almost a year after that. Our relationship was unsustainable and that we lasted as long as we did is a tribute to how far two people can go on passion alone. Before I met her I began my novel. Ironically, or maybe not, she left me to pursue a relationship that was more stable. It took me a little while to accept that and let her go but eventually I did. A month before we broke up *Happy Baby* came out and she decided she liked it after all.

———◆———

THE LADY OR THE TIGER?

Credit: Anonymous

In the very olden time there lived a semi-barbaric king, whose ideas, though somewhat polished and sharpened by the progressiveness of distant Latin neighbors, were still large, florid, and untrammeled, as became the half of him which was barbaric. He was a man of exuberant fancy, and, withal, of an authority so irresistible that, at his will, he turned his varied fancies into facts. He was greatly given to self-communing, and, when he and himself agreed upon anything, the thing was done. When every member of his domestic and political systems moved smoothly in its appointed course, his nature was bland and genial; but, whenever there was a little hitch, and some of his orbs got out of their orbits, he was blander and more genial still, for nothing pleased him so much as to make the crooked straight and crush down uneven places.

Among the borrowed notions by which his barbarism had become semified was that of the public arena, in which, by exhibitions of manly and beastly valor, the minds of his subjects were refined and cultured.

But even here the exuberant and barbaric fancy asserted itself. The arena of the king was built, not to give the people an opportunity of hearing the rhapsodies of dying gladiators, nor to enable them to view the inevitable conclusion of a conflict between religious opinions and hungry jaws, but for purposes far better adapted to widen and develop the mental energies of the people. This vast amphitheater, with its encircling galleries, its mysterious vaults, and its unseen passages, was an agent of poetic justice, in which crime was punished, or virtue rewarded, by the decrees of an impartial and incorruptible chance.

When a subject was accused of a crime of sufficient importance to interest the king, public notice was given that on an appointed day the fate of the accused person would be decided in the king's arena, a structure which well deserved its name, for, although its form and plan were borrowed from afar, its purpose emanated solely from the brain of this man, who, every barleycorn a king, knew no tradition to which he owed more allegiance than pleased his fancy, and who ingrafted on every adopted form of human thought and action the rich growth of his barbaric idealism.

When all the people had assembled in the galleries, and the king, surrounded by his court, sat high up on his throne of royal state on one side of the arena, he gave a signal, a door beneath him opened, and the accused subject stepped out into the amphitheater. Directly opposite him, on the other side of the enclosed space, were two doors, exactly alike and side by side. It was the duty and the privilege of the person on trial to walk directly to these doors and open one of them. He could open either door he pleased; he was subject to no guidance or influence but that of the aforementioned impartial and incorruptible chance. If he opened the one, there came out of it a hungry tiger, the fiercest and most cruel that could be procured, which immediately sprang upon him and tore him to pieces as a punishment for his guilt. The moment that the case of the criminal was thus decided, doleful iron bells were clanged, great wails went up from the hired mourners posted on the outer rim of the arena, and the vast audience, with bowed heads and downcast hearts, wended slowly their homeward way, mourning greatly that one so young and fair, or so old and respected, should have merited so dire a fate.

But, if the accused person opened the other door, there came forth from it a lady, the most suitable to his years and station that his majesty could select among his fair subjects, and to this lady he was immediately married, as a reward of his innocence. It mattered not that he might already possess a wife and family, or that his affections might be engaged upon an object of his own selection; the king allowed no such subordinate arrangements to interfere with his great scheme of retribution and reward. The exercises, as in the other instance, took place immediately, and in the arena. Another door opened beneath the king, and a priest, followed by a band of choristers, and dancing maidens blowing joyous airs on golden horns and treading an epithalamic measure, advanced to where the pair stood, side by side, and the wedding was promptly and cheerily solemnized. Then the gay brass bells rang forth their merry peals, the people shouted glad hurrahs, and the innocent man, preceded by children strewing flowers on his path, led his bride to his home.

This was the king's semi-barbaric method of administering justice. Its perfect fairness is obvious. The criminal could not know out of which door would come the lady; he opened either he pleased, without having the slightest idea whether, in the next instant, he was to be devoured or married. On some occasions the tiger came out of one door, and on some out of the other. The decisions of this tribunal were not only fair, they were positively determinate: the accused person was instantly punished if he found himself guilty, and, if innocent, he was rewarded on the spot, whether he liked it or not. There was no escape from the judgments of the king's arena.

The institution was a very popular one. When the people gathered together on one of the great trial days, they never knew whether they were to witness a bloody slaughter or a hilarious wedding. This element of uncertainty lent an interest to the occasion which it could not otherwise have attained. Thus, the masses were entertained and pleased, and the thinking part of the community could bring no charge of unfairness against this plan, for did not the accused person have the whole matter in his own hands?

This semi-barbaric king had a daughter as blooming as his most florid fancies, and with a soul as fervent and imperious as his own. As is usual in such cases, she was the apple of his eye, and was loved by him above all humanity. Among his courtiers was a young man of that fineness of blood and lowness of station common to the conventional heroes of romance who love royal maidens. This royal maiden was well satisfied with her lover, for he was handsome and brave to a degree unsurpassed in all this kingdom, and she loved him with an ardor that had enough of barbarism in it to make it exceedingly warm and strong. This love affair moved on happily for many months, until one day the king happened to discover its existence. He did not hesitate nor waver in regard to his duty in the premises. The youth was immediately cast into prison, and a day was appointed for his trial in the king's arena. This, of course, was an especially important occasion, and his majesty, as well as all the people, was greatly interested in the workings and development of this trial. Never before had such a case occurred; never before had a subject dared to love the daughter of the king. In after years such things became commonplace enough, but then they were in no slight degree novel and startling.

The tiger-cages of the kingdom were searched for the most savage and relentless beasts, from which the fiercest monster might be selected for the arena; and the ranks of maiden youth and beauty throughout the land were carefully surveyed by competent judges in order that the young man might have a fitting bride in case fate did not determine for him a different destiny. Of course, everybody knew that the deed with which the accused was charged had been done. He had loved the princess, and neither he, she, nor any one else, thought of denying the fact; but the king would not think of allowing any fact of this kind to interfere with the workings of the tribunal, in which he took such great delight and satisfaction. No matter how the affair turned out, the youth would be disposed of, and the king would take an aesthetic pleasure in watching the course of events, which would determine whether or not the young man had done wrong in allowing himself to love the princess.

The appointed day arrived. From far and near the people gathered, and thronged the great galleries of the arena, and crowds, unable to gain admittance, massed themselves against its outside walls. The king and his court were in their places, opposite the twin doors, those fateful portals, so terrible in their similarity.

All was ready. The signal was given. A door beneath the royal party opened, and the lover of the princess walked into the arena. Tall, beautiful, fair, his appearance was greeted with a low hum of admiration and anxiety. Half the audience had not known so grand a youth had lived among them. No wonder the princess loved him! What a terrible thing for him to be there!

As the youth advanced into the arena he turned, as the custom was, to bow to the king, but he did not think at all of that royal personage. His eyes were fixed upon the princess, who sat to the right of her father. Had it not been for the moiety of barbarism in her nature it is probable that lady would not have been there, but her intense and fervid soul would not allow her to be absent on an occasion in which she was so terribly interested. From the moment that the decree had gone forth that her lover should decide his fate in the king's arena, she had thought of nothing, night or day, but this great event and the various subjects connected with it. Possessed of more power, influence, and force of character than any one who had ever before been interested in such a case, she had done what no other person had done - she had possessed herself of the secret of the doors. She knew in which of the two rooms, that lay behind those doors, stood the cage of the tiger, with its open front, and in which waited the lady. Through these thick doors, heavily curtained with skins on the inside, it was impossible that any noise or suggestion should come from within to the person who should approach to raise the latch of one of them. But gold, and the power of a woman's will, had brought the secret to the princess.

And not only did she know in which room stood the lady ready to emerge, all blushing and radiant, should her door be opened, but she knew who the lady was. It was one of the fairest and loveliest of the damsels of the court who had been selected as the reward of the accused youth, should he be proved innocent of the crime of aspiring to one so far above him; and the princess hated her. Often had she seen, or imagined that she had seen, this fair creature throwing glances of admiration upon the person of her lover, and sometimes she thought these glances were perceived, and even returned. Now and then she had seen them talking together; it was but for a moment or two, but much can be said in a brief space; it may have been on most unimportant topics, but how could she know that? The girl was lovely, but she had dared to raise her eyes to the loved one of the princess; and, with all the intensity of the savage blood transmitted to her through long lines of wholly barbaric ancestors, she hated the woman who blushed and trembled behind that silent door.

When her lover turned and looked at her, and his eye met hers as she sat there, paler and whiter than any one in the vast ocean of anxious faces about her, he saw, by that power of quick perception which is given to those whose souls are one, that she knew behind which door

119

crouched the tiger, and behind which stood the lady. He had expected her to know it. He understood her nature, and his soul was assured that she would never rest until she had made plain to herself this thing, hidden to all other lookers-on, even to the king. The only hope for the youth in which there was any element of certainty was based upon the success of the princess in discovering this mystery; and the moment he looked upon her, he saw she had succeeded, as in his soul he knew she would succeed.

Then it was that his quick and anxious glance asked the question: "Which?" It was as plain to her as if he shouted it from where he stood. There was not an instant to be lost. The question was asked in a flash; it must be answered in another.Her right arm lay on the cushioned parapet before her. She raised her hand, and made a slight, quick movement toward the right. No one but her lover saw her. Every eye but his was fixed on the man in the arena.

He turned, and with a firm and rapid step he walked across the empty space. Every heart stopped beating, every breath was held, every eye was fixed immovably upon that man. Without the slightest hesitation, he went to the door on the right, and opened it.

Now, the point of the story is this: Did the tiger come out of that door, or did the lady?

The more we reflect upon this question, the harder it is to answer. It involves a study of the human heart which leads us through devious mazes of passion, out of which it is difficult to find our way. Think of it, fair reader, not as if the decision of the question depended upon yourself, but upon that hot-blooded, semi-barbaric princess, her soul at a white heat beneath the combined fires of despair and jealousy. She had lost him, but who should have him?

How often, in her waking hours and in her dreams, had she started in wild horror, and covered her face with her hands as she thought of her lover opening the door on the other side of which waited the cruel fangs of the tiger!

But how much oftener had she seen him at the other door! How in her grievous reveries had she gnashed her teeth, and torn her hair, when she saw his start of rapturous delight as he opened the door of the lady! How her soul had burned in agony when she had seen him rush to meet that woman, with her flushing cheek and sparkling eye of triumph; when she had seen him lead her forth, his whole frame kindled with the joy of recovered life; when she had heard the glad shouts from the multitude, and the wild ringing of the happy bells; when she had seen the priest, with his joyous followers, advance to the couple, and make them man and wife before her very eyes; and when she had seen them walk away together upon their path of flowers, followed by the tremendous shouts of the hilarious multitude, in which her one despairing shriek was lost and drowned! Would it not be better for him to die at once, and go to wait for her in the blessed regions of semi-barbaric futurity?

And yet, that awful tiger, those shrieks, that blood!

Her decision had been indicated in an instant, but it had been made after days and nights of anguished deliberation. She had known she would be asked, she had decided what she would answer, and, without the slightest hesitation, she had moved her hand to the right.

The question of her decision is one not to be lightly considered, and it is not for me to presume to set myself up as the one person able to answer it. And so I leave it with all of you: Which came out of the opened door - the lady, or the tiger?

———————◆———————

WHAT I SAW ON THE COUNTRY ROAD

Credit: Anonymous

While in University, I loved finding snakes (I was a biology student). So a friend from herpetology club showed me this road that he would "cruise" for snakes. Cruising is when you drive slowly down old back roads after dark looking for snakes that have slithered onto the warmer road to heat up. The road we took was about 4 miles and had around 4 houses on its entirety. We had taken a few laps on this road, and we were making our final pass. There are two houses near the beginning of the road, one at the end and one near the middle. We were getting close to the center house when we see movement on the left side of the road. There are a lot of animals (obviously) on this road so we aren't surprised to see this. However what shoots out is this kid, probably around 8 or 9 in torn blue jeans and a ripped dark t shirt.

He takes one look at us, and his face is a mix of fear and pain. He looked back really quickly from where he had come out of then booked it across the road. The guy I'm with gets out of the car chasing to see if he's alright and I pull the car up to the point where the boy went into the woods. I am starting to get out of the car when my friend walks quickly back from the trail and just says, "lets go, now!" We hop in the car and tear out of there. He says there is a grave yard about 10 yards into the woods where there are 5 grave stones with the same death date. They all had the same last name, and one was a boy who was 9. We never came back the rest of the summer to that road (we usually would go out once or twice a week).

The next year when my friend had graduated I took my girlfriend out to the road. We had gone early to try to find different types of snakes (different snakes tend to move at different points of dusk/night). We got to the house near the graveyard and these 3 men doing some yard work. I rolled down the window explained what I was doing and asked them about the graveyard. Apparently their Dad's brother's family had all died when their space heater caught fire around 20 years ago. I kept pushing and asking about it, and they told me the firemen or whoever does it had found all the bodies in the rubble except for the youngest son but they assumed he was too far burned. I asked if they had a little brother, and the 6'4" 250 pound man said he was the youngest. When I gave the description of the kid I saw and they all went white.

They all have individually seen the kid I was talking about. And he always runs to the gravesite. I have never been down that road again.

———————◆———————

A BEDTIME STORY
FOR ADULTS

Credit: Roxane Gay

Once upon a time in a far away place far away from anything there lived a boy and a girl.

No.

This is an adult story.

Once upon a time in a far away place, far away from anything, there lived a man and a woman. His name was Johann and hers was Elise. Johann had white skin and Elise's was brown. This didn't matter in the beginning, but over time, it would, first in small ways, tiny little cracks, and then in ways they could no longer ignore. Johann first saw Elise in a smoke filled room, and decided he wanted her, wanted to know the taste of her brown skin, wanted to run his hands over the soft curves of her ample body. Elise didn't believe him. She didn't believe in fairy tales or herself or much of anything. Johann chased her and chased her and finally, she let him take her to dinner because she was hungry. Elise let him have a drink at her house because she was lonely. She let him touch her because she was another kind of hungry. She lay with him and enjoyed the meat of his body against hers, how his rough hands held her sweetly, how his lips brushed her shoulder. Johann brought her pleasure and she brought him pleasure and after, he lay next to her, breathing heavy. Elise thanked him. She told him to leave. He did so but vowed to return, ignoring her protests.

Johann sent Elise a beautiful bouquet of fragrant wildflowers. She called and said thank you and please don't do that again but she set the flowers on the coffee table in her living room and smiled at them each day. He continued to call and sometimes she answered and they talked about all manner of things. Johann persisted in his pursuit and Elise finally relented and accompanied him to more dinners and sometimes, they had drinks and sometimes they saw moving pictures and she always let him spend the night. Soon, Elise had forgotten there ever was a time when she didn't want Johann around.

The man was so different. Elise often worried he was too different. Johann worked with his hands and had never been beyond the borders of the far away place far from anything. He knew things about the stars and the position of the sun. He knew about secret waterfalls in the heart of the deep woods and he showed them to her, let her drink that cool clean water from his rough, calloused hands. Elise worked with her mind and sometimes her heart. She knew about words and spent her days studying books. She spoke different languages and had traveled to lands across oceans and further even still. She longed to be closer to places where she could find bright lights and crowded streets and where once in a while she might see someone who looked like her. But Elise had a job to do and studies to complete. She would bide her time. Johann and Elise knew little of the same things but he knew how to touch her and how to press his lips to her neck and how to hold her as she slept and if all that mattered was the moments shared between them, they could have easily found a happily ever after.

There were, however, other things that mattered. Johann had a wicked mother who lived in a grand house high on a hill. She kept an extravagant garden and enjoyed receiving visitors in a large living room filled with large, imposing furniture. The wicked mother scowled more than she smiled. The wicked mother thought her son a king and wanted nothing but the best for her oldest boy. She did not think Elise was any kind of good enough and she let that be known throughout the land. Elise brought Johann's wicked mother gifts and kind words. She said please and thank you and when invited to dinner, she offered to wash the dishes. None of her gestures could sway the wicked mother who did not want Johann to love a woman with such different skin. It was a scandal, she said. Think of the family name, she said. Soon, Elise stopped going to the grand house high on the hill. She and Johann pretended the wicked mother didn't matter. Her displeasure was an unfortunate detail, they told themselves. They ignored the harsh words and the harsh thoughts. They pretended nothing could get in the way of their happy and ever after. On festive days though, when there was much to celebrate, Elise often found herself alone and waiting while Johann paid his respects and feted with his family. In those lonely moments, Elise wanted Johann to make a choice but she didn't dare ask, couldn't bear knowing he might not choose her.

There came a day when Elise learned she was carrying Johann's child. It was an unexpected but welcome blessing. When she told the Johann, he said his heart was so full it ached. He offered his hand in marriage and a place in his kingdom, at his side. Elise told him they would wait and see. She wanted to say yes. They began planning for a future and when they saw the doctor and heard the beating heart of their unborn child, they looked at each other and discovered they did share one thing—love. Johann and Elise were so blinded by their joy, they shared their good news with Johann's wicked mother who, upon hearing the news of a new heir in the kingdom, a bastard heir, she said, she narrowed her eyes into hard, black slits. She said no such child, a child from two terribly different worlds, would ever be recognized or loved by anyone under her reign. Elise held her hands against her stomach, tried to shield her beloved unborn child from such venomous words. The wicked mother banished Elise from her home and Johann stood by and said nothing, torn between his mother and would be wife. Elise hoped to find a way to forgive his silence. She would never forget.

It happened on an ordinary day full of extraordinary moments, a day when Johann painted the nursery a soft shade of pink for the child who would be a girl who would be named Emma. He stood in the room admiring his work, picturing his woman holding their child near the large window, perhaps staring up at the sky. Elise stood in the kitchen preparing her man a fine meal, humming to her baby, trusting in her joy. She was overcome by a sudden, terrible pain in the seat of her womb. It was a pain so sharp and precise, she couldn't make a single sound. The last moment Elise remembered was falling to her knees and thinking, "I cannot bear to lose this." Johann found her, on the floor, bleeding slowly, breathing shallow after their home filled with the smell of burning meat. They both mourned the loss of the child but instead of tearing them apart, their sorrow made them love each other better and more fiercely.

When she finished her studies, Elise told Johann she had to leave the far away place, far away from anything. She had been offered a position for which she had prepared her entire life. It was too hard to live amongst so many memories of what should have been. She didn't want to raise children in a place where its citizens would always look upon them as more hers than his. Johann said he understood. He said they would find a way to love each other across an impossible distance. She believed him. She trusted in her joy.

On the eve of her departure, Johann sat next to Elise on a wooden pier. They looked out on moonlit waters, their heads dizzy with wine. He said the most beautiful things she had ever heard a man say to a woman. He presented her with a ring, a beautiful diamond in the shape of a tear. He tried to slide the ring on her finger but it did not fit. Elise laughed, nervously, said it was a bad omen. Johann said they would fix the ring. He said it was just a detail, and details didn't matter. He said, please, take this ring, please stay here, with me, in my kingdom. Elise looked at the beautiful ring and thought of how she had never shared how much she loved him. She thought about how he made her forget all the tragedies that had befallen her before he loved her. She tried to stop herself but she cried and felt her heart falling apart.

Johann thought her tears meant she was saying yes. Elise handed Johann his ring, her hands shaking. She said, I can't stay; I cannot believe you asked. She said you do not know me at all; the details do matter. She said you should have asked if you could leave this place with me. Johann said he had never known any other kind of life. He said these were his people and this was his land. He said he would spend his life making her love that land the way he did, that his family would grow to accept her. He grew angry, said she was his, said he would never let her go. Elise held her stomach, remembered the child once growing there and how the loss of her bound them together so tightly. They sat together in silence, the night air cooling everything between them. She understood she had been right about fairy tales all along.

———◆———

A HUGE DINOSAURS IN MY BED

Credit: Richard & Esther Provencher

Andrew lay shivering in his bed. The sky was alive with booming sounds and brilliant flashes just outside his window.

Fifteen minutes ago he asked, "Mom, will the storm last long?"

"Please, don't worry," she said. "The weatherman promised it would pass over Truro quickly. Now get some sleep."

Except it didn't; and he couldn't.

Andrew listened to his alarm clock. "Tick…Tick…Tock." The night seemed to go on forever. Seconds turned into minutes.

Then into what seemed like hours.

Above the house, loud lightning crashes made him duck further under the blankets. Outside thunder even rattled his window.

Should he go into his parent's room? But then he was a big boy now. And he had to be brave. Dad even helped him prepare for this bad weather.

Just in case it lasted all night.

Now his backpack was hidden under the blankets. It was filled with favorite toys, games and comic books. Even "Panda" bear he had since the age of two.

Mom made sure Andrew also had a few goodies. A huge bag of popcorn was close to his right side. And a bag of rippled chips was on the other.

His family had gone tenting in Cape Breton, last weekend. So he was now a boy with camping experience. And he knew how to be brave.

What was moving around his toes? "Ouch, that hurt," his trembling voice, whispered. The noise outside was so loud Andrew could hardly think.

Through the window, a dark sky blocked out the stars.

The boy was suddenly nervous. What was under the blanket? He was curious and rummaged through his backpack.

"OMIGOSH," Andrew said. "I forgot my flashlight."

He slid out of bed and hurled himself across the floor. Andrew hunted around until he found it in the top dresser drawer.

Quickly jumping back into bed, he forced cold feet down to the very end. Bare toes rested on something rough and sharp. Now it seemed to be crawling around his ankles.

Yikes! He wasn't alone in bed!

He checked under the covers where it was black as coal, almost like being outside. Instead of gleaming stars lit up, spots looked more like eyes.

Roaring came from behind his left leg.

Andrew chewed on his left thumb and turned on the flashlight. "That terrifying sound couldn't be...?" he hesitated.

Yes, a dinosaur! But that was impossible, wasn't it? Dinosaurs couldn't fit under bed covers belonging to a little boy, living inside his house. Right?

Wrong. Staring back at him was a Stegosaurus. And it tasted his Hostess vinegar chips, the one small bag with a few morsels left.

"Get away, you!" Andrew bellowed, trying to be brave. The animal rumbled something back under the blanket-sky and hurried into a shadowy corner.

New noises caught the boy's attention. His flashlight helped pick out moving shadows. What was going on? he wondered. There was a Triceratops and a Deinonychus.

And a Tyranosaurus!

"Run!" Andrew yelled. Suddenly he felt like he was the only one alive on the planet. But he was still under his blanket that seemed to expand in the distance and even high above him.

He searched for somewhere to hide.

Cold feet could barely move. It was like a different world under the blankets. His heart marched to the beat of a drum. Lightning zipped then zapped under his blanket-sky.

Large animals began to chase smaller ones.

Racing toward him was a Dicraeosaurus. This was a peaceful plant eater and would not hurt him. But, Andrew couldn't take any chances.

He pulled a fire engine from his backpack. Jumping into the front seat, Andrew turned the siren on full velocity. All it did was hurt his ears.

A Ceratosaurus and Albertosaurus bounded after him. They were like large friendly dogs wanting to play. But Andrew didn't wish to get crushed.

He stepped on the gas pedal. And the fire engine leaped forward.

Soon, the road became a narrow path, aiming straight for the forest. Andrew quickly parked. Then he laced on new sneakers from his backpack.

He also brought his whistle. Shrill blowing warned everything to get out of his way. A flurry of feet escaped down the trail, each step pounding hard.

One arm held tightly to 'Panda.'

The wind blew off his cap sending it into the distance. Branches snatched at his face. He didn't want to get squashed or eaten by those dinosaurs.

The storm outside was nothing compared to wild animals chasing him under his blanket. How did all of this happen anyhow?

Growls and speeding feet kept pace behind him. Reaching into his backpack Andrew grabbed his roller blades. Now, he thought, it should be easy to skate away safely.

That is, until a sneaky tree root sent him headfirst into the mud.

Now it was hurry-up time to climb a tree.

"Mom, where are you?" Andrew shouted. "Daddd!" Skinny legs scrambled up the trunk. And like a monkey climbed higher from branch to branch.

Suddenly between two limbs was the head of a Brontosaurus. It smiled as it chewed a mouthful of leaves. "What's your problem?" it seemed to say.

"Andrew! ANDREWWW!" someone called. Voices seemed to move back and forth and around like echoes. Yes, people were shouting his name!

The boy hastily threw off his blankets, sat up, and stared at mom and dad. He blinked as morning's sun peeked between Venetian blinds.

"Panda" was still tucked securely under his arm.

"I see you found our surprises under your blankets," mom said.

Andrew looked blankly at his mom.

"You know. Remember the dinosaur models you asked for last week?"

"And I'm proud of you," dad said. "Look how neatly you stacked them on your dresser."

Andrew felt weird as dad pointed.

In a neat row was a parade of colorful dinosaurs. They were following a friendly Dicraeosaurus, with a ferocious looking Tyrannosaurus Rex at the end of the line.

Leading the whole group was a figure of a little boy. And he was holding tightly to a teddy bear.

———•◆•———

THE SWEET NIGHT DREAM

Credit: Richard & Esther Provencher

"If you're that worn out, then go to bed," mom said. And I did, even if darkness didn't come creeping yet outside my window. My arms were so weak I couldn't get my socks off. They kept sticking to my feet. So I crawled under the covers. When I'm very tired, I dream...

I have to go to the bank to get some money. Dad's birthday is tomorrow. And I want to buy him something super-dooper special.

"Hurry up," mom said, "before the bank closes." She always reminds me I have my own money. Sometimes I forget my bankbook says I still have $36 dollars left. The bus driver is very nice when I tell him I have no money. "But, I'll pay you back when I get some from the bank," I say.

We travel down busy streets, past tall buildings and I jump off the three steps from the bus. There is a long line of people at the bank. And the Teller's wicket looks like it is a mile away. So I count bushels of butterflies while waiting. Finally it's my turn. And I look up at this man behind the counter. He must be ten feet tall. At first I thought he was very nice.

"There's no money here for you," he said. "You must have spent it all."

"But...but, my mother said there's some left," I answered. "I saved it all myself, from my paper route."

"Then you should check with her again," said the man sternly. "Or, you must have come to the wrong bank," he said, showing off his teeth.

I looked into his eyes. And watched his smile. Was he pretending to be a sly coyote? Last summer, I saw one in a field near my house. The animal looked sneaky with his bushy tail.

On the way home I met a nice lady. When I told her my sad story, she felt sorry for me. She must have been rich because she gave me a whole suitcase full of money. I couldn't carry it all. So I gave her back one stack of paper money. In case she needed to buy a bag of chips, or go to a movie.

Now I don't have to go home. I have enough money to get an awesome gift for my dad. "Something really special," I say to a white rabbit, sitting on the seat beside me. I think he is following me home.

"You be careful, the coyote doesn't try to eat you," I say. I show him my teeth. But it doesn't scare him.

Around the corner, there is a little girl standing on the sidewalk. I get off the bus to see why she is crying. "My hands are cold," she said. So I bought her a pair of red mittens. She is so surprised she forgets to thank me.

Now I am hungry, and tired. So I sit down on the sidewalk and open my birthday gift knapsack. There is half an apple, a mustard sandwich, and two chocolate chip cookies. Soon my knapsack is empty, except for one crust of bread. It tries to hide in the corner.

"If only I had some blueberry jam," I told the bus driver waiting for me. "It would be delicious on this crust of bread."

"I'll take you to where blueberries are large. And juicy," he said.

The bus brought me far from the city, and across a busy highway. Even past fishing boats in the harbor. Then the bus drove up a gravel road. I watched a pheasant hurry across the road. We went past fields of hay and a high hill, and we finally stopped. The bus had a flat tire.

I got off and looked across a valley filled with blueberries. And waiting beside the first bush was that white rabbit. "How did he find me?" I wondered.

I quickly filled up my knapsack with juicy berries. My hands look like they are painted blue. And my back is sore from bending over so much. So I sat on a log and took off my right shoe and sock. Then I began to cry. I was afraid the coyote would come and bite my toe.

What was I doing here? I thought. There are no gifts for dad here. Besides, that sly coyote might find me. After running like thunder across a field I tripped over a log. Then fell into a little creek, with squishy mud. Was something chasing me? Maybe it was that white rabbit. I shook myself dry, the way my friend's dog does. Spotty is his name. I mean that's the dog's name. I heard more crying. But it sounded far away. My eyes were closed tightly. Just like the front door when I slam it.

Then I open my eyes, one at a time. Mom and dad are staring at me. The cat is on my bed. And I am too.

When I look out the window, the coyote's face is there. And he is laughing. I hug my mother. She begins to laugh too. Oh…Oh. I forgot to get Dad's present. Closing my eyes, I hurry back to my dreaming.

———•◆•———

THE VELVETEEN RABBIT

Credit: Margery Williams

This famous children's story starts out on Christmas morning. A young boy finds a stuffed rabbit nestled in his stocking. He loves the rabbit but forgets about him when more glamorous and expensive Christmas presents arrive. But chance will intervene twice in this magical story about childhood toys and the transformative power of love.

There was once a velveteen rabbit, and in the beginning he was really splendid. He was fat and bunchy, as a rabbit should be; his coat was spotted brown and white, he had real thread whiskers, and his ears were lined with pink sateen. On Christmas morning, when he sat wedged in the top of the Boy's stocking, with a sprig of holly between his paws, the effect was charming.

There were other things in the stocking, nuts and oranges and a toy engine, and chocolate almonds and a clockwork mouse, but the Rabbit was quite the best of all. For at least two hours the Boy loved him, and then Aunts and Uncles came to dinner, and there was a great rustling of tissue paper and unwrapping of parcels, and in the excitement of looking at all the new presents the Velveteen Rabbit was forgotten.

For a long time he lived in the toy cupboard or on the nursery floor, and no one thought very much about him. He was naturally shy, and being only made of velveteen, some of the more expensive toys quite snubbed him. The mechanical toys were very superior, and looked down upon every one else; they were full of modern ideas, and pretended they were real. The model boat, who had lived through two seasons and lost most of his paint, caught the tone from them and never missed an opportunity of referring to his rigging in technical terms. The Rabbit could not claim to be a model of anything, for he didn't know that real rabbits existed; he thought they were all stuffed with sawdust like himself, and he understood that sawdust was quite out-of-date and should never be mentioned in modern circles. Even Timothy, the jointed wooden lion, who was made by the disabled soldiers, and should have had broader views, put on airs and pretended he was connected with Government. Between them all the poor little Rabbit was made to feel himself very insignificant and commonplace, and the only person who was kind to him at all was the Skin Horse.

The Skin Horse had lived longer in the nursery than any of the others. He was so old that his brown coat was bald in patches and showed the seams underneath, and most of the hairs in his tail had been pulled out to string bead necklaces. He was wise, for he had seen a long succession of mechanical toys arrive to boast and swagger, and by-and-by break their mainsprings and pass away, and he knew that they were only toys, and would never turn into anything else. For nursery magic is very strange and wonderful, and only those playthings that are old and wise and experienced like the Skin Horse understand all about it.

"What is REAL?" asked the Rabbit one day, when they were lying side by side near the nursery fender, before Nana came to tidy the room. "Does it mean having things that buzz inside you and a stick-out handle?"

"Real isn't how you are made," said the Skin Horse. "It's a thing that happens to you. When a child loves you for a long, long time, not just to play with, but REALLY loves you, then you become Real."

"Does it hurt?" asked the Rabbit.

"Sometimes," said the Skin Horse, for he was always truthful. "When you are Real you don't mind being hurt."

"Does it happen all at once, like being wound up," he asked, "or bit by bit?"

"It doesn't happen all at once," said the Skin Horse. "You become. It takes a long time. That's why it doesn't often happen to people who break easily, or have sharp edges, or who have to be carefully kept. Generally, by the time you are Real, most of your hair has been loved off and your eyes drop out and you get loose in the joints and very shabby. But these things don't matter at all, because once you are Real you can't be ugly, except to people who don't understand."

"I suppose *you* are Real?" said the Rabbit. And then he wished he had not said it, for he thought the Skin Horse might be sensitive. But the Skin Horse only smiled. "The Boy's Uncle made me Real", he said. "That was a great many years ago; but once you are Real you can't become unreal again. It lasts for always."

The Rabbit sighed. He thought it would be a long time before this magic called Real happened to him. He longed to become Real, to know what it felt like; and yet the idea of growing shabby and losing his eyes and whiskers was rather sad. He wished that he could become it without these uncomfortable things happening to him.

There was a person called Nana who ruled the nursery. Sometimes she took no notice of the playthings lying about, and sometimes, for no reason whatever, she went swooping about like a great wind and hustled them away in cupboards. She called this "tidying up," and the playthings all hated it, especially the tin ones. The Rabbit didn't mind it so much, for wherever he was thrown he came down soft.

One evening, when the Boy was going to bed, he couldn't find the china dog that always slept with him. Nana was in a hurry, and it was too much trouble to hunt for china dogs at bedtime, so she simply looked about her, and seeing that the toy cupboard door stood open, she made a swoop.

"Here", she said, "take your old Bunny! He'll do to sleep with you!" And she dragged the Rabbit out by one ear, and put him into the Boy's arms.

That night, and for many nights after, the Velveteen Rabbit slept in the Boy's bed. At first he found it rather uncomfortable, for the Boy hugged him very tight, and sometimes he rolled over on him, and sometimes he pushed him so far under the pillow that the Rabbit could scarcely breathe. And he missed, too, those long moonlight hours in the nursery, when all the house was silent, and his talks with the Skin Horse. But very soon he grew to like it, for the Boy used to talk to him, and made nice tunnels for him under the bedclothes that he said were like the burrows the real rabbits lived in. And they had splendid games together, in whispers, when Nana had gone away to her supper and left the nightlight burning on the mantelpiece. And when the Boy dropped off to sleep, the Rabbit would snuggle down close under his little warm chin and dream, with the Boy's hands clasped close round him all night long.

And so time went on, and the little Rabbit was very happy—so happy that he never noticed how his beautiful velveteen fur was getting shabbier and shabbier, and his tail coming unsewn, and all the pink rubbed off his nose where the Boy had kissed him.

Spring came, and they had long days in the garden, for wherever the Boy went the Rabbit went too. He had rides in the wheelbarrow, and picnics on the grass, and lovely fairy huts built for him under the raspberry canes behind the flower border. And once, when the Boy was called away suddenly to go out to tea, the Rabbit was left out on the lawn until long after dusk, and Nana had to come and look for him with the candle because the Boy couldn't go to sleep unless he was there. He was wet through with the dew and quite earthy from diving into the burrows the Boy had made for him in the flower bed, and Nana grumbled as she rubbed him off with a corner of her apron.

"You must have your old Bunny!" she said. "Fancy all that fuss for a toy!"

The Boy sat up in bed and stretched out his hands.

"Give me my Bunny!" he said. "You mustn't say that. He isn't a toy. He's REAL!"

When the little Rabbit heard that he was happy, for he knew that what the Skin Horse had said was true at last. The nursery magic had happened to him, and he was a toy no longer. He was Real. The Boy himself had said it.

That night he was almost too happy to sleep, and so much love stirred in his little sawdust heart that it almost burst. And into his boot-button eyes, that had long ago lost their polish, there came a look of wisdom and beauty, so that even Nana noticed it next morning when she picked him up, and said, "I declare if that old Bunny hasn't got quite a knowing expression!"

That was a wonderful Summer!

Near the house where they lived there was a wood, and in the long June evenings the Boy liked to go there after tea to play. He took the Velveteen Rabbit with him, and before he wandered off to pick flowers, or play at brigands among the trees, he always made the Rabbit a little nest somewhere among the bracken, where he would be quite cosy, for he was a kind-hearted little boy and he liked Bunny to be comfortable. One evening, while the Rabbit was lying there alone, watching the ants that ran to and fro between his velvet paws in the grass, he saw two strange beings creep out of the tall bracken near him.

They were rabbits like himself, but quite furry and brand-new. They must have been very well made, for their seams didn't show at all, and they changed shape in a queer way when they moved; one minute they were long and thin and the next minute fat and bunchy, instead of always staying the same like he did. Their feet padded softly on the ground, and they crept quite close to him, twitching their noses, while the Rabbit stared hard to see which side the clockwork stuck out, for he knew that people who jump generally have something to wind them up. But he couldn't see it. They were evidently a new kind of rabbit altogether.

They stared at him, and the little Rabbit stared back. And all the time their noses twitched.

"Why don't you get up and play with us?" one of them asked.

"I don't feel like it," said the Rabbit, for he didn't want to explain that he had no clockwork.

"Ho!" said the furry rabbit. "It's as easy as anything." And he gave a big hop sideways and stood on his hind legs.

"I don't believe you can!" he said.

"I can!" said the little Rabbit. "I can jump higher than anything!" He meant when the Boy threw him, but of course he didn't want to say so.

"Can you hop on your hind legs?" asked the furry rabbit.

That was a dreadful question, for the Velveteen Rabbit had no hind legs at all! The back of him was made all in one piece, like a pincushion. He sat still in the bracken, and hoped that the other rabbits wouldn't notice.

"I don't want to!" he said again.

But the wild rabbits have very sharp eyes. And this one stretched out his neck and looked.

"He hasn't got any hind legs!" he called out. "Fancy a rabbit without any hind legs!" And he began to laugh.

"I have!" cried the little Rabbit. "I have got hind legs! I am sitting on them!"

"Then stretch them out and show me, like this!" said the wild rabbit. And he began to whirl round and dance, till the little Rabbit got quite dizzy.

"I don't like dancing," he said. "I'd rather sit still!"

But all the while he was longing to dance, for a funny new tickly feeling ran through him, and he felt he would give anything in the world to be able to jump about like these rabbits did.

The strange rabbit stopped dancing, and came quite close. He came so close this time that his long whiskers brushed the Velveteen Rabbit's ear, and then he wrinkled his nose suddenly and flattened his ears and jumped backwards.

"He doesn't smell right!" he exclaimed. "He isn't a rabbit at all! He isn't real!"

"I *am* Real!" said the little Rabbit, "I am Real! The Boy said so!" And he nearly began to cry.

Just then there was a sound of footsteps, and the Boy ran past near them, and with a stamp of feet and a flash of white tails the two strange rabbits disappeared.

"Come back and play with me!" called the little Rabbit. "Oh, do came back! I *know* I am Real!"

But there was no answer, only the little ants ran to and fro, and the bracken swayed gently where the two strangers had passed. The Velveteen Rabbit was all alone.

"Oh, dear!" he thought. "Why did they run away like that? Why couldn't they stop and talk to me?" For a long time he lay very still, watching the bracken, and hoping that they would come back. But they never returned, and presently the sun sank lower and the little white moths fluttered out, and the Boy came and carried him home.

Weeks passed, and the little Rabbit grew very old and shabby, but the Boy loved him just as much. He loved him so hard that he loved all his whiskers off, and the pink lining to his ears turned grey, and his brown spots faded. He even began to lose his shape, and he scarcely looked like a rabbit any more, except to the Boy. To him he was always beautiful, and that was all that the little Rabbit cared about. He didn't mind how he looked to other people, because the nursery magic had made him Real, and when you are Real shabbiness doesn't matter.

And then, one day, the Boy was ill.

His face grew very flushed, and he talked in his sleep, and his little body was so hot that it burned the Rabbit when he held him close. Strange people came and went in the nursery, and a light burned all night, and through it all the little Velveteen Rabbit lay there, hidden from sight under the bedclothes, and he never stirred, for he was afraid that if they found him someone might take him away, and he knew that the Boy needed him.

It was a long weary time, for the Boy was too ill to play, and the little Rabbit found it rather dull with nothing to do all day long. But he snuggled down patiently, and looked forward to the time when the Boy should be well again, and they would go out in the garden amongst the flowers and the butterflies and play splendid games in the raspberry thicket like they used to. All sorts of delightful things he planned, and while the Boy lay half asleep he crept up close to the pillow and whispered them in his ear. And presently the fever turned, and the Boy got better. He was able to sit up in bed and look at picture books, while the little Rabbit cuddled close at his side. And one day, they let him get up and dress.

It was a bright, sunny morning, and the windows stood wide open. They had carried the Boy out on to the balcony, wrapped in a shawl, and the little Rabbit lay tangled up among the bedclothes, thinking.

The Boy was going to the seaside to-morrow. Everything was arranged, and now it only remained to carry out the doctor's orders. They talked about it all, while the little Rabbit lay under the bedclothes, with just his head peeping out, and listened. The room was to be disinfected, and all the books and toys that the Boy had played with in bed must be burnt.

"Hurrah!" thought the little Rabbit. "To-morrow we shall go to the seaside!" For the Boy had often talked of the seaside, and he wanted very much to see the big waves coming in, and the tiny crabs, and the sand castles.

Just then Nana caught sight of him.

"How about his old Bunny?" she asked.

"*That?*" said the doctor. "Why, it's a mass of scarlet fever germs!—Burn it at once. What? Nonsense! Get him a new one. He mustn't have that anymore!"

And so the little Rabbit was put into a sack with the old picture-books and a lot of rubbish, and carried out to the end of the garden behind the fowl-house. That was a fine place to make a bonfire, only the gardener was too busy just then to attend to it. He had the potatoes to dig and the green peas to gather, but next morning he promised to come quite early and burn the whole lot.

That night the Boy slept in a different bedroom, and he had a new bunny to sleep with him. It was a splendid bunny, all white plush with real glass eyes, but the Boy was too excited to care very much about it. For to-morrow he was going to the seaside, and that in itself was such a wonderful thing that he could think of nothing else.

And while the Boy was asleep, dreaming of the seaside, the little Rabbit lay among the old picture-books in the corner behind the fowl house, and he felt very lonely. The sack had been left untied, and so by wriggling a bit he was able to get his head through the opening and look out. He was shivering a little, for he had always been used to sleeping in a proper bed, and by this time his coat had worn so thin and threadbare from hugging that it was no longer any protection to him. Near by he could see the thicket of raspberry canes, growing tall and close like a tropical jungle, in whose shadow he had played with the Boy on bygone mornings. He thought of those long sunlit hours in the garden—how happy they were—and a great sadness came over him. He seemed to see them all pass before him, each more beautiful than the other, the fairy huts in the flower-bed, the quiet evenings in the wood when he lay in the bracken and the little ants ran over his paws; the wonderful day when he first knew that he was Real. He thought of the Skin Horse, so wise and gentle, and all that he had told him. Of what use was it to be loved and lose one's beauty and become Real if it all ended like this? And a tear, a real tear, trickled down his little shabby velvet nose and fell to the ground.

And then a strange thing happened. For where the tear had fallen a flower grew out of the ground, a mysterious flower, not at all like any that grew in the garden. It had slender green leaves the colour of emeralds, and in the centre of the leaves a blossom like a golden cup. It was so beautiful that the little Rabbit forgot to cry, and just lay there watching it. And presently the blossom opened, and out of it there stepped a fairy.

She was quite the loveliest fairy in the whole world. Her dress was of pearl and dewdrops, and there were flowers round her neck and in her hair, and her face was like the most perfect flower of all. And she came close to the little Rabbit and gathered him up in her arms and kissed him on his velveteen nose that was all damp from crying.

"Little Rabbit," she said, "don't you know who I am?"

The Rabbit looked up at her, and it seemed to him that he had seen her face before, but he couldn't think where.

"I am the nursery magic Fairy," she said. "I take care of all the playthings that the children have loved. When they are old and worn out and the children don't need them any more, then I come and take them away with me and turn them into Real."

"Wasn't I Real before?" asked the little Rabbit.

"You were Real to the Boy," the Fairy said, "because he loved you. Now you shall be real to every one."

And she held the little Rabbit close in her arms and flew with him into the wood.

It was light now, for the moon had risen. All the forest was beautiful, and the fronds of the bracken shone like frosted silver. In the open glade between the tree-trunks the wild rabbits danced with their shadows on the velvet grass, but when they saw the Fairy they all stopped dancing and stood round in a ring to stare at her.

"I've brought you a new playfellow," the Fairy said. "You must be very kind to him and teach him all he needs to know in Rabbitland, for he is going to live with you for ever and ever!"

And she kissed the little Rabbit again and put him down on the grass.

"Run and play, little Rabbit!" she said.

But the little Rabbit sat quite still for a moment and never moved. For when he saw all the wild rabbits dancing around him he suddenly remembered about his hind legs, and he didn't want them to see that he was made all in one piece. He did not know that when the Fairy kissed him that last time she had changed him altogether. And he might have sat there a long time, too shy to move, if just then something hadn't tickled his nose, and before he thought what he was doing he lifted his hind toe to scratch it.

And he found that he actually had hind legs! Instead of dingy velveteen he had brown fur, soft and shiny, his ears twitched by themselves, and his whiskers were so long that they brushed the grass. He gave one leap and the joy of using those hind legs was so great that he went springing about the turf on them, jumping sideways and whirling round as the others did, and he grew so excited that when at last he did stop to look for the Fairy she had gone.

He was a Real Rabbit at last, at home with the other rabbits.

Autumn passed and Winter, and in the Spring, when the days grew warm and sunny, the Boy went out to play in the wood behind the house. And while he was playing, two rabbits crept out from the bracken and peeped at him. One of them was brown all over, but the other had strange markings under his fur, as though long ago he had been spotted, and the spots still showed through. And about his little soft nose and his round black eyes there was something familiar, so that the Boy thought to himself:

"Why, he looks just like my old Bunny that was lost when I had scarlet fever!"

But he never knew that it really was his own Bunny, come back to look at the child who had first helped him to be Real.

———— ♦ ————

THE THREE LITTLE PIGS

Credit: Flora Annie Steel

Once upon a time there was an old mother pig that had three little pigs and not enough food to feed them. So when they were old enough, she sent them out into the world to seek their fortunes.

The first little pig was very lazy. He didn't want to work at all and he built his house out of straw. The second little pig worked a little bit harder but he was somewhat lazy too and he built his house out of sticks. Then, they sang and danced and played together the rest of the day.

The third little pig worked hard all day and built his house with bricks. It was a sturdy house complete with a fine fireplace and chimney. It looked like it could withstand the strongest winds.

The next day, a wolf happened to pass by the lane where the three little pigs lived; and he saw the straw house, and he smelled the pig inside. He thought the pig would make a mighty fine meal and his mouth began to water.

So he knocked on the door and said:

"Little pig! Little pig!

Let me in! Let me in!"

But the little pig saw the wolf's big paws through the keyhole, so he answered back:

"No! No! No!

Not by the hairs on my chinny chin chin!"

Then the wolf showed his teeth and said:

"Then I'll huff

and I'll puff

and I'll blow your house down."

So he huffed and he puffed and he blew the house down! The wolf opened his jaws very wide and bit down as hard as he could, but the first little pig escaped and ran away to hide with the second little pig.

The wolf continued down the lane and he passed by the second house made of sticks; and he saw the house, and he smelled the pigs inside, and his mouth began to water as he thought about the fine dinner they would make.

So he knocked on the door and said:

"Little pigs! Little pigs!

Let me in! Let me in!"

But the little pigs saw the wolf's pointy ears through the keyhole, so they answered back:

"No! No! No!

Not by the hairs on our chinny chin chin!"

So the wolf showed his teeth and said:

"Then I'll huff

and I'll puff

and I'll blow your house down."

So he huffed and he puffed and he blew the house down! The wolf was greedy and he tried to catch both pigs at once, but he was too greedy and got neither! His big jaws clamped down on nothing but air and the two little pigs scrambled away as fast as their little hooves would carry them.

The wolf chased them down the lane and he almost caught them. But they made it to the brick house and slammed the door closed before the wolf could catch them. The three little pigs they were very frightened, they knew the wolf wanted to eat them. And that was very, very true. The wolf hadn't eaten all day and he had worked up a large appetite chasing the pigs around and now he could smell all three of them inside and he knew that the three little pigs would make a lovely feast.

So the wolf knocked on the door and said:

"Little pigs! Little pigs!

Let me in! Let me in!"

But the little pigs saw the wolf's narrow eyes through the keyhole, so they answered back:

"No! No! No!

Not by the hairs on our chinny chin chin!"

So the wolf showed his teeth and said:

"Then I'll huff

and I'll puff

and I'll blow your house down."

Well! he huffed and he puffed. He puffed and he huffed. And he huffed, huffed, and he puffed, puffed;

but he could not blow the house down. At last, he was so out of breath that he couldn't huff and he couldn't puff anymore. So he stopped to rest and thought a bit.

But this was too much. The wolf danced about with rage and swore he would come down the chimney and eat up the little pig for his supper. But while he was climbing on to the roof the little pig made up a blazing fire and put on a big pot full of water to boil. Then, just as the wolf was coming down the chimney, the little piggy pulled off the lid, and plop! in fell the wolf into the scalding water.

So the little piggy put on the cover again, boiled the wolf up, and the three little pigs ate him for supper.

———————♦———————

THE GINGERBREAD MAN

Credit: Anonymous

ONE day, the cook went into the kitchen to make some gingerbread. She took some flour and water, and treacle and ginger, and mixed them all well together, and she put in some more water to make it thin, and then some more flour to make it thick, and a little salt and some spice, and then she rolled it out into a beautiful, smooth, dark-yellow dough.

Then she took the square tins and cut out some square cakes for the little boys, and with some round tins she cut out some round cakes for the little girls, and then she said, "I'm going to make a little gingerbread man for little Bobby." So she took a nice round lump of dough for his body, and a smaller lump for his head, which she pulled out a little for the neck. Two other lumps were stuck on beneath for the legs, and were pulled out into proper shape, with feet and toes all complete, and two still smaller pieces were made into arms, with dear little hands and fingers.

But the nicest work was done on the head, for the top was frizzed up into a pretty sugary hat; on either side was made a dear little ear, and in front, after the nose had been carefully moulded, a beautiful mouth was made out of a big raisin, and two bright little eyes with burnt almonds and caraway seeds.

Then the gingerbread man was finished ready for baking, and a very jolly little man he was. In fact, he looked so sly that the cook was afraid he was plotting some mischief, and when the batter was ready for the oven, she put in the square cakes and she put in the round cakes; and then she put in the little gingerbread man in a far back corner, where he couldn't get away in a hurry.

Then she went up to sweep the parlor, and she swept and she swept till the clock struck twelve, when she dropped her broom in a hurry, and exclaiming, "Lawks! the gingerbread will be all baked to a cinder," she ran down into the kitchen, and threw open the oven door. And the square cakes were all done, nice and hard and brown, and the round cakes were all done, nice and hard and brown, and the gingerbread man was all done too, nice and hard and brown; and he was standing up in his corner, with his little caraway-seed eyes sparkling, and his raisin mouth bubbling over with mischief, while he waited for the oven door to be opened. The instant the door was opened, with a hop, skip, and a jump, he went right over the square cakes and the round cakes, and over the cook's arm, and before she could say "Jack Robinson" he was running across the kitchen floor, as fast as his little legs would carry him, towards the back door, which was standing wide open, and through which he could see the garden path.

"Run, Run, Fast As You Can. You Can't Catch Me, I'm The Gingerbread Man!"

The old cook turned round as fast as she could, which wasn't very fast, for she was rather a heavy woman and she had been quite taken by surprise, and she saw lying right across the door-way, fast asleep in the sun, old Mouser, the cat.

"Mouser, Mouser," she cried, "stop the gingerbread man! I want him for little Bobby." When the cook first called, Mouser thought it was only some one calling in her dreams, and simply rolled over lazily; and the cook called again, "Mouser, Mouser!" The old cat sprang up with a jump, but just as she turned round to ask the cook what all the noise was about, the little gingerbread man cleverly jumped under her tail, and in an instant was trotting down the garden walk. Mouser turned in a hurry and ran after, although she was still rather too sleepy to know what it was she was trying to catch, and after the cat came the cook, lumbering along rather heavily, but also making pretty good speed.

Now at the bottom of the walk, lying fast asleep in the sun against the warm stones of the garden wall, was Towser, the dog.

And the cook called out: "Towser, Towser, stop the gingerbread man! I want him for little Bobby."

And when Towser first heard her calling he thought it was some one speaking in his dreams, and he only turned over on his side, with another snore, and then the cook called again, "Towser, Towser, stop him, stop him!"

Then the dog woke up in good earnest, and jumped up on his feet to see what it was that he should stop. But just as the dog jumped up, the little gingerbread man, who had been watching for the chance, quietly slipped between his legs, and climbed up on the top of the stone wall, so that Towser saw nothing but the cat running

162

towards him down the walk, and behind the cat the cook, now quite out of breath.

"Run, Run, Fast As You Can. You Can't Catch Me, I'm The Gingerbread Man!"

He thought at once that the cat must have stolen something, and that it was the cat the cook wanted him to stop. Now, if there was anything that Towser liked, it was going after the cat, and he jumped up the walk so fiercely that the poor cat did not have time to stop herself or to get out of his way, and they came together with a great fizzing, and barking, and meowing, and howling, and scratching, and biting, as if a couple of Catherine-wheels had gone off in the wrong way and had got mixed up with one another.

But the old cook had been running so hard that she was not able to stop herself any better than the cat had done, and she fell right on top of the mixed up dog and cat, so that all three rolled over on the walk in a heap together.

And the cat scratched whichever came nearest, whether it was a piece of the dog or of the cook, and the dog bit at whatever came nearest, whether it was a piece of the cat or of the cook, so that the poor cook was badly pummelled on both sides.

Meanwhile, the gingerbread man had climbed up on the garden wall, and stood on the top with his hands in his pockets, looking at the scrimmage, and laughing till the tears ran down from his little caraway-seed eyes and his raisin mouth was bubbling all over with fun.

"Run, Run, Fast As You Can. You Can't Catch Me, I'm The Gingerbread Man!"

After a little while, the cat managed to pull herself out from under the cook and the dog, and a very cast-down and crumpled-up-looking cat she was. She had had enough of hunting gingerbread men, and she crept back to the kitchen to repair damages.

The dog, who was very cross because his face had been badly scratched, let go of the cook, and at last, catching sight of the gingerbread man, made a bolt for the garden wall. The cook picked herself up, and although her face was also badly scratched and her dress was torn, she was determined to see the end of the chase, and she followed after the dog, though this time more slowly.

When the gingerbread man saw the dog coming, he jumped down on the farther side of the wall, and began running across the field. Now in the middle of the field was a tree, and at the foot of the tree was lying Jocko, the monkey. He wasn't asleep—monkeys never are— and when he saw the little man running across the field and heard the cook calling, "Jocko, Jocko, stop the gingerbread man," he at once gave one big jump. But he jumped so fast and so far that he went right over the gingerbread man, and as luck would have it, he came down on the back of Towser, the dog, who had just scrambled over the wall, and whom he had not before noticed. Towser was naturally taken by surprise, but he turned his head around and promptly bit off the end of the monkey's tail, and Jocko quickly jumped off again, chattering his indignation.

Meanwhile, the gingerbread man had got to the bottom of the tree, and was saying to himself: "Now, I know the dog can't climb a tree, and I don't believe the old cook can climb a tree; and as for the monkey I'm not sure, for I've never seen a monkey before, but I am going up."

So he pulled himself up hand over hand until he had got to the topmost branch.

"Climb, Climb, Fast As You Can. You Can't Catch Me, I'm The Gingerbread Man!"

But the monkey had jumped with one spring onto the lowest branch, and in an instant he also was at the top of the tree.The gingerbread man crawled out to the furthermost end of the branch, and hung by one hand, but the monkey swung himself under the branch, and stretching out his long arm, he pulled the gingerbread man in. Then he held him up and looked at him so hungrily that the little raisin mouth began to pucker down at the corners, and the caraway-seed eyes filled with tears.And then what do you think happened? Why, little Bobby himself came running up. He had been taking his noon-day nap upstairs, and in his dreams it seemed as if he kept hearing people call "Little Bobby, little Bobby!" until finally he jumped up with a start, and was so sure that some one was calling him that he ran down-stairs, without even waiting to put on his shoes.

As he came down, he could see through the window in the field beyond the garden the cook, and the dog, and the monkey, and could even hear the barking of Towser and the chattering of Jocko. He scampered down the walk, with his little bare feet pattering against the warm gravel, climbed over the wall, and in a few seconds arrived under the tree, just as Jocko was holding up the poor little gingerbread man."Drop it, Jocko!" cried Bobby, and drop it Jocko did, for he always had to mind Bobby. He dropped it so straight that the gingerbread man fell right into Bobby's uplifted pinafore.Then Bobby held him up and looked at him, and the little raisin mouth puckered down lower than ever, and the tears ran right out of the caraway-seed eyes.But Bobby was too hungry to mind gingerbread tears, and he gave one big bite, and swallowed down both legs and a piece of the body.

"OH!" said the gingerbread man, "I'm One-Third Gone!"

Bobby gave a second bite, and swallowed the rest of the body and the arms.

"OH!" said the gingerbread man, "I'm Two-Thirds Gone!"

Bobby gave a third bite, and gulped down the head.

"OH!" said the gingerbread man, "I'm All Gone!"

And so he was—and that is the end of the story.

THE HORRIBLE DRAGON'S TEETH

Credit: Nathaniel Hawthorne

Cadmus, Phoenix, and Cilix, the three sons of King Agenor, and their little sister Europa (who was a very beautiful child), were at play together near the seashore in their father's kingdom of Phoenicia. They had rambled to some distance from the palace where their parents dwelt, and were now in a verdant meadow, on one side of which lay the sea, all sparkling and dimpling in the sunshine, and murmuring gently against the beach. The three boys were very happy, gathering flowers, and twining them into garlands, with which they adorned the little Europa. Seated on the grass, the child was almost hidden under an abundance of buds and blossoms, whence her rosy face peeped merrily out, and, as Cadmus said, was the prettiest of all the flowers.

Just then, there came a splendid butterfly, fluttering along the meadow; and Cadmus, Phoenix, and Cilix set off in pursuit of it, crying out that it was a flower with wings. Europa, who was a little wearied with playing all day long, did not chase the butterfly with her brothers, but sat still where they had left her, and closed her eyes. For a while, she listened to the pleasant murmur of the sea, which was like a voice saying "Hush!" and bidding her go to sleep. But the pretty child, if she slept at all, could not have slept more than a moment, when she heard something trample on the grass, not far from her, and, peeping out from the heap of flowers, beheld a snow-white bull.

And whence could this bull have come? Europa and her brothers had been a long time playing in the meadow, and had seen no cattle, nor other living thing, either there or on the neighboring hills.

"Brother Cadmus!" cried Europa, starting up out of the midst of the roses and lilies. "Phoenix! Cilix! Where are you all? Help! Help! Come and drive away this bull!"

But her brothers were too far off to hear; especially as the fright took away Europa's voice, and hindered her from calling very loudly. So there she stood, with her pretty mouth wide open, as pale as the white lilies that were twisted among the other flowers in her garlands.

Nevertheless, it was the suddenness with which she had perceived the bull, rather than anything frightful in his appearance, that caused Europa so much alarm. On looking at him more attentively, she began to see that he was a beautiful animal, and even fancied a particularly amiable expression in his face. As for his breath--the breath of cattle, you know, is always sweet--it was as fragrant as if he had been grazing on no other food than rosebuds, or at least, the most delicate of clover blossoms. Never before did a bull have such bright and tender eyes, and such smooth horns of ivory, as this one. And the bull ran little races, and capered sportively around the child; so that she quite forgot how big and strong he was, and, from the gentleness and playfulness of his actions, soon came to consider him as innocent a creature as a pet lamb.

Thus, frightened as she at first was, you might by and by have seen Europa stroking the bull's forehead with her small white hand, and taking the garlands off her own head to hang them on his neck and ivory horns. Then she pulled up some blades of grass, and he ate them out of her hand, not as if he were hungry, but because he wanted to be friends with the child, and took pleasure in eating what she had touched. Well, my stars! was there ever such a gentle, sweet, pretty, and amiable creature as this bull, and ever such a nice playmate for a little girl?

When the animal saw (for the bull had so much intelligence that it is really wonderful to think of), when he saw that Europa was no longer afraid of him, he grew overjoyed, and could hardly contain himself for delight. He frisked about the meadow, now here, now there, making sprightly leaps, with as little effort as a bird expends in hopping from twig to twig. Indeed, his motion was as light as if he were flying through the air, and his hoofs seemed hardly to leave their print in the grassy soil over which he trod. With his spotless hue, he resembled a snow drift, wafted along by the wind. Once he galloped so far away that Europa feared lest she might never see him again; so, setting up her childish voice, called him back.

"Come back, pretty creature!" she cried. "Here is a nice clover blossom."

And then it was delightful to witness the gratitude of this amiable bull, and how he was so full of joy and thankfulness that he capered higher than ever. He came running, and bowed his head before Europa, as if he knew her to be a king's daughter, or else recognized the important truth that a little girl is everybody's queen. And not only did the bull bend his neck, he absolutely knelt down at her feet, and made such intelligent nods, and other inviting gestures, that Europa understood what he meant just as well as if he had put it in so many words.

"Come, dear child," was what he wanted to say, "let me give you a ride on my back."

At the first thought of such a thing, Europa drew back. But then she considered in her wise little head that there could be no possible harm in taking just one gallop on the back of this docile and friendly animal, who would certainly set her down the very instant she desired it. And how it would surprise her brothers to see her riding across the green meadow! And what merry times they might have, either taking turns for a gallop, or clambering on the gentle creature, all four children together, and careering round the field with shouts of laughter that would be heard as far off as King Agenor's palace!

"I think I will do it," said the child to herself.

And, indeed, why not? She cast a glance around, and caught a glimpse of Cadmus, Phoenix, and Cilix, who were still in pursuit of the butterfly, almost at the other end of the meadow. It would be the quickest way of rejoining them, to get upon the white bull's back. She came a step nearer to him therefore; and--sociable creature that he was--he showed so much joy at this mark of her confidence, that the child could not find in her heart to hesitate any longer. Making one bound (for this little princess was as active as a squirrel), there sat Europa on the beautiful bull, holding an ivory horn in each hand, lest she should fall off.

"Softly, pretty bull, softly!" she said, rather frightened at what she had done. "Do not gallop too fast."

Having got the child on his back, the animal gave a leap into the air, and came down so like a feather that Europa did not know when his hoofs touched the ground. He then began a race to that part of the flowery plain where her three brothers were, and where they had just caught their splendid butterfly. Europa screamed with delight; and Phoenix, Cilix, and Cadmus stood gaping at the spectacle of their sister mounted on a white bull, not knowing whether to be frightened or to wish the same good luck for themselves. The gentle and innocent creature (for who could possibly doubt that he was so?) pranced round among the children as sportively as a kitten. Europa all the while looked down upon her brothers, nodding and laughing, but yet with a sort of stateliness in her rosy little face. As the bull wheeled about to take another gallop across the meadow, the child waved her hand, and said, "Good-bye," playfully pretending that she was now bound on a distant journey, and might not see her brothers again for nobody could tell how long.

"Good-bye," shouted Cadmus, Phoenix, and Cilix, all in one breath.

But, together with her enjoyment of the sport, there was still a little remnant of fear in the child's heart; so that her last look at the three boys was a troubled one, and made them feel as if their dear sister were really leaving them forever. And what do you think the snowy bull did next? Why, he set off, as swift as the wind, straight down to the seashore, scampered across the sand, took an airy leap, and plunged right in among the foaming billows. The white spray rose in a shower over him and little Europa, and fell spattering down upon the water.

Then what a scream of terror did the poor child send forth! The three brothers screamed manfully, likewise, and ran to the shore as fast as their legs would carry them, with Cadmus at their head. But it was too late. When they reached the margin of the sand, the treacherous animal was already far away in the wide blue sea, with only his snowy head and tail emerging, and poor little Europa between them, stretching out one hand towards her dear brothers, while she grasped the bull's ivory horn with the other. And there stood Cadmus, Phoenix, and Cilix, gazing at this sad spectacle, through their tears, until they could no longer distinguish the bull's snowy head from the white-capped billows that seemed to boil up out of the sea's depths around him. Nothing more was ever seen of the white bull--nothing more of the beautiful child.

This was a mournful story, as you may well think, for the three boys to carry home to their parents. King

Agenor, their father, was the ruler of the whole country; but he loved his little daughter Europa better than his kingdom, or than all his other children, or than anything else in the world. Therefore, when Cadmus and his two brothers came crying home, and told him how that a white bull had carried off their sister, and swam with her over the sea, the king was quite beside himself with grief and rage. Although it was now twilight, and fast growing dark, he bade them set out instantly in search of her.

"Never shall you see my face again," he cried, "unless you bring me back my little Europa, to gladden me with her smiles and her pretty ways. Begone, and enter my presence no more, till you come leading her by the hand."

As King Agenor said this, his eyes flashed fire (for he was a very passionate king), and he looked so terribly angry that the poor boys did not even venture to ask for their suppers, but slunk away out of the palace, and only paused on the steps a moment to consult whither they should go first. While they were standing there, all in dismay, their mother, Queen Telephassa (who happened not to be by when they told the story to the king), came hurrying after them, and said that she too would go in quest of her daughter.

"O, no, mother!" cried the boys. "The night is dark, and there is no knowing what troubles and perils we may meet with."

"Alas! my dear children," answered poor Queen Telephassa; weeping bitterly, "that is only another reason why I should go with you. If I should lose you, too, as well as my little Europa, what would become of me!"

"And let me go likewise!" said their playfellow Thasus, who came running to join them.

Thasus was the son of a seafaring person in the neighborhood; he had been brought up with the young princes, and was their intimate friend, and loved Europa very much; so they consented that he should accompany them. The whole party, therefore, set forth together. Cadmus, Phoenix, Cilix, and Thasus clustered round Queen Telephassa, grasping her skirts, and begging her to lean upon their shoulders whenever she felt weary. In this manner they went down the palace steps, and began a journey, which turned out to be a great deal longer than they dreamed of. The last that they saw of King Agenor, he came to the door, with a servant holding a torch beside him, and called after them into the gathering darkness:

"Remember! Never ascend these steps again without the child!"

"Never!" sobbed Queen Telephassa; and the three brothers and Thasus answered, "Never! Never! Never! Never!"

And they kept their word. Year after year, King Agenor sat in the solitude of his beautiful palace, listening in vain for their returning footsteps, hoping to hear the familiar voice of the queen, and the cheerful talk of his sons and their playfellow Thasus, entering the door together, and the sweet, childish accents of little Europa in the midst of them. But so long a time went by, that, at last, if they had really come, the king would not have known that this was the voice of Telephassa, and these the younger voices that used to make such joyful echoes, when the children were playing about the palace. We must now leave King Agenor to sit on his throne, and must go along with Queen Telephassa, and her four youthful companions.

They went on and on, and traveled a long way, and passed over mountains and rivers, and sailed over seas. Here, and there, and everywhere, they made continual inquiry if any person could tell them what had become of Europa. The rustic people, of whom they asked this question, paused a little while from their labors in the field, and looked very much surprised. They thought it strange to behold a woman in the garb of a queen (for Telephassa in her haste had forgotten to take off her crown and her royal robes), roaming about the country, with four lads around her, on such an errand as this seemed to be. But nobody could give them any tidings of Europa; nobody had seen a little girl dressed like a princess, and mounted on a snow-white bull, which galloped as swiftly as the wind.

I cannot tell you how long Queen Telephassa, and Cadmus, Phoenix, and Cilix, her three sons, and Thasus, their playfellow, went wandering along the highways and bypaths, or through the pathless wildernesses of the earth, in this manner. But certain it is, that, before they reached any place of rest, their splendid garments were quite worn out. They all looked very much travel-stained, and would have had the dust of many countries on their shoes, if the streams, through which they waded, had not washed it all away. When they had been gone a year, Telephassa threw away her crown, because it chafed her forehead.

"It has given me many a headache," said the poor queen, "and it cannot cure my heartache."

As fast as their princely robes got torn and tattered, they exchanged them for such mean attire as ordinary people wore. By and by, they come to have a wild and homeless aspect; so that you would much sooner have taken them for a gypsy family than a queen and three princes, and a young nobleman, who had once a palace for a home, and a train of servants to do their bidding. The four boys grew up to be tall young men, with sunburnt faces. Each of them girded on a sword, to defend themselves against the perils of the way. When the husbandmen, at whose farmhouses they sought hospitality, needed their assistance in the harvest field, they gave it willingly; and Queen Telephassa (who had done no work in her palace, save to braid silk threads with golden ones) came behind them to bind the sheaves. If payment was offered, they shook their heads, and only asked for tidings of Europa.

"There are bulls enough in my pasture," the old farmers would reply; "but I never heard of one like this you tell me of. A snow-white bull with a little princess on his back! Ho! ho! I ask your pardon, good folks; but there never such a sight seen hereabouts."

At last, when his upper lip began to have the down on it, Phoenix grew weary of rambling hither and thither to no purpose. So one day, when they happened to be passing through a pleasant and solitary tract of country, he sat himself down on a heap of moss.

"I can go no farther," said Phoenix. "It is a mere foolish waste of life, to spend it as we do, always wandering up and down, and never coming to any home at nightfall. Our sister is lost, and never will be found. She probably perished in the sea; or, to whatever shore the white bull may have carried her, it is now so many years ago, that there would be neither love nor acquaintance between us, should we meet again. My father has forbidden us to return to his palace, so I shall build me a hut of branches, and dwell here."

"Well, son Phoenix," said Telephassa, sorrowfully, "you have grown to be a man, and must do as you judge best. But, for my part, I will still go in quest of my poor child."

"And we three will go along with you!" cried Cadmus and Cilix, and their faithful friend Thasus.

But, before setting out, they all helped Phoenix to build a habitation. When completed, it was a sweet rural bower, roofed overhead with an arch of living boughs. Inside there were two pleasant rooms, one of which had a soft heap of moss for a bed, while the other was furnished with a rustic seat or two, curiously fashioned out of the crooked roots of trees. So comfortable and home-like did it seem, that Telephassa and her three companions could not help sighing, to think that they must still roam about the world, instead of spending the remainder of their lives in some such cheerful abode as they had here built for Phoenix. But, when they bade him farewell, Phoenix shed tears, and probably regretted that he was no longer to keep them company.

However, he had fixed upon an admirable place to dwell in. And by and by there came other people, who chanced to have no homes; and, seeing how pleasant a spot it was, they built themselves huts in the neighborhood of Phoenix's habitation. Thus, before many years went by, a city had grown up there, in the center of which was seen a stately palace of marble, wherein dwelt Phoenix, clothed in a purple robe, and wearing a golden crown upon his head. For the inhabitants of the new city, finding that he had royal blood in his veins, had chosen him to be their king. The very first decree of state which King Phoenix issued was, that, if a maiden happened to arrive in the kingdom, mounted on a snow-white bull, and calling herself Europa, his subjects should treat her with the greatest kindness and respect, and immediately bring her to the palace. You may see, by this, that Phoenix's conscience never quite ceased to trouble him, for giving up the quest of his dear sister, and sitting himself down to be comfortable, while his mother and her companions went onward.

But often and often, at the close of a weary day's journey, did Telephassa and Cadmus, Cilix, and Thasus, remember the pleasant spot in which they had left Phoenix. It was a sorrowful prospect for these wanderers, that on the morrow they must again set forth, and that, after many nightfalls, they would perhaps be no nearer the close of their toilsome pilgrimage than now. These thoughts made them all melancholy at times, but appeared to torment Cilix more than the rest of the party. At length, one morning, when they were taking their staffs in hand to set out, he thus addressed them:

"My dear mother, and you, good brother Cadmus, and my friend Thasus, methinks we are like people in a dream. There is no substance in the life which we are leading. It is such a dreary length of time since the white bull carried off my sister Europa, that I have quite forgotten how she looked, and the tones of her voice, and, indeed, almost doubt whether such a little girl ever lived in the world. And whether she once lived or no, I am convinced that she no longer survives, and that therefore it is the merest folly to waste our own lives and happiness in seeking her. Were we to find her, she would now be a woman grown, and would look upon us all as strangers. So, to tell you the truth, I have resolved to take up my abode here; and I entreat you, mother, brother, and friend, to follow my example."

"Not I, for one," said Telephassa; although the poor queen, firmly as she spoke, was so travel-worn that she could hardly put her foot to the ground. "Not I, for one! In the depths of my heart, little Europa is still the rosy child who ran to gather flowers so many years ago. She has not grown to womanhood, nor forgotten me. At noon, at night, journeying onward, sitting down to rest, her childish voice is always in my ears, calling, 'Mother! mother!' Stop here who may, there is no repose for me."

"Nor for me," said Cadmus, "while my dear mother pleases to go onward."

And the faithful Thasus, too, was resolved to bear them company. They remained with Cilix a few days, however, and helped him to build a rustic bower, resembling the one which they had formerly built for Phoenix.

When they were bidding him farewell Cilix burst into tears, and told his mother that it seemed just as melancholy a dream to stay there, in solitude, as to go onward. If she really believed that they would ever find Europa, he was willing to continue the search with them, even now. But Telephassa bade him remain there, and be happy, if his own heart would let him. So the pilgrims took their leave of him, and departed, and were hardly out of sight before some other wandering people came along that way, and saw Cilix's habitation, and were greatly delighted with the appearance of the place. There being abundance of unoccupied ground in the neighborhood, these strangers built huts for themselves, and were soon joined by a multitude of new settlers, who quickly formed a city. In the middle of it was seen a magnificent palace of colored marble, on the balcony of which, every noontide, appeared Cilix, in a long purple robe, and with a jeweled crown upon his head; for the inhabitants, when they found out that he was a king's son, had considered him the fittest of all men to be a king himself.

One of the first acts of King Cilix's government was to send out an expedition, consisting of a grave ambassador, and an escort of bold and hardy young men, with orders to visit the principal kingdoms of the earth, and inquire whether a young maiden had passed through those regions, galloping swiftly on a white bull. It is, therefore, plain to my mind, that Cilix secretly blamed himself for giving up the search for Europa, as long as he was able to put one foot before the other.

As for Telephassa, and Cadmus, and the good Thasus, it grieves me to think of them, still keeping up that weary pilgrimage. The two young men did their best for the poor queen, helping her over the rough places, often carrying her across rivulets in their faithful arms and seeking to shelter her at nightfall, even when they themselves lay on the ground. Sad, sad it was to hear them asking of every passer-by if he had seen Europa, so long after the white bull had carried her away. But, though the gray years thrust themselves between, and made the child's figure dim in their remembrance, neither of these true-hearted three ever dreamed of giving up the search.

One morning, however, poor Thasus found that he had sprained his ankle, and could not possibly go a step farther.

"After a few days, to be sure," said he, mournfully, "I might make shift to hobble along with a stick. But that would only delay you, and perhaps hinder you from finding dear little Europa, after all your pains and trouble. Do you go forward, therefore, my beloved companions, and leave me to follow as I may."

"Thou hast been a true friend, dear Thasus," said Queen Telephassa, kissing his forehead. "Being neither my son, nor the brother of our lost Europa, thou hast shown thyself truer to me and her than Phoenix and Cilix did, whom we have left behind us. Without thy loving help, and that of my son Cadmus, my limbs could not have borne me half so far as this. Now, take thy rest, and be at peace. For--and it is the first time I have owned it to myself--I begin to question whether we shall ever find my beloved daughter in this world."

Saying this, the poor queen shed tears, because it was a grievous trial to the mother's heart to confess that her hopes were growing faint. From that day forward, Cadmus noticed that she never traveled with the same alacrity of spirit that had heretofore supported her. Her weight was heavier upon his arm.

Before setting out, Cadmus helped Thasus build a bower; while Telephassa, being too infirm to give any great assistance, advised them how to fit it up and furnish it, so that it might be as comfortable as a hut of branches could. Thasus, however, did not spend all his days in this green bower. For it happened to him, as to Phoenix and Cilix, that other homeless people visited the spot, and liked it, and built themselves habitations in the neighborhood. So here, in the course of a few years, was another thriving city, with a red freestone palace in the center of it, where Thasus sat upon a throne, doing justice to the people, with a purple robe over his shoulders, a sceptre in his hand, and a crown upon his head. The inhabitants had made him king, not for the sake of any royal blood (for none was in his veins), but because Thasus was an upright, true-hearted, and courageous man, and therefore fit to rule.

But when the affairs of his kingdom were all settled, King Thasus laid aside his purple robe and crown, and sceptre, and bade his worthiest subjects distribute justice to the people in his stead. Then, grasping the pilgrim's staff that had supported him so long, he set forth again, hoping still to discover some hoof-mark of the snow-white bull, some trace of the vanished child. He returned after a lengthened absence, and sat down wearily upon his throne. To his latest hour, nevertheless, King Thasus showed his true-hearted remembrance of Europa, by ordering that a fire should always be kept burning in his palace, and a bath steaming hot, and food ready to be served up, and a bed with snow-white sheets, in case the maiden should arrive, and require immediate refreshment. And, though Europa never came, the good Thasus had the blessings of many a poor traveler, who profited by the food and lodging which were meant for the little playmate of the king's boyhood.

Telephassa and Cadmus were now pursuing their weary way, with no companion but each other. The queen leaned heavily upon her son's arm, and could walk only a few miles a day. But for all her weakness and weariness, she would not be persuaded to give up the search. It was enough to bring tears into the eyes of bearded men to hear the melancholy tone with which she inquired of every stranger whether he could not tell her any news of the lost child.

"Have you seen a little girl--no, no, I mean a young maiden of full growth--passing by this way, mounted on a snow-white bull, which gallops as swiftly as the wind?"

"We have seen no such wondrous sight," the people would reply; and very often, taking Cadmus aside, they whispered to him, "Is this stately and sad-looking woman your mother? Surely she is not in her right mind; and you ought to take her home, and make her comfortable, and do your best to get this dream out of her fancy."

"It is no dream," said Cadmus. "Everything else is a dream, save that."

But, one day, Telephassa seemed feebler than usual, and leaned almost her whole weight on the arm of Cadmus, and walked more slowly than ever before. At last they reached a solitary spot, where she told her son that she must needs lie down, and take a good long rest.

"A good long rest!" she repeated, looking Cadmus tenderly in the face. "A good long rest, thou dearest one!"

"As long as you please, dear mother," answered Cadmus.

Telephassa bade him sit down on the turf beside her, and then she took his hand.

"My son," said she, fixing her dim eyes most lovingly upon him, "this rest that I speak of will be very long indeed! You must not wait till it is finished. Dear Cadmus, you do not comprehend me. You must make a grave here, and lay your mother's weary frame into it. My pilgrimage is over."

Cadmus burst into tears, and, for a long time, refused to believe that his dear mother was now to be taken from him. But Telephassa reasoned with him, and kissed him, and at length made him discern that it was better for her spirit to pass away out of the toil, the weariness, and grief, and disappointment which had burdened her on earth, ever since the child was lost. He therefore repressed his sorrow, and listened to her last words.

"Dearest Cadmus," said she, "thou hast been the truest son that ever mother had, and faithful to the very last. Who else would have borne with my infirmities as thou hast! It is owing to thy care, thou tenderest child, that my grave was not dug long years ago, in some valley, or on some hillside, that lies far, far behind us. It is enough. Thou shalt wander no more on this hopeless search. But, when thou hast laid thy mother in the earth, then go, my son, to Delphi, and inquire of the oracle what thou shalt do next."

"O mother, mother," cried Cadmus, "couldst thou but have seen my sister before this hour!"

"It matters little now," answered Telephassa, and there was a smile upon her face. "I go now to the better world, and, sooner or later, shall find my daughter there."

I will not sadden you, my little hearers, with telling how Telephassa died and was buried, but will only say, that her dying smile grew brighter, instead of vanishing from her dead face; so that Cadmus left convinced that, at her very first step into the better world, she had caught Europa in her arms. He planted some flowers on his mother's grave, and left them to grow there, and make the place beautiful, when he should be far away.

After performing this last sorrowful duty, he set forth alone, and took the road towards the famous oracle of Delphi, as Telephassa had advised him. On his way thither, he still inquired of most people whom he met whether they had seen Europa; for, to say the truth, Cadmus had grown so accustomed to ask the question, that it came to his lips as readily as a remark about the weather. He received various answers. Some told him one thing, and some another. Among the rest, a mariner affirmed, that, many years before, in a distant country, he had heard a rumor about a white bull, which came swimming across the sea with a child on his back, dressed up in flowers that were blighted by the sea water. He did not know what had become of the child or the bull; and Cadmus suspected, indeed, by a queer twinkle in the mariner's eyes, that he was putting a joke upon him, and had never really heard anything about the matter.

Poor Cadmus found it more wearisome to travel alone than to bear all his dear mother's weight, while she had kept him company. His heart, you will understand, was now so heavy that it seemed impossible, sometimes, to carry it any farther. But his limbs were strong and active, and well accustomed to exercise. He walked swiftly along, thinking of King Agenor and Queen Telephassa, and his brothers, and the friendly Thasus, all of whom he had left behind him, at one point of his pilgrimage or another, and never expected to see them any more. Full of these remembrances, he came within sight of a lofty mountain, which the people thereabouts told him was called Parnassus. On the slope of Mount

Parnassus was the famous Delphi, whither Cadmus was going.

This Delphi was supposed to be the very midmost spot of the whole world. The place of the oracle was a certain cavity in the mountain side, over which, when Cadmus came thither, he found a rude bower of branches. It reminded him of those which he had helped to build for Phoenix and Cilix, and afterwards for Thasus. In later times, when multitudes of people came from great distances to put questions to the oracle, a spacious temple of marble was erected over the spot. But in the days of Cadmus, as I have told you, there was only this rustic bower, with its abundance of green foliage, and a tuft of shrubbery, that ran wild over the mysterious hole in the hillside.

When Cadmus had thrust a passage through the tangled boughs, and made his way into the bower, he did not at first discern the half-hidden cavity. But soon he felt a cold stream of air rushing out of it, with so much force that it shook the ringlets on his cheek. Pulling away the shrubbery which clustered over the hole, he bent forward, and spoke in a distinct but reverential tone, as if addressing some unseen personage inside of the mountain.

"Sacred oracle of Delphi," said he, "whither shall I go next in quest of my dear sister Europa?"

There was at first a deep silence, and then a rushing sound, or a noise like a long sigh, proceeding out of the interior of the earth. This cavity, you must know, was looked upon as a sort of fountain of truth, which sometimes gushed out in audible words; although, for the most part, these words were such a riddle that they might just as well have staid at the bottom of the hole. But Cadmus was more fortunate than many others who went to Delphi in search of truth. By and by, the rushing noise began to sound like articulate language. It repeated, over and over again, the following sentence, which, after all, was so like the vague whistle of a blast of air, that Cadmus really did not quite know whether it meant anything or not:

"Seek her no more! Seek her no more! Seek her no more!"

"What, then, shall I do?" asked Cadmus.

For, ever since he was a child, you know, it had been the great object of his life to find his sister. From the very hour that he left following the butterfly in the meadow, near his father's palace, he had done his best to follow Europa, over land and sea. And now, if he must give up the search, he seemed to have no more business in the world.

But again the sighing gust of air grew into something like a hoarse voice.

"Follow the cow!" it said. "Follow the cow! Follow the cow!"

And when these words had been repeated until Cadmus was tired of hearing them (especially as he could not imagine what cow it was, or why he was to follow her), the gusty hole gave vent to another sentence.

"Where the stray cow lies down, there is your home."

These words were pronounced but a single time, and died away into a whisper before Cadmus was fully satisfied that he had caught the meaning. He put other questions, but received no answer; only the gust of wind sighed continually out of the cavity, and blew the withered leaves rustling along the ground before it.

"Did there really come any words out of the hole?" thought Cadmus; "or have I been dreaming all this while?"

He turned away from the oracle, and thought himself no wiser than when he came thither. Caring little what might happen to him, he took the first path that offered itself, and went along at a sluggish pace; for, having no object in view, nor any reason to go one way more than another, it would certainly have been foolish to make haste. Whenever he met anybody, the old question was at his tongue's end.

"Have you seen a beautiful maiden, dressed like a king's daughter, and mounted on a snow-white bull, that gallops as swiftly as the wind?"

But, remembering what the oracle had said, he only half uttered the words, and then mumbled the rest indistinctly; and from his confusion, people must have imagined that this handsome young man had lost his wits.

I know not how far Cadmus had gone, nor could he himself have told you, when at no great distance before him, he beheld a brindled cow. She was lying down by the wayside, and quietly chewing her cud; nor did she take any notice of the young man until he had approached pretty nigh. Then, getting leisurely upon her feet, and giving her head a gentle toss, she began to move along at a moderate pace, often pausing just long enough to crop a mouthful of grass. Cadmus loitered behind, whistling idly to himself, and scarcely noticing the cow; until the thought occurred to him, whether this could possibly be the animal which, according to the oracle's response, was to serve him for a guide. But he smiled at himself for fancying such a thing. He could not seriously think that this was the cow, because she went along so quietly, behaving just like any other cow. Evidently she neither knew nor cared so much as a wisp of hay about Cadmus, and was only thinking how to get her living along the wayside, where the herbage was green and fresh. Perhaps she was going home to be milked.

"Cow, cow, cow!" cried Cadmus. "Hey, Brindle, hey! Stop, my good cow!"

He wanted to come up with the cow, so as to examine her, and see if she would appear to know him, or whether there were any peculiarities to distinguish her from a thousand other cows, whose only business is to fill the milk-pail, and sometimes kick it over. But still the brindled cow trudged on, whisking her tail to keep the flies away, and taking as little notice of Cadmus as she well could. If he walked slowly, so did the cow, and seized the opportunity to graze. If he quickened his pace, the cow went just so much the faster; and once, when Cadmus tried to catch her by running, she threw out her heels, stuck her tail straight on end, and set off at a gallop, looking as queerly as cows generally do, while putting themselves to their speed.

When Cadmus saw that it was impossible to come up with her, he walked on moderately, as before. The cow, too, went leisurely on, without looking behind. Wherever the grass was greenest, there she nibbled a mouthful or two. Where a brook glistened brightly across the path, there the cow drank, and breathed a comfortable sigh, and drank again. and trudged onward at the pace that best suited herself and Cadmus.

"I do believe," thought Cadmus, "that this may be the cow that was foretold me. If it be the one, I suppose she will lie down somewhere hereabouts."

Whether it were the oracular cow or some other one, it did not seem reasonable that she should travel a great way farther. So, whenever they reached a particularly pleasant spot on a breezy hillside, or in a sheltered vale, or flowery meadow, on the shore of a calm lake, or along the bank of a clear stream, Cadmus looked eagerly around to see if the situation would suit him for a home. But still, whether he liked the place or no, the brindled cow never offered to lie down. On she went at the quiet pace of a cow going homeward to the barn yard; and, every moment, Cadmus expected to see a milkmaid approaching with a pail, or a herdsman running to head the stray animal, and turn her back towards the pasture. But no milkmaid came; no herdsman drove her back; and Cadmus followed the stray Brindle till he was almost ready to drop down with fatigue.

"O brindled cow," cried he, in a tone of despair, "do you never mean to stop?"

He had now grown too intent on following her to think of lagging behind, however long the way, and whatever might be his fatigue. Indeed, it seemed as if there were something about the animal that bewitched people. Several persons who happened to see the brindled cow, and Cadmus following behind, began to trudge after her, precisely as he did. Cadmus was glad of somebody to converse with, and therefore talked very freely to these good people. He told them all his adventures, and how he had left King Agenor in his palace, and Phoenix at one place, and Cilix at another, and Thasus at a third, and his dear mother, Queen Telephassa, under a flowery sod; so that now he was quite alone, both friendless and homeless. He mentioned, likewise, that the oracle had bidden him be guided by a cow, and inquired of the strangers whether they supposed that this brindled animal could be the one.

"Why, 'tis a very wonderful affair," answered one of his new companions. "I am pretty well acquainted with the ways of cattle, and I never knew a cow, of her own accord, to go so far without stopping. If my legs will let me, I'll never leave following the beast till she lies down."

"Nor I!" said a second.

"Nor I!" cried a third. "If she goes a hundred miles farther, I am determined to see the end of it."

The secret of it was, you must know, that the cow was an enchanted cow, and that, without their being conscious of it, she threw some of her enchantment over everybody that took so much as half a dozen steps behind her. They could not possibly help following her, though all the time they fancied themselves doing it of their own accord. The cow was by no means very nice in choosing her path; so that sometimes they had to scramble over rocks, or wade through mud and mire, and all in a terribly bedraggled condition, and tired to death, and very hungry, into the bargain. What a weary business it was!

But still they kept trudging stoutly forward, and talking as they went. The strangers grew very fond of Cadmus, and resolved never to leave him, but to help him build a city wherever the cow might lie down. In the center of it there should be a noble palace, in which Cadmus might dwell, and be their king, with a throne, a crown, a sceptre, a purple robe, and everything else that a king ought to have; for in him there was the royal blood, and the royal heart, and the head that knew how to rule.

While they were talking of these schemes, and beguiling the tediousness of the way with laying out the plan of the new city, one of the company happened to look at the cow.

"Joy! joy!" cried he, clapping his hands. "Brindle is going to lie down."

They all looked; and, sure enough, the cow had stopped, and was staring leisurely about her, as other cows do when on the point of lying down. And slowly, slowly did she recline herself on the soft grass, first bending her forelegs, and then crouching her hind ones. When Cadmus and his companions came up with her, there was the brindled cow taking her ease, chewing her cud, and looking them quietly in the face; as if this was just the spot she had been seeking for, and as if it were all a matter of course.

"This, then," said Cadmus, gazing around him, "this is to be my home."

It was a fertile and lovely plain, with great trees flinging their sun-speckled shadows over it, and hills fencing it in from the rough weather. At no great distance, they beheld a river gleaming in the sunshine. A home feeling stole into the heart of poor Cadmus. He was very glad to know that here he might awake in the morning without the necessity of putting on his dusty sandals to travel farther and farther. The days and the years would pass over him, and find him still in this pleasant spot. If he could have had his brothers with him, and his friend Thasus, and could have seen his dear mother under a roof of his own, he might here have been happy after all their disappointments. Some day or other, too, his sister Europa might have come quietly to the door of his home, and smiled round upon the familiar faces. But, indeed, since there was no hope of regaining the friends of his boyhood, or ever seeing his dear sister again, Cadmus resolved to make himself happy with these new companions, who had grown so fond of him while following the cow.

"Yes, my friends," said he to them, "this is to be our home. Here we will build our habitations. The brindled cow, which has led us hither, will supply us with milk.

We will cultivate the neighboring soil. and lead an innocent and happy life."

His companions joyfully assented to this plan; and, in the first place, being very hungry and thirsty, they looked about them for the means of providing a comfortable meal. Not far off they saw a tuft of trees, which appeared as if there might be a spring of water beneath them. They went thither to fetch some, leaving Cadmus stretched on the ground along with the brindled cow; for, now that he had found a place of rest, it seemed as if all the weariness of his pilgrimage, ever since he left King Agenor's palace, had fallen upon him at once. But his new friends had not long been gone, when he was suddenly startled by cries, shouts, and screams, and the noise of a terrible struggle, and in the midst of it all, a most awful hissing, which went right through his ears like a rough saw.

Running towards the tuft of trees, he beheld the head and fiery eyes of an immense serpent or dragon, with the widest jaws that ever a dragon had, and a vast many rows of horribly sharp teeth. Before Cadmus could reach the spot, this pitiless reptile had killed his poor companions, and was busily devouring them, making but a mouthful of each man.

It appears that the fountain of water was enchanted, and that the dragon had been set to guard it, so that no mortal might ever quench his thirst there. As the neighboring inhabitants carefully avoided the spot, it was now a long time (not less than a hundred years or thereabouts) since the monster had broken his fast; and, as was natural enough, his appetite had grown to be enormous, and was not half satisfied by the poor people whom he had just eaten up. When he caught sight of Cadmus, therefore, he set up another abominable hiss, and flung back his immense jaws, until his mouth looked like a great red cavern, at the farther end of which were seen the legs of his last victim, whom he had hardly had time to swallow.

But Cadmus was so enraged at the destruction of his friends that he cared neither for the size of the dragon's jaws nor for his hundreds of sharp teeth. Drawing his sword, he rushed at the monster, and flung himself right into his cavernous mouth. This bold method of attacking him took the dragon by surprise; for, in fact, Cadmus had leaped so far down into his throat, that the rows of terrible teeth could not close upon him, nor do him the least harm in the world. Thus, though the struggle was a tremendous one, and though the dragon shattered the tuft of trees into small splinters by the lashing of his tail, yet, as Cadmus was all the while slashing and stabbing at his very vitals, it was not long before the scaly wretch bethought himself of slipping away. He had not gone his length, however, when the brave Cadmus gave him a sword thrust that finished the battle; and creeping out of the gateway of the creature's jaws, there he beheld him still wriggling his vast bulk, although there was no longer life enough in him to harm a little child.

But do not you suppose that it made Cadmus sorrowful to think of the melancholy fate which had befallen those poor, friendly people, who had followed the cow along with him? It seemed as if he were doomed to lose everybody whom he loved, or to see them perish in one way or another. And here he was, after all his toils and troubles, in a solitary place, with not a single human being to help him build a hut.

"What shall I do?" cried he aloud. "It were better for me to have been devoured by the dragon, as my poor companions were."

"Cadmus," said a voice but whether it came from above or below him, or whether it spoke within his own breast, the young man could not tell--"Cadmus, pluck out the dragon's teeth, and plant them in the earth."

This was a strange thing to do; nor was it very easy, I should imagine, to dig out all those deep-rooted fangs from the dead dragon's jaws. But Cadmus toiled and tugged, and after pounding the monstrous head almost to pieces with a great stone, he at last collected as many teeth as might have filled a bushel or two. The next thing was to plant them. This, likewise, was a tedious piece of work, especially as Cadmus was already exhausted with killing the dragon and knocking his head to pieces, and had nothing to dig the earth with, that I know of, unless it were his sword blade. Finally, however, a sufficiently large tract o ground was turned up, and sown with this new kind of seed; although half of the dragon's teeth still remained to be planted some other day.

Cadmus, quite out of breath, stood leaning upon his sword, and wondering what was to happen next. He had waited but a few moments, when he began to see a sight, which was as great a marvel as the most marvelous thing I ever told you about.

The sun was shining slantwise over the field, and showed all the moist, dark soil just like any other newly-planted piece of ground. All at once, Cadmus fancied he saw something glisten very brightly, first at one spot, then at another, and then at a hundred and a thousand spots together. Soon he perceived them to be the steel heads of spears, sprouting up everywhere like so many stalks of grain, and continually growing taller and taller. Next appeared a vast number of bright sword blades, thrusting themselves up in the same way. A moment afterwards, the whole surface of the ground was broken by a multitude of polished brass helmets, coming up like a crop of enormous beans. So rapidly did they grow, that Cadmus now discerned the fierce countenance of a man beneath every one. In short, before he had time to think what a wonderful affair it was, he beheld an abundant harvest of what looked like human beings, armed with helmets and breastplates, shields, swords, and spears; and before they were well out of the earth, they brandished their weapons, and clashed them one against another, seeming to think, little while as they had yet lived, that they had wasted too much of life without a battle. Every tooth of the dragon had produced one of these sons of deadly mischief.

Up sprouted also a great many trumpeters; and with the first breath that they drew, they put their brazen trumpets to their lips, and sounded a tremendous and ear-shattering blast, so that the whole space, just now so quiet and solitary, reverberated with the clash and clang of arms, the bray of warlike music, and the shouts of angry men. So enraged did they all look, that Cadmus fully expected them to put the whole world to the sword. How fortunate would it be for a great conqueror, if he could get a bushel of the dragon's teeth to sow!

"Cadmus," said the same voice which he had before heard, "throw a stone into the midst of the armed men."

So Cadmus seized a large stone, and flinging it into the middle of the earth army, saw it strike the breastplate of a gigantic and fierce-looking warrior. Immediately on feeling the blow, he seemed to take it for granted that somebody had struck him; and, uplifting his weapon, he smote his next neighbor a blow that cleft his helmet asunder, and stretched him on the ground. In an instant, those nearest the fallen warrior began to strike at one another with their swords, and stab with their spears. The confusion spread wider and wider. Each man smote down his brother, and was himself smitten down before he had time to exult in his victory. The trumpeters, all the while, blew their blasts shriller and shriller; each soldier shouted a battle cry, and often fell with it on his lips. It was the strangest spectacle of causeless wrath, and of mischief for no good end, that had ever been witnessed; but, after all, it was neither more foolish nor more wicked than a thousand battles that have since been fought, in which men have slain their brothers with just as little reason as these children of the dragon's teeth. It ought to be considered, too, that the dragon people were made for nothing else; whereas other mortals were born to love and help one another.

Well, this memorable battle continued to rage until the ground was strewn with helmeted heads that had been cut off. Of all the thousands that began the fight, there were only five left standing. These now rushed from different parts of the field, and, meeting in the middle of it, clashed their swords, and struck at each other's hearts as fiercely as ever.

"Cadmus," said the voice again, "bid those five warriors sheathe their swords. They will help you to build the city."

Without hesitating an instant, Cadmus stepped forward, with the aspect of a king and a leader, and extending his drawn sword amongst them, spoke to the warriors in a stern and commanding voice.

"Sheathe your weapons!" said he.

And forthwith, feeling themselves bound to obey him, the five remaining sons of the dragon's teeth made him a military salute with their swords, returned them to the scabbards, and stood before Cadmus in a rank, eyeing him as soldiers eye their captain, while awaiting the word of command.

These five men had probably sprung from the biggest of the dragon's teeth, and were the boldest and strongest of the whole army. They were almost giants indeed, and had good need to be so, else they never could have lived through so terrible a fight. They still had a very furious look, and, if Cadmus happened to glance aside, would glare at one another, with fire flashing out of their eyes. It was strange, too, to observe how the earth, out of which they had so lately grown, was incrusted, here and there, on their bright breastplates, and even, begrimed their faces; just as you may have seen it clinging to beets and carrots, when pulled out of their native soil. Cadmus hardly knew whether to consider them as men, or some odd kind of vegetable; although, on the whole, he concluded that there was human nature in them, because they were so fond of trumpets and weapons, and so ready to shed blood.

They looked him earnestly in the face, waiting for his next order, and evidently desiring no other employment than to follow him from one battlefield to another, all over the wide world. But Cadmus was wiser than these earth-born creatures, with the dragon's fierceness in them, and knew better how to use their strength and hardihood.

"Come!" said he. "You are sturdy fellows. Make yourselves useful! Quarry some stones with those great swords of yours, and help me to build a city."

The five soldiers grumbled a little, and muttered that it was their business to overthrow cities, not to build them up. But Cadmus looked at them with a stern eye, and spoke to them in a tone of authority, so that they knew him for their master, and never again thought of disobeying his commands. They set to work in good earnest, and toiled so diligently, that, in a very short time, a city began to make its appearance. At first, to be sure, the workmen showed a quarrelsome disposition. Like savage beasts, they would doubtless have done one another a mischief, if Cadmus had not kept watch over them, and quelled the fierce old serpent that lurked in their hearts, when he saw it gleaming out of their wild eyes. But, in course of time, they got accustomed to honest labor, and had sense enough to feel that there was more true enjoyment in living at peace, and doing good to one's neighbor, than in striking at him with a two-edged sword. It may not be too much to hope that the rest of mankind will by and by grow as wise and peaceable as these five earth-begrimed warriors, who sprang from the dragon's teeth.

And now the city was built, and there was a home in it for each of the workmen. But the palace of Cadmus was not yet erected, because they had left it till the last, meaning to introduce all the new improvements of architecture, and make it very commodious, as well as stately and beautiful. After finishing the rest of their labors, they all went to bed betimes, in order to rise in the gray of the morning, and get at least the foundation of the edifice laid before nightfall. But, when Cadmus arose, and took his way towards the site where the palace was to be built, followed by his five sturdy workmen marching all in a row, what do you think he saw?

What should it be but the most magnificent palace that had ever been seen in the world. It was built of marble and other beautiful kinds of stone, and rose high into the air, with a splendid dome and a portico along the front, and carved pillars, and everything else that befitted the habitation of a mighty king. It had grown up out of the earth in almost as short a time as it had taken the armed host to spring from the dragon's teeth; and what made the matter more strange, no seed of this stately edifice ever had been planted.

When the five workmen beheld the dome, with the morning sunshine making it look golden and glorious, they gave a great shout.

"Long live King Cadmus," they cried, "in his beautiful palace."

And the new king, with his five faithful followers at his heels, shouldering their pickaxes and marching in a rank (for they still had a soldier-like sort of behavior, as their nature was), ascended the palace steps. Halting at the entrance, they gazed through a long vista of lofty pillars, that were ranged from end to end of a great hall. At the farther extremity of this hall, approaching slowly towards him, Cadmus beheld a female figure, wonderfully beautiful, and adorned with a royal robe, and a crown of diamonds over her golden ringlets, and the richest necklace that ever a queen wore. His heart thrilled with delight. He fancied it his long-lost sister Europa, now grown to womanhood, coming to make him happy, and to repay him with her sweet sisterly affection, for all those weary wonderings in quest of her since he left King Agenor's palace--for the tears that he had shed, on parting with Phoenix, and Cilix, and Thasus--for the heart-breakings that had made the whole world seem dismal to him over his dear mother's grave.

But, as Cadmus advanced to meet the beautiful stranger, he saw that her features were unknown to him, although, in the little time that it required to tread along the hall, he had already felt a sympathy betwixt himself and her.

"No, Cadmus," said the same voice that had spoken to him in the field of the armed men, "this is not that dear sister Europa whom you have sought so faithfully all over the wide world. This is Harmonia, a daughter of the sky, who is given you instead of sister, and brothers, and friend, and mother. You will find all those dear ones in her alone."

So King Cadmus dwelt in the palace, with his new friend Harmonia, and found a great deal of comfort in his magnificent abode, but would doubtless have found as much, if not more, in the humblest cottage by the wayside. Before many years went by, there was a group of rosy little children (but how they came thither has always been a mystery to me) sporting in the great hall, and on the marble steps of the palace, and running joyfully to meet King Cadmus when affairs of state left him at leisure to play with them. They called him father, and Queen Harmonia mother. The five old soldiers of the dragon's teeth grew very fond of these small urchins, and were never weary of showing them how to shoulder sticks, flourish wooden swords, and march in military order, blowing a penny trumpet, or beating an abominable rub-a-dub upon a little drum.

But King Cadmus, lest there should be too much of the dragon's tooth in his children's disposition, used to find time from his kingly duties to teach them their A B C--which he invented for their benefit, and for which many little people, I am afraid, are not half so grateful to him as they ought to be.

THE STORY OF LITTLE BOY BLUE

Credit: Frank Baum

Little Boy Blue, come blow your horn.

The sheep 's in the meadow, the cow 's in the corn;

Where 's the little boy that minds the sheep?

He's under the haystack, fast asleep!

There once lived a poor widow who supported herself and her only son by gleaning in the fields the stalks of grain that had been missed by the reapers. Her little cottage was at the foot of a beautiful valley, upon the edge of the river that wound in and out among the green hills; and although poor, she was contented with her lot, for her home was pleasant and her lovely boy was a constant delight to her.

He had big blue eyes, and fair golden curls, and he loved his good mother very dearly, and was never more pleased than when she allowed him to help her with her work.

And so the years passed happily away till the boy was eight years old, but then the widow fell sick, and their little store of money melted gradually away.

"I do n't know what we shall do for bread," she said, kissing her boy with tears in her eyes, "for I am not yet strong enough to work, and we have no money left."

"But I can work," answered the boy; "and I 'm sure if I go to the Squire up at the Hall he will give me something to do."

At first the widow was reluctant to consent to this, since she loved to keep her child at her side, but finally, as nothing else could be done, she decided to let him go to see the Squire.

Being too proud to allow her son to go to the great house in his ragged clothes, she made him a new suit out of a pretty blue dress she had herself worn in happier times, and when it was finished and the boy dressed in it, he looked as pretty as a prince in a fairy tale. For the bright blue jacket set off his curls to good advantage, and the color just matched the blue of his eyes. His trousers were blue, also, and she took the silver buckles from her own shoes and put them on his, that he might appear the finer. And then she brushed his curls and placed his big straw hat upon them and sent him away with a kiss to see the Squire.

It so happened that the great man was walking in his garden with his daughter Madge that morning, and was feeling in an especially happy mood, so that when he suddenly looked up and saw a little boy before him, he said, kindly,

"Well, my child, what can I do for you?"

"If you please, sir," said the boy, bravely, although he was frightened at meeting the Squire face to face, "I want you to give me some work to do, so that I can earn money."

"Earn money!" repeated the Squire, "why do you wish to earn money?"

"To buy food for my mother, sir. We are very poor, and since she is no longer able to work for me I wish to work for her."

"But what can you do?" asked the Squire; "you are too small to work in the fields."

"I could earn something, sir, couldn't I?"

His tone was so pleading that mistress Madge was unable to resist it, and even the Squire was touched. The young lady came forward and took the boy's hand in her own, and pressing back his curls, she kissed his fair cheek.

"You shall be our shepherd," she said, pleasantly, "and keep the sheep out of the meadows and the cows from getting in to the corn. You know, father," she continued, turning to the Squire, "it was only yesterday you said you must get a boy to tend the sheep, and this little boy can do it nicely."

"Very well," replied the Squire, "it shall be as you say, and if he is attentive and watchful he will be able to save me a good bit of trouble and so really earn his money."

Then he turned to the child and said,

"Come to me in the morning, my little man, and I will give you a silver horn to blow, that you may call the sheep and the cows whenever they go astray. What is your name?"

"Oh, never mind his name, papa!" broke in the Squire's daughter; "I shall call him Little Boy Blue, since he is dressed in blue from head to foot, and his dress but matches his eyes. And you must give him a good wage, also, for surely no Squire before ever had a prettier shepherd boy than this."

"Very good," said the Squire, cheerfully, as he pinched his daughter's rosy cheek; "be watchful, Little Boy Blue, and you shall be well paid."

Then Little Boy Blue thanked them both very sweetly and ran back over the hill and into the valley where his home lay nestled by the riverside, to tell the good news to his mother.

The poor widow wept tears of joy when she heard his story, and smiled when he told her that his name was to be Little Boy Blue. She knew the Squire was a kind master and would be good to her darling son.

Early the next morning Little Boy Blue was at the Hall, and the Squire's steward gave him a new silver horn, that glistened brightly in the sunshine, and a golden cord to fasten it around his neck. And then he was given charge of the sheep and the cows, and told to keep them from straying into the meadowlands and the fields of grain.

It was not hard work, but just suited to Little Boy Blue's age, and he was watchful and vigilant and made a very good shepherd boy indeed. His mother needed food no longer, for the Squire paid her son liberally, and the Squire's daughter made a favorite of the small shepherd and loved to hear the call of his silver horn echoing amongst the hills. Even the sheep and the cows were fond of him, and always obeyed the sound of his horn; therefore the Squire's corn thrived finely, and was never trampled.

Little Boy Blue was now very happy, and his mother was proud and contented and began to improve in health. After a few weeks she became strong enough to leave the cottage and walk a little in the fields each day; but she could not go far, because her limbs were too feeble to support her long, so the most she could attempt was to walk as far as the stile to meet Little Boy Blue as he came home from work in the evening. Then she would lean on his shoulder and return to the cottage with him, and the boy was very glad he could thus support his darling mother and assist her faltering steps.

But one day a great misfortune came upon them, since it is true that no life can be so happy but that sorrow will creep in to temper it.

Little Boy Blue came homeward one evening very light of heart and whistled merrily as he walked, for he thought he should find his mother awaiting him at the stile and a good supper spread upon the table in the little cottage. But when he came to the stile his mother was not in sight, and in answer to his call a low moan of pain reached his ears.

Little Boy Blue sprang over the stile and found lying upon the ground his dear mother, her face white and drawn with suffering, and tears of anguish running down her cheeks. For she had slipped upon the stile and fallen, and her leg was broken!

Little Boy Blue ran to the cottage for water and bathed the poor woman's face, and raised her head that she might drink. There were no neighbors, for the cottage stood all alone by the river, so the child was obliged to support his mother in his arms as best he could while she crawled painfully back to the cottage. Fortunately, it was not far, and at last she was safely laid upon her bed. Then Little Boy Blue began to think what he should do next.

"Can I leave you alone while I go for the doctor, mamma?" he asked, anxiously, as he held her clasped hands tightly in his two little ones. His mother drew him towards her and kissed him.

"Take the boat, dear," she said, "and fetch the doctor from the village. I shall be patient till you return."

Little Boy Blue rushed away to the river bank and unfastened the little boat; and then he pulled sturdily down the river until he passed the bend and came to the pretty village below. When he had found the doctor and told of his mother's misfortune, the good man promised to attend him at once, and very soon they were seated in the boat and on their way to the cottage.

It was very dark by this time, but Little Boy Blue knew every turn and bend in the river, and the doctor helped him pull at the oars, so that at last they came to the place where a faint light twinkled through the cottage window. They found the poor woman in much pain, but the doctor quickly set and bandaged her leg, and gave her some medicine to ease her suffering. It was nearly midnight when all was finished and the doctor was ready to start back to the village.

"Take good care of your mother," he said to the boy, "and do n't worry about her, for it is not a bad break and the leg will mend nicely in time; but she will be in bed many days, and you must nurse her as well as you are able."

All through the night the boy sat by the bedside, bathing his mother's fevered brow and ministering to her wants. And when the day broke she was resting easily and the pain had left her, and she told Little Boy Blue he must go to his work.

"For," said she, "more than ever now we need the money you earn from the Squire, as my misfortune will add to the expenses of living, and we have the doctor to pay. Do not fear to leave me, for I shall rest quietly and sleep most of the time while you are away."

Little Boy Blue did not like to leave his mother all alone, but he knew of no one he could ask to stay with her; so he placed food and water by her bedside, and ate a little breakfast himself, and started off to tend his sheep.

The sun was shining brightly, and the birds sang sweetly in the trees, and the crickets chirped just as merrily as if this great trouble had not come to Little Boy Blue to make him sad.

But he went bravely to his work, and for several hours he watched carefully; and the men at work in the fields, and the Squire's daughter, who sat embroidering upon the porch of the great house, heard often the sound of his horn as he called the straying sheep to his side.

But he had not slept the whole night, and he was tired with his long watch at his mother's bedside, and so in spite of himself the lashes would droop occasionally over his blue eyes, for he was only a child, and children feel the loss of sleep more than older people.

Still, Little Boy Blue had no intention of sleeping while he was on duty, and bravely fought against the drowsiness that was creeping over him. The sun shone very hot that day, and he walked to the shady side of a big haystack and sat down upon the ground, leaning his back against the stack.

The cows and sheep were quietly browsing near him, and he watched them earnestly for a time, listening to the singing of the birds, and the gentle tinkling of the bells upon the weathers, and the faraway songs of the reapers that the breeze brought to his ears.

And before he knew it the blue eyes had closed fast, and the golden head lay back upon the hay, and Little Boy Blue was fast asleep and dreaming that his mother was well again and had come to the stile to meet him.

The sheep strayed near the edge of the meadow and paused, waiting for the warning sound of the horn. And the breeze carried the fragrance of the growing corn to the nostrils of the browsing cows and tempted them nearer and nearer to the forbidden feast. But the silver horn was silent, and before long the cows were feeding upon the Squire's pet cornfield and the sheep were enjoying themselves amidst the juicy grasses of the meadows.

The Squire himself was returning from a long, weary ride over his farms, and when he came to the cornfield and saw the cows trampling down the grain and feeding upon the golden stalks he was very angry.

"Little Boy Blue!" he cried; "ho! Little Boy Blue, come blow your horn!" But there was no reply. He rode on a way and now discovered that the sheep were deep within the meadows, and that made him more angry still.

"Here, Isaac," he said to a farmer's lad who chanced to pass by, "where is Little Boy Blue?"

"He's under the haystack, your honor, fast asleep!" replied Isaac with a grin, for he had passed that way and seen that the boy was lying asleep.

"Will you go and wake him?" asked the Squire; "for he must drive out the sheep and the cows before they do more damage."

"Not I," replied Isaac, "if I wake him he 'll surely cry, for he is but a baby, and not fit to mind the sheep. But I myself will drive them out for your honor," and away he ran to do so, thinking that now the Squire would give him Little Boy Blue's place, and make him the shepherd boy, for Isaac had long coveted the position.

The Squire's daughter, hearing the angry tones of her father's voice, now came out to see what was amiss, and when she heard that Little Boy Blue had failed in his trust she was deeply grieved, for she had loved the child for his pretty ways.

The Squire dismounted from his horse and came to where the boy was lying.

"Awake!" said he, shaking him by the shoulder, "and depart from my lands, for you have betrayed my trust, and let the sheep and the cows stray into the fields and meadows!"

Little Boy Blue started up at once and rubbed his eyes; and then he did as Isaac prophesied, and began to weep bitterly, for his heart was sore that he had failed in his duty to the good Squire and so forfeited his confidence.

But the Squire's daughter was moved by the child's tears, so she took him upon her lap and comforted him, asking,

"Why did you sleep, Little Boy Blue, when you should have watched the cows and the sheep?"

"My mother has broken her leg," answered the boy, between his sobs, "and I did not sleep all last night, but sat by her bedside nursing her. And I tried hard not to fall asleep, but could not help myself; and oh, Squire! I hope you will forgive me this once, for my poor mother's sake!"

"Where does your mother live?" asked the Squire, in a kindly tone, for he had already forgiven Little Boy Blue.

"In the cottage down by the river," answered the child; "and she is all alone, for there is no one near to help us in our trouble."

"Come," said Mistress Madge, rising to her feet and taking his hand; "lead us to your home, and we will see if we cannot assist your poor mother."

So the Squire and his daughter and Little Boy Blue all walked down to the little cottage, and the Squire had a long talk with the poor widow. And that same day a big basket of dainties was sent to the cottage, and Mistress Madge bade her own maid go to the widow and nurse her carefully until she recovered.So that after all Little Boy Blue did more for his dear mother by falling asleep than he could had he kept wide awake; for after his mother was well again the Squire gave them a pretty cottage to live in very near to the great house itself, and the Squire's daughter was ever afterward their good friend, and saw that they wanted for no comforts of life.And Little Boy Blue did not fall asleep again at his post, but watched the cows and the sheep faithfully for many years, until he grew up to manhood and had a farm of his own.He always said his mother's accident had brought him good luck, but I think it was rather his own loving heart and his devotion to his mother that made him friends. For no one is afraid to trust a boy who loves to serve and care for his mother.

———— • ————

FIVE LITTLE PIGS

Credit: Joseph Martin Kronheim

The Little Pig who went to Market

There was once a family of Five Little Pigs, and Mrs. Pig, their mother, loved them all very dearly. Some of these little pigs were very good, and took a great deal of trouble to please her. The eldest pig was so active and useful that he was called Mr. Pig. One day he went to market with his cart full of vegetables, but Rusty, the donkey, began to show his bad temper before he had gone very far on the road. All the coaxing and whipping would not make him move. So Mr. Pig took him out of the shafts, and being very strong, drew the cart to market himself. When he got there, all the other pigs began to laugh. But they did not laugh so loudly when Mr. Pig told them all his struggles on the road. Mr. Pig lost no time in selling his vegetables, and very soon after Rusty came trotting into the market-place, and as he now seemed willing to take his place in the cart, Mr. Pig started for home without delay. When he got there, he told Mrs. Pig his story, and she called him her best and most worthy son.

The Little Pig who stayed at Home

This little pig very much wanted to go with his brother, but as he was so mischievous that he could not be trusted far away, his mother made him stay at home, and told him to keep a good fire while she went out to the miller's to buy some flour. But as soon as he was alone, instead of learning his lessons, he began to tease the poor cat.

216

Then he got the bellows, and cut the leather with a knife, so as to see where the wind came from: and when he could not find this out, he began to cry. After this he broke all his brother's toys; he forced the drum-stick through the drum, he tore off the tail from the kite, and then pulled off the horse's head. And then he went to the cupboard and ate the jam. When Mrs. Pig came home, she sat down by the fire, and being very tired, she soon fell asleep. No sooner had she done so, than this bad little pig got a long handkerchief and tied her in her chair. But soon she awoke and found out all the mischief that he had been doing. She saw at once the damage that he had done to his brother's playthings. So she quickly brought out her thickest and heaviest birch, and gave this naughty little pig such a beating as he did not forget for a long time.

The Little Pig who had Roast Beef

This little pig was a very good and careful fellow. He gave his mother scarcely any trouble, and always took a pleasure in doing all she bade him. Here you see him sitting down with clean hands and face, to some nice roast beef, while his brother, the idle pig, who is standing on a stool in the corner, with the dunce's cap on, has none. He sat down and quietly learned his lesson, and asked his mother to hear him repeat it. And thishe did so well that Mrs. Pig stroked him on the ears and forehead, and called him a good little pig. After this he asked her to allow him to help her make tea. He brought everything she wanted, and lifted off the kettle from the fire, without spilling a drop either on his toes or the carpet. By-and-bye he went out, after asking his mother's leave, to play with his hoop. He had not gone far when he saw an old blind pig, who, with his hat in his hand was crying at the loss of his dog; so he put his hand in his pocket and found a halfpenny which he gave to the poor old pig. It was for such thoughtful conduct as this that his mother often gave this little pig roast beef. We now come to the little pig who had none.

The Little Pig who had None

This was a most obstinate and willful little pig. His mother had set him to learn his lesson, but no sooner had she gone out into the garden, than he tore his book into pieces. When his mother came back he ran off into the streets to play with other idle little pigs like himself. After this he quarrelled with one of the pigs and got a sound thrashing. Being afraid to go home, he stayed out till it was quite dark and caught a severe cold. So he was taken home and put to bed, and had to take a lot of nasty physic.

The Little Pig who Cried "Wee, wee," all the Way Home

This little pig went fishing. Now he had been told not to go into Farmer Grumpey's grounds, who did not allow any one to fish in his part of the river. But in spite of what he had been told, this foolish little pig went there. He soon caught a very large fish, and while he was trying to carry it home, Farmer Grumpey came running along with his great whip. He quickly dropped the fish, but the farmer caught him, and as he laid his whip over his back for some time, the little pig ran off, crying, "Wee, wee, wee," all the way home.

THE LITTLE RED RIDING HOOD

Credit: Anonymous

Once upon a time there was a dear little girl who was loved by every one who looked at her, but most of all by her grandmother, and there was nothing that she would not have given to the child. Once she gave her a little cap of red velvet, which suited her so well that she would never wear anything else. So she was always called Little Red Riding Hood.

One day her mother said to her, "Come, Little Red Riding Hood, here is a piece of cake and a bottle of wine. Take them to your grandmother, she is ill and weak, and they will do her good. Set out before it gets hot, and when you are going, walk nicely and quietly and do not run off the path, or you may fall and break the bottle, and then your grandmother will get nothing. And when you go into her room, don't forget to say, good-morning, and don't peep into every corner before you do it."

I will take great care, said Little Red Riding Hood to her mother, and gave her hand on it.

The grandmother lived out in the wood, half a league from the village, and just as Little Red Riding Hood entered the wood, a wolf met her. Little Red Riding Hood did not know what a wicked creature he was, and was not at all afraid of him.

"Good-day, Little Red Riding Hood," said he.

"Thank you kindly, wolf."

"Whither away so early, Little Red Riding Hood?"

"To my grandmother's."

"What have you got in your apron?"

"Cake and wine. Yesterday was baking-day, so poor sick grandmother is to have something good, to make her stronger."

"Where does your grandmother live, Little Red Riding Hood?"

"A good quarter of a league farther on in the wood. Her house stands under the three large oak-trees, the nut-trees are just below. You surely must know it," replied Little Red Riding Hood.

The wolf thought to himself, "What a tender young creature. What a nice plump mouthful, she will be better to eat than the old woman. I must act craftily, so as to catch both." So he walked for a short time by the side of Little Red Riding Hood, and then he said, "see Little Red Riding Hood, how pretty the flowers are about here. Why do you not look round. I believe, too, that you do not hear how sweetly the little birds are singing. You walk gravely along as if you were going to school, while everything else out here in the wood is merry."

Little Red Riding Hood raised her eyes, and when she saw the sunbeams dancing here and there through the trees, and pretty flowers growing everywhere, she thought, suppose I take grandmother a fresh nosegay. That would please her too. It is so early in the day that I shall still get there in good time. And so she ran from the path into the wood to look for flowers. And whenever she had picked one, she fancied that she saw a still prettier one farther on, and ran after it, and so got deeper and deeper into the wood.

Meanwhile the wolf ran straight to the grandmother's house and knocked at the door.

"Who is there?"

"Little Red Riding Hood," replied the wolf. "She is bringing cake and wine. Open the door."

"Lift the latch," called out the grandmother, "I am too weak, and cannot get up."

The wolf lifted the latch, the door sprang open, and without saying a word he went straight to the grandmother's bed, and devoured her. Then he put on her clothes, dressed himself in her cap, laid himself in bed and drew the curtains.

Little Red Riding Hood, however, had been running about picking flowers, and when she had gathered so many that she could carry no more, she remembered her grandmother, and set out on the way to her.

She was surprised to find the cottage-door standing open, and when she went into the room, she had such a strange feeling that she said to herself, oh dear, how uneasy I feel to-day, and at other times I like being with grandmother so much.

She called out, "Good morning," but received no answer. So she went to the bed and drew back the curtains. There lay her grandmother with her cap pulled far over her face, and looking very strange.

"Oh, grandmother," she said, "what big ears you have."

"The better to hear you with, my child," was the reply.

"But, grandmother, what big eyes you have," she said.

"The better to see you with, my dear."

"But, grandmother, what large hands you have."

"The better to hug you with."

"Oh, but, grandmother, what a terrible big mouth you have."

"The better to eat you with."

And scarcely had the wolf said this, than with one bound he was out of bed and swallowed up Little Red Riding Hood.

When the wolf had appeased his appetite, he lay down again in the bed, fell asleep and began to snore very loud. The huntsman was just passing the house, and thought to himself, how the old woman is snoring. I must just see if she wants anything.

So he went into the room, and when he came to the bed, he saw that the wolf was lying in it. "Do I find you here, you old sinner," said he. "I have long sought you."

Then just as he was going to fire at him, it occurred to him that the wolf might have devoured the grandmother, and that she might still be saved, so he did not fire, but took a pair of scissors, and began to cut open the stomach of the sleeping wolf.

When he had made two snips, he saw the Little Red Riding Hood shining, and then he made two snips more, and the little girl sprang out, crying, "Ah, how frightened I have been. How dark it was inside the wolf."

And after that the aged grandmother came out alive also, but scarcely able to breathe. Little Red Riding Hood, however, quickly fetched great stones with which they filled the wolf's belly, and when he awoke, he wanted to run away, but the stones were so heavy that he collapsed at once, and fell dead.

Then all three were delighted. The huntsman drew off the wolf's skin and went home with it. The grandmother ate the cake and drank the wine which Little Red Riding Hood had brought, and revived, but Little Red Riding Hood thought to herself, as long as I live, I will never by myself leave the path, to run into the wood, when my mother has forbidden me to do so.

It is also related that once when Little Red Riding Hood was again taking cakes to the old grandmother, another wolf spoke to her, and tried to entice her from the path. Little Red Riding Hood, however, was on her guard, and went straight forward on her way, and told her grandmother that she had met the wolf, and that he had said good-morning to her, but with such a wicked look in his eyes, that if they had not been on the public road she was certain he would have eaten her up. "Well," said the grandmother, "we will shut the door, that he may not come in."

Soon afterwards the wolf knocked, and cried, "open the door, grandmother, I am Little Red Riding Hood, and am bringing you some cakes."

But they did not speak, or open the door, so the grey-beard stole twice or thrice round the house, and at last jumped on the roof, intending to wait until Little Red Riding Hood went home in the evening, and then to steal after her and devour her in the darkness. But the grandmother saw what was in his thoughts. In front of the house was a great stone trough, so she said to the child, take the pail, Little Red Riding Hood. I made some sausages yesterday, so carry the water in which I boiled them to the trough. Little Red Riding Hood carried until the great trough was quite full. Then the smell of the sausages reached the wolf, and he sniffed and peeped down, and at last stretched out his neck so far that he could no longer keep his footing and began to slip, and slipped down from the roof straight into the great trough, and was drowned. But Little Red Riding Hood went joyously home, and no one ever did anything to harm her again.

————————◆————————

OLD MOTHER GOOSE AND HER SON JACK

Credit: Joseph Martin Kronheim

Old Mother Goose lived in a cottage with her son Jack. Jack was a very good lad, and although he was not handsome, he was good-tempered and industrious, and this made him better-looking than half the other boys. Old Mother Goose carried a long stick, she wore a high-crowned hat, and high-heeled shoes, and her kerchief was as white as snow. Then there was the Gander that swam in the pond, and the Owl that sat on the wall. So you see they formed a very happy family. But what a fine strong fellow the Gander was! Whenever Old Mother Goose wanted to take a journey, she would mount upon his broad strong back, and away he would fly and carry her swiftly to any distance.

Now Old Mother Goose thought her Gander often looked sad and lonely; so one day she sent Jack to market to buy the finest Goose he could find. It was early in the morning when he started, and his way lay through a wood. He was not afraid of robbers; so on he went, with his Mother's great clothes-prop over his shoulder. The fresh morning air caused Jack's spirits to rise. He left the road, and plunged into the thick of the wood, where he amused himself by leaping with his clothes-prop till he found he had lost himself. After he had made many attempts to find the path again, he heard a scream. He jumped up and ran boldly towards the spot from which the sound came. Through an opening in the trees he saw a young lady trying to get away from a ruffian who wanted to steal her mantle. With one heavy blow of his staff Jack sent the thief howling away, and then went back to the young lady, who was lying on the ground, crying.

She soon dried her tears when she found that the robber had made off, and thanked Jack for his help. The young lady told Jack that she was the daughter of the Squire, who lived in the great white house on the hill-top. She knew the path out of the wood quite well, and when they reached the border, she said that Jack must come soon to her father's house, so that he might thank him for his noble conduct.

When Jack was left alone, he made the best of his way to the market-place. He found little trouble in picking out the best Goose, for when he got there he was very late, and there was but one left. But as it was a prime one, Jack bought it at once, and keeping to the road, made straight for home. At first the Goose objected to be carried; and then, when she had walked along slowly and gravely for a short time, she tried to fly away; so Jack seized her in his arms and kept her there till he reached home.

Old Mother Goose was greatly pleased when she saw what a fine bird Jack had bought; and the Gander showed more joy than I can describe. And then they all lived very happily for a long time. But Jack would often leave off work to dream of the lovely young lady whom he had rescued in the forest, and soon began to sigh all day long. He neglected the garden, cared no more for the Gander, and scarcely even noticed the beautiful Goose.

But one morning, as he was walking by the pond, he saw both the Goose and the Gander making a great noise, as though they were in the utmost glee. He went up to them and was surprised to find on the bank a large golden egg. He ran with it to his mother, who said, "Go to market, my son; sell your egg, and you will soon be rich enough to pay a visit to the Squire." So to market Jack went, and sold his golden egg; but the rogue who bought it of him cheated him out of half his due. Then he dressed himself in his finest clothes, and went up to the Squire's house. Two footmen stood at the door, one looking very stout and saucy, and the other sleepy and stupid.

When Jack asked to see the Squire, they laughed at him, and made sport of his fine clothes; but Jack had wit enough to offer them each a guinea, when they at once showed him to the Squire's room.

Now the Squire, who was very rich, was also very proud and fat, and scarcely turned his head to notice Jack; but when he showed him his bag of gold, and asked for his daughter to be his bride, the Squire flew into a rage, and ordered his servants to throw him into the horse-pond. But this was not so easy to do, for Jack was strong and active; and then the young lady come out and begged her father to release him. This made Jack more deeply in love with her than ever, and he went home determined to win her in spite of all. And well did his wonderful Goose aid him in his design. Almost every morning she would lay him a golden egg, and Jack, grown wiser, would no longer sell them at half their value to the rogue who had before cheated him. So Jack soon grew to be a richer man than the Squire himself.

His wealth became known to all the country round, and the Squire at length consented to accept Jack as his son-in-law. Then Old Mother Goose flew away into the woods on the back of her strong Gander, leaving the cottage and the Goose to Jack and his bride, who lived happily ever afterwards.

————————•◆•————————

THE TALE OF HUCKLEBERRY

Credit: Frank Stockton

MORE than a hundred and sixty-eight years ago, there lived a curious personage called "Old Riddler." His real name was unknown to the people in that part of the country where he dwelt; but this made no difference, for the name given him was probably just as good as his own. Indeed, I am quite sure that it was better, for it meant something, and very few people have names that mean anything.

He was called Old Riddler for two reasons. In the first place, he was an elderly man; secondly, he was the greatest fellow to ask riddles that you ever heard of. So this name fitted him very well.

Old Riddler had some very peculiar characteristics,—among others, he was a gnome. Living underground for the greater part of his time, he had ample opportunities of working out curious and artful riddles, which he used to try on his fellow-gnomes; and if they liked them, he would go above ground and propound his conundrums to the country people, who sometimes guessed them, but not often.

The fact is, that those persons who wished to be on good terms with the old gnome never guessed his riddles. They knew that they would please him better by giving them up.

He took such a pleasure in telling the answers to his riddles that no truly kind-hearted person would deprive him of it by trying to solve them.

"You see," as Old Riddler used to say, when talked to on the subject, "if I take all the trouble to make up these riddles, it's no more than fair that I should be allowed to give the answers."

So the old gnome, who was not much higher than a two-year old child, though he had quite a venerable head and face, was very much encouraged by the way the people treated him, and when a person happened to be very kind and appreciative, and gave a good deal of attention to one of his conundrums, that person would be pretty sure, before long, to feel glad that he had met Old Riddler.

There were thousands of ways in which the gnomes could benefit the country-folks, especially those who had little farms or gardens. Sometimes Old Riddler, who was a person of great influence in his tribe, would take a company of gnomes under the garden of some one to whom he wished to do a favor, and they would put their little hands up through the earth and pull down all the weeds, root-foremost, so that when the owner went out in the morning, he would find his garden as clear of weeds as the bottom of a dinner-plate.

Of course, any one who has habits of this kind must eventually become a general favorite, and this was the case with Old Riddler.

One day he made up a splendid riddle, and, after he had told it to all the gnomes, he hurried up to propound it to some human person.

He was in such haste that he actually forgot his hat, although it was late in the fall, and he wore his cloak. He had not gone far through the fields before he met a young goose-girl, named Lois. She was a poor girl, and was barefooted; and as Old Riddler saw her in her scanty dress, standing on the cold ground, watching her geese, he thought to himself: "Now I do hope that girl has wit enough to understand my riddle, for I feel that I would like to get interested in her."

So, approaching Lois, he made a bow and politely asked her: "Can you tell me, my good little girl, why a ship full of sailors, at the bottom of the sea, is like the price of beef?"

The goose-girl began to scratch her head, through the old handkerchief she wore instead of a bonnet, and tried to think of the answer.

"Because it's 'low'," said she, after a minute or two.

"Oh, no!" said the gnome. "That's not it. You can give it up, you know, if you can't think of the answer."

"I know!" said Lois. "Because it's sunk."

"Not at all," said Old Riddler, a little impatiently. "Now come, my good girl, you'd much better give it up. You will just hack at the answer until you make it good for nothing."

"Well, what is it?" said Lois.

"I will tell you," said the gnome. "Now, pay attention to the answer: Because it has gone down. Don't you see?" asked the old fellow, with a gracious smile.

"Yes, I see," said the goose-girl, scratching her head again; "but my answer was nearly as good as yours."

"Oh, dear me!" said Old Riddler, "that won't do. It's of no use at all to give an answer that is nearly good enough. It must be exactly right, or it's worthless. I am afraid, young girl, that you don't care much for riddles."

"Yes I do," said the goose girl; "I make 'em."

"Make them?" exclaimed Old Riddler, in great surprise.

"Yes," replied Lois, "I'm out here all day with these geese, and I haven't anything else to do, and so I make riddles. Do you want to hear one of them?"

"Yes, I would like it very much indeed," said the gnome.

"Well, then, here's one: "If the roofs of houses were flat instead of slanting, why would the rain be like a chained dog?"

"Give it up," said Old Riddler.

"Because it couldn't run off," answered Lois.

"Very good, very good," said the gnome. "Why, that's nearly as good as some of mine. And now, my young friend, did n't you feel pleased to have me give up that riddle and let you tell me the answer, straight and true, just as you knew it ought to be?"

"Oh, yes!" said the goose-girl.

"Well, then," continued Old Riddler, "remember this: What pleases you will often please other people. And never guess another riddle."

Lois, although a rough country girl, was touched by the old man's earnestness and his gentle tones.

"I never will," said she.

"That's a very well-meaning girl," said Old Riddler to himself as he walked away, "although she hasn't much polish. I'll come sometimes and help her a little with her conundrums."

Old Riddler had a son named Huckleberry. He was a smart, bright young fellow, and resembled his father in many respects. When he went home, the old gnome told his son about Lois, and tried to impress on his mind the same lesson he had taught the young girl. Huckleberry was a very good little chap, but he was quick-witted and rather forward, and often made his father very angry by guessing his riddles; and so he needed a good deal of parental counsel.

Nearly all that night Huckleberry thought about what his father had told him. But not at all as Old Riddler intended he should.

"What a fine thing it must be," said Huckleberry to himself "to go out into the world and teach people things. I'm going to try it myself."

So, the next day, he started off on his mission. The first person he saw was a very small girl playing under a big oak-tree.

When the small girl saw the young gnome, she was frightened and drew back, standing up as close against the tree as she could get.

But up stepped Master Huckleberry, with all the airs and graces he could command.

"Can you tell me, my little miss," said he, "why an elephant with a glass globe of gold-fish tied to his tail is like a monkey with one pink eye and one of a mazarine blue?"

"No," said the small girl, "I don't know. Go away!"

"Oh," said Huckleberry, "perhaps that's too hard for you. I know some nice little ones, in words of one syllable. Why is a red man with a green hat like a good boy who has a large duck in a small pond?"

"Go away!" said the small girl. "I came here to pick flowers. I don't know riddles."

"Perhaps that one was too easy," said Huckleberry, kindly. "I have all sorts. Here is one with longer words, divided into syllables. I'll say it slowly for you: What is the dif-fer-ence be-tween a mag-nan-i-mous ship-mate and the top-most leaf-let on your grand-mo-ther's bar-ber-ry bush?"

"I haven't got any grandmother," said she.

"Oh, well!" any grandmother will do," said Huckleberry.

"I can't guess it," said the small girl, who was now beginning to lose her fear of the funny little fellow. "I never guessed any riddles. I'm not old enough."

"Very well, then," said Huckleberry, "I'll tell you what I'll do. Let's sit down here under the tree, and I'll tell you one of father's riddles, and give you the answer. His riddles are better than mine, because none of mine have any answers. I don't put answers to them, for I can never think of any good ones. I met a boy once, and told him a lot of my riddles; and he learned them and went about asking people to guess them; and when the people gave them up, he couldn't tell them the answers, because there were none, and that made everybody mad. He told one of the riddles to his grandmother,—I think it was the one about the pink-eyed monkey and the wagon-load of beans——"

"No," said the small girl; "the elephant and the gold-fish was the other part of the pink-eyed monkey one."

"Oh, it don't make any difference," said Huckleberry. "I don't join my riddles together the same way every time. Sometimes I use the gold-fish and elephant with the last part of one riddle, and sometimes with another. As there's no answer, it don't matter. I begin a good many of my best riddles with the elephant, for it makes a fine opening. But, as I was going to tell you, this boy told one of my riddles to his grandmother, and she liked it very much; but when she found out that there was no answer to it, she gave him a good box on the ear, and that boy has never liked me since. But now I'll tell you a story. That is, it's like a story, but it's really a riddle. Father made it, and everybody thinks it's one of his best. There was once a fair lady of renown who was engaged to be married to a prince. And when the wedding day came round—they were to be married in one of the prince's palaces in the mountains—she was so long getting dressed—you see she dressed in one of her father's palaces, down in the valley—that she was afraid she would be late; so as soon as her veil was pinned on, she ran down to the stables, threw a wolf-skin on the back of one of the fieriest of the chargers, and springing on him, she dashed away. She was n't used to harnessing horses, and was in such a hurry that she forgot all about the bridle, and so, as she was dashing away, she found she couldn't steer the animal, and he didn't go any where near the prince's palace, but galloped on, and on, and on, every minute taking her farther and farther away from where she wanted to go. She could n't turn the charger, and she could n't stop him, though she tore off pieces of her veil and tried to put them around his nose, but it was no good. So when the wedding-party had waited, and waited, and waited, the prince got angry and married another lady, and nobody knows where the fair lady of renown went to, although there are some people who say that she's a-galloping yet, and trying to get her veil around the charger's nose. Now, why was it that that fair lady of renown never married? Answer: Because she had no bridal. You can say either bri-d-a-l or bri-d-l-e, because they both sound alike, and if she had had either one of them, she would have been married. This is a pretty long riddle, but it's easier than mine, because it's all fixed up right, with the answer to it and everything. You like it better than mine, don't you?"

The small girl did not answer, and when Huckleberry looked around, he saw that she was asleep.

"Poor little thing!" said Huckleberry, softly, to himself. "I guess I gave her a little too much riddle to begin with. Her mind isn't formed enough yet. But it's pretty hard on me. I wanted to teach somebody something, and here she's gone to sleep. I wish I could find that goose-girl. If father could teach her something, I'm sure I could."

So he went walking through the fields, and pretty soon he saw Lois, standing among her geese, who were feeding on the grass.

Huckleberry skipped up to her as lively as a cricket.

"Can you tell me," said he, "why an elephant with a glass globe of gold-fish tied to his tail is like the Lord High Admiral of the British Isles?"

"Was the globe of gold-fish all the elephant owned?" asked the goose-girl, thoughfully.

"Yes," said Huckleberry. "But I don't see what that's got to do with it."

"Then the answer is," said Lois, without noticing this last remark, "because all his property is entailed."

"Well, I de-clare!" cried Huckleberry, opening his eyes as wide as they would go, "if you didn't guess it! Why, I didn't know it had an answer."

"I wish it hadn't had an answer," said the goose-girl, suddenly stamping her foot. "I wish there had never been any answer to it in the whole world. It was only yesterday that I promised Old Riddler that I would never guess another riddle, and here I've done it! It's too bad!"

"I don't think it is," cried Huckleberry, waving his little cap around by the tassel. "It's all very well for father not to want people to guess his riddles, because they've got answers and he knows what they are. But I would never have known that any of mine had an answer if you hadn't guessed this one. If you had had a riddle like this one, wouldn't you have been glad to have some one tell you the answer?"

"Yes, I would," said Lois.

"Well, then, my good girl, remember this: If a thing gives you pleasure, it's very likely that it will give somebody else pleasure. So let somebody else have a chance, and the next time you hear a riddle that you think the owner has no answer for, guess it for him, if you can." Good-by!"

And away went Master Huckleberry, skipping and singing and snapping his fingers and twirling his cap, until he came to a wide crack in the ground, when he rolled himself up like a huckleberry dumpling, and went tumbling and bouncing down into the underground home of the gnomes.

"Get out of the way!" said he to the gnomes he passed, as he proudly strode to his father's apartments. "I'm going to make a report. For the first time in my life I've taught somebody something."

When Huckleberry left her, the goose-girl stood silently in the midst of her geese. Her brow was overcast.

"How's anybody to do two things that can't both be done?" she exclaimed at last. "I'll have nothing more to do with riddles as long as I live."

———————◆———————

GOLDILOCKS AND THE THREE BEARS

Credit: Arthur Rackham

Once upon a time there were three Bears, who lived together in a house of their own, in a wood. One of them was a Little Wee Bear, and one was a Middle-sized Bear, and the other was a Great Big Bear. They had each a bowl for their porridge; a little bowl for the Little Wee Bear; and a middle-sized bowl for the Middle-sized Bear; and a great bowl for the Great Big Bear. And they had each a chair to sit in; a little chair for the Little Wee Bear; and a middle-sized chair for the Middle-sized Bear; and a great chair for the Great Big Bear. And they had each a bed to sleep in; a little bed for the Little Wee Bear; and a middle-sized bed for the Middle-sized Bear; and a great bed for the Great Big Bear.

One day, after they had made the porridge for their breakfast, and poured it into their porridge-bowls, they walked out into the wood while the porridge was cooling, that they might not burn their mouths by beginning too soon, for they were polite, well-brought-up Bears. And while they were away a little girl called Goldilocks, who lived at the other side of the wood and had been sent on an errand by her mother, passed by the house, and looked in at the window. And then she peeped in at the keyhole, for she was not at all a well-brought-up little girl. Then seeing nobody in the house she lifted the latch. The door was not fastened, because the Bears were good Bears, who did nobody any harm, and never suspected that anybody would harm them. So Goldilocks opened the door and went in; and well pleased was she when she saw the porridge on the table. If she had been a well-brought-up little girl she would have waited till the Bears came home, and then, perhaps, they would have asked her to breakfast; for they were good Bears—a little rough or so, as the manner of Bears is, but for all that very good-natured and hospitable. But she was an impudent, rude little girl, and so she set about helping herself.

First she tasted the porridge of the Great Big Bear, and that was too hot for her. Next she tasted the porridge of the Middle-sized Bear, but that was too cold for her. And then she went to the porridge of the Little Wee Bear, and tasted it, and that was neither too hot nor too cold, but just right, and she liked it so well that she ate it all up, every bit!

Then Goldilocks, who was tired, for she had been catching butterflies instead of running on her errand, sat down in the chair of the Great Big Bear, but that was too hard for her. And then she sat down in the chair of the Middle-sized Bear, and that was too soft for her. But when she sat down in the chair of the Little Wee Bear, which was neither too hard nor too soft, but just right. So she seated herself in it, and there she sate till the bottom of the chair came out, and down she came, plump upon the ground; and that made her very cross, for she was a bad-tempered little girl.

Now, being determined to rest, Goldilocks went upstairs into the bedchamber in which the Three Bears slept. And first she lay down upon the bed of the Great

Big Bear, but that was too high at the head for her. And next she lay down upon the bed of the Middle-sized Bear, and that was too high at the foot for her. And then she lay down upon the bed of the Little Wee Bear, and that was neither too high at the head nor at the foot, but just right. So she covered herself up comfortably, and lay there till she fell fast asleep.

By this time the Three Bears thought their porridge would be cool enough for them to eat it properly; so they came home to breakfast. Now careless Goldilocks had left the spoon of the Great Big Bear standing in his porridge.

"Somebody Has Been At My Porridge!"

said the Great Big Bear in his great, rough, gruff voice.

Then the Middle-sized Bear looked at his porridge and saw the spoon was standing in it too.

"Somebody Has Been At My Porridge!"

said the Middle-sized Bear in his middle-sized voice.

Then the Little Wee Bear looked at his, and there was the spoon in the porridge-bowl, but the porridge was all gone!

"Somebody Has Been At My Porridge, And Has Eaten It All Up!"

said the Little Wee Bear in his little wee voice.

Upon this the Three Bears, seeing that some one had entered their house, and eaten up the Little Wee Bear's breakfast, began to look about them. Now the careless

Goldilocks had not put the hard cushion straight when she rose from the chair of the Great Big Bear.

"Somebody Has Been Sitting In My Chair!"

said the Great Big Bear in his great, rough, gruff voice.

And the careless Goldilocks had squatted down the soft cushion of the Middle-sized Bear.

"Somebody Has Been Sitting In My Chair!"

said the Middle-sized Bear in his middle-sized voice.

"Somebody Has Been Sitting In My Chair, And Has Sate The Bottom Through!"

said the Little Wee Bear in his little wee voice.

Then the Three Bears thought they had better make further search in case it was a burglar, so they went upstairs into their bedchamber. Now Goldilocks had pulled the pillow of the Great Big Bear out of its place.

"Somebody Has Been Lying In My Bed!"

said the Great Big Bear in his great, rough, gruff voice.

And Goldilocks had pulled the bolster of the Middle-sized Bear out of its place.

"Somebody Has Been Lying In My Bed!"

said the Middle-sized Bear in his middle-sized voice.

But when the Little Wee Bear came to look at his bed, there was the bolster in its place! And the pillow was in its place upon the bolster!

And upon the pillow——?

There was Goldilocks's yellow head—which was not in its place, for she had no business there.

"Somebody Has Been Lying In My Bed,—And Here She Is Still!"

said the Little Wee Bear in his little wee voice.

Now Goldilocks had heard in her sleep the great, rough, gruff voice of the Great Big Bear; but she was so fast asleep that it was no more to her than the roaring of wind, or the rumbling of thunder. And she had heard the middle-sized voice of the Middle-sized Bear, but it was only as if she had heard some one speaking in a dream. But when she heard the little wee voice of the Little Wee Bear, it was so sharp, and so shrill, that it awakened her at once. Up she started, and when she saw the Three Bears on one side of the bed, she tumbled herself out at the other, and ran to the window. Now the window was open, because the Bears, like good, tidy Bears, as they were, always opened their bedchamber window when they got up in the morning. So naughty, frightened little Goldilocks jumped; and whether she broke her neck in the fall, or ran into the wood and was lost there, or found her way out of the wood and got whipped for being a bad girl and playing truant, no one can say. But the Three Bears never saw anything more of her.

THE ANDROCLUS AND THE LION

Credit: James Baldwin

In Rome there was once a poor slave whose name was Androclus. His master was a cruel man, and so unkind to him that at last Androclus ran away.

He hid himself in a wild wood for many days; but there was no food to be found, and he grew so weak and sick that he thought he should die. So one day he crept into a cave and lay down, and soon he was fast asleep.

After a while a great noise woke him up. A lion had come into the cave, and was roaring loudly. Androclus was very much afraid, for he felt sure that the beast would kill him. Soon, however, he saw that the lion was not angry, but that he limped as though his foot hurt him.

Then Androclus grew so bold that he took hold of the lion's lame paw to see what was the matter. The lion stood quite still, and rubbed his head against the man's shoulder. He seemed to say,--

"I know that you will help me."

Androclus lifted the paw from the ground, and saw that it was a long, sharp thorn which hurt the lion so much. He took the end of the thorn in his fingers; then he gave a strong, quick pull, and out it came. The lion was full of joy. He jumped about like a dog, and licked the hands and feet of his new friend.

Androclus was not at all afraid after this; and when night came, he and the lion lay down and slept side by side.

For a long time, the lion brought food to Androclus every day; and the two became such good friends, that Androclus found his new life a very happy one.

One day some soldiers who were passing through the wood found Androclus in the cave. They knew who he was, and so took him back to Rome.

It was the law at that time that every slave who ran away from his master should be made to fight a hungry lion. So a fierce lion was shut up for a while without food, and a time was set for the fight.

When the day came, thousands of people crowded to see the sport. They went to such places at that time very much as people now-a-days go to see a circus show or a game of baseball.

The door opened, and poor Androclus was brought in. He was almost dead with fear, for the roars of the lion could already be heard. He looked up, and saw that there was no pity in the thousands of faces around him.

Then the hungry lion rushed in. With a single bound he reached the poor slave. Androclus gave a great cry, not of fear, but of gladness. It was his old friend, the lion of the cave.

The people, who had expected to see the man killed by the lion, were filled with wonder. They saw Androclus put his arms around the lion's neck; they saw the lion lie down at his feet, and lick them lovingly; they saw the great beast rub his head against the slave's face as though he wanted to be petted. They could not understand what it all meant.

After a while they asked Androclus to tell them about it. So he stood up before them, and, with his arm around the lion's neck, told how he and the beast had lived together in the cave.

"I am a man," he said; "but no man has ever befriended me. This poor lion alone has been kind to me; and we love each other as brothers."

The people were not so bad that they could be cruel to the poor slave now. "Live and be free!" they cried. "Live and be free!"

Others cried, "Let the lion go free too! Give both of them their liberty!"

And so Androclus was set free, and the lion was given to him for his own. And they lived together in Rome for many years.

———•◆•———

THE STORY OF UGLY DUCKLING

Credit: Hans Christian Andersen

IT was lovely summer weather in the country, and the golden corn, the green oats, and the haystacks piled up in the meadows looked beautiful. The stork walking about on his long red legs chattered in the Egyptian language, which he had learnt from his mother. The corn-fields and meadows were surrounded by large forests, in the midst of which were deep pools. It was, indeed, delightful to walk about in the country. In a sunny spot stood a pleasant old farm-house close by a deep river, and from the house down to the water side grew great burdock leaves, so high, that under the tallest of them a little child could stand upright. The spot was as wild as the centre of a thick wood. In this snug retreat sat a duck on her nest, watching for her young brood to hatch; she was beginning to get tired of her task, for the little ones were a long time coming out of their shells, and she seldom had any visitors. The other ducks liked much better to swim about in the river than to climb the slippery banks, and sit under a burdock leaf, to have a gossip with her. At length one shell cracked, and then another, and from each egg came a living creature that lifted its head and cried, "Peep, peep." "Quack, quack," said the mother, and then they all quacked as well as they could, and looked about them on every side at the large green leaves. Their mother allowed them to look as much as they liked, because green is good for the eyes. "How large the world is," said the young ducks, when they found how much more room they now had than while they were inside the egg-shell. "Do you imagine this is the whole world?" asked the mother; "Wait till you have seen the garden; it stretches far beyond that to the parson's field, but I have never ventured to such a distance. Are you all out?" she continued, rising; "No, I declare, the largest egg lies there still. I wonder how long this is to last, I am quite tired of it;" and she seated herself again on the nest.

"Well, how are you getting on?" asked an old duck, who paid her a visit.

"One egg is not hatched yet," said the duck, "it will not break. But just look at all the others, are they not the prettiest little ducklings you ever saw? They are the image of their father, who is so unkind, he never comes to see."

"Let me see the egg that will not break," said the duck; "I have no doubt it is a turkey's egg. I was persuaded to hatch some once, and after all my care and trouble with the young ones, they were afraid of the water. I quacked and clucked, but all to no purpose. I could not get them to venture in. Let me look at the egg. Yes, that is a turkey's egg; take my advice, leave it where it is and teach the other children to swim."

"I think I will sit on it a little while longer," said the duck; "as I have sat so long already, a few days will be nothing."

"Please yourself," said the old duck, and she went away.

At last the large egg broke, and a young one crept forth crying, "Peep, peep." It was very large and ugly. The duck stared at it and exclaimed, "It is very large and not at all like the others. I wonder if it really is a turkey. We shall soon find it out, however when we go to the water. It must go in, if I have to push it myself."

On the next day the weather was delightful, and the sun shone brightly on the green burdock leaves, so the mother duck took her young brood down to the water, and jumped in with a splash. "Quack, quack," cried she, and one after another the little ducklings jumped in. The water closed over their heads, but they came up again in an instant, and swam about quite prettily with their legs paddling under them as easily as possible, and the ugly duckling was also in the water swimming with them.

"Oh," said the mother, "that is not a turkey; how well he uses his legs, and how upright he holds himself! He is my own child, and he is not so very ugly after all if you look at him properly. Quack, quack! come with me now, I will take you into grand society, and introduce you to the farmyard, but you must keep close to me or you may be trodden upon; and, above all, beware of the cat."

When they reached the farmyard, there was a great disturbance, two families were fighting for an eel's head, which, after all, was carried off by the cat. "See, children, that is the way of the world," said the mother duck, whetting her beak, for she would have liked the eel's head herself. "Come, now, use your legs, and let me see how well you can behave. You must bow your heads prettily to that old duck yonder; she is the highest born of them all, and has Spanish blood, therefore, she is well off. Don't you see she has a red flag tied to her leg, which is something very grand, and a great honor for a duck; it shows that every one is anxious not to lose her, as she can be recognized both by man and beast. Come, now, don't turn your toes, a well-bred duckling spreads his feet wide apart, just like his father and mother, in this way; now bend your neck, and say 'quack.'"

The ducklings did as they were bid, but the other duck stared, and said, "Look, here comes another brood, as if there were not enough of us already! and what a queer looking object one of them is; we don't want him here," and then one flew out and bit him in the neck.

"Let him alone," said the mother; "he is not doing any harm."

"Yes, but he is so big and ugly," said the spiteful duck "and therefore he must be turned out."

"The others are very pretty children," said the old duck, with the rag on her leg, "all but that one; I wish his mother could improve him a little."

"That is impossible, your grace," replied the mother; "he is not pretty; but he has a very good disposition, and swims as well or even better than the others. I think he will grow up pretty, and perhaps be smaller; he has remained too long in the egg, and therefore his figure is not properly formed;" and then she stroked his neck and smoothed the feathers, saying, "It is a drake, and therefore not of so much consequence. I think he will grow up strong, and able to take care of himself."

"The other ducklings are graceful enough," said the old duck. "Now make yourself at home, and if you can find an eel's head, you can bring it to me."

And so they made themselves comfortable; but the poor duckling, who had crept out of his shell last of all, and looked so ugly, was bitten and pushed and made fun of, not only by the ducks, but by all the poultry. "He is too big," they all said, and the turkey cock, who had been born into the world with spurs, and fancied himself really an emperor, puffed himself out like a vessel in full sail, and flew at the duckling, and became quite red in the head with passion, so that the poor little thing did not know where to go, and was quite miserable because he was so ugly and laughed at by the whole farmyard. So it went on from day to day till it got worse and worse. The poor duckling was driven about by every one; even his brothers and sisters were unkind to him, and would say, "Ah, you ugly creature, I wish the cat would get you," and his mother said she wished he had never been born. The ducks pecked him, the chickens beat him, and the girl who fed the poultry kicked him with her feet. So at last he ran away, frightening the little birds in the hedge as he flew over the palings.

"They are afraid of me because I am ugly," he said. So he closed his eyes, and flew still farther, until he came out on a large moor, inhabited by wild ducks. Here he remained the whole night, feeling very tired and sorrowful.

In the morning, when the wild ducks rose in the air, they stared at their new comrade. "What sort of a duck are you?" they all said, coming round him.

He bowed to them, and was as polite as he could be, but he did not reply to their question. "You are exceedingly ugly," said the wild ducks, "but that will not matter if you do not want to marry one of our family."

Poor thing! he had no thoughts of marriage; all he wanted was permission to lie among the rushes, and drink some of the water on the moor. After he had been on the moor two days, there came two wild geese, or rather goslings, for they had not been out of the egg long, and were very saucy. "Listen, friend," said one of them to the duckling, "you are so ugly, that we like you very well. Will you go with us, and become a bird of passage? Not far from here is another moor, in which there are some pretty wild geese, all unmarried. It is a chance for you to get a wife; you may be lucky, ugly as you are."

"Pop, pop," sounded in the air, and the two wild geese fell dead among the rushes, and the water was tinged with blood. "Pop, pop," echoed far and wide in the distance, and whole flocks of wild geese rose up from the rushes. The sound continued from every direction, for the sportsmen surrounded the moor, and some were even seated on branches of trees, overlooking the rushes. The blue smoke from the guns rose like clouds over the dark trees, and as it floated away across the water, a number of sporting dogs bounded in among the rushes, which bent beneath them wherever they went. How they terrified the poor duckling! He turned away his head to hide it under his wing, and at the same moment a large terrible dog passed quite near him. His jaws were open, his tongue hung from his mouth, and his eyes glared fearfully. He thrust his nose close to the duckling, showing his sharp teeth, and then, "splash, splash," he went into the water without touching him, "Oh," sighed the duckling, "how thankful I am for being so ugly; even a dog will not bite me." And so he lay quite still, while the shot rattled through the rushes, and gun after gun was fired over him. It was late in the day before all became quiet, but even then the poor young thing did not dare to move. He waited quietly for several hours, and then, after looking carefully around him, hastened away from the moor as fast as he could. He ran over field and meadow till a storm arose, and he could hardly struggle against it. Towards evening, he reached a poor little cottage that seemed ready to fall, and only remained standing because it could not decide on which side to fall first. The storm continued so violent, that the duckling could go no farther; he sat down by the cottage, and then he noticed that the door was not quite closed in consequence of one of the hinges having given way. There was therefore a narrow opening near the bottom large enough for him to slip through, which he did very quietly, and got a shelter for the night. A woman, a tom cat, and a hen lived in this cottage. The tom cat, whom the mistress called, "My little son," was a great favorite; he could raise his back, and purr, and could even throw out sparks from his fur if it were stroked the wrong way. The hen had very short legs, so she was called "Chickie short legs." She laid good eggs, and her mistress loved her as if she had been her own child. In the morning, the strange visitor was discovered, and the tom cat began to purr, and the hen to cluck.

"What is that noise about?" said the old woman, looking round the room, but her sight was not very good; therefore, when she saw the duckling she thought it must be a fat duck, that had strayed from home. "Oh what a prize!" she exclaimed, "I hope it is not a drake, for then I shall have some duck's eggs. I must wait and see." So the duckling was allowed to remain on trial for three weeks, but there were no eggs. Now the tom cat was the master of the house, and the hen was mistress, and they always said, "We and the world," for they believed themselves to be half the world, and the better half too. The duckling thought that others might hold a different opinion on the subject, but the hen would not listen to such doubts. "Can you lay eggs?" she asked. "No." "Then have the goodness to hold your tongue." "Can you raise your back, or purr, or throw out sparks?" said the tom cat. "No." "Then you have no right to express an opinion when sensible people are speaking." So the duckling sat in a corner, feeling very low spirited, till the sunshine and the fresh air came into the room through the open door, and then he began to feel such a great longing for a swim on the water, that he could not help telling the hen.

"What an absurd idea," said the hen. "You have nothing else to do, therefore you have foolish fancies. If you could purr or lay eggs, they would pass away."

"But it is so delightful to swim about on the water," said the duckling, "and so refreshing to feel it close over your head, while you dive down to the bottom."

"Delightful, indeed!" said the hen, "why you must be crazy! Ask the cat, he is the cleverest animal I know, ask him how he would like to swim about on the water, or to dive under it, for I will not speak of my own opinion; ask our mistress, the old woman- there is no one in the world more clever than she is. Do you think she would like to swim, or to let the water close over her head?"

"You don't understand me," said the duckling.

"We don't understand you? Who can understand you, I wonder? Do you consider yourself more clever than the cat, or the old woman? I will say nothing of myself. Don't imagine such nonsense, child, and thank your good fortune that you have been received here. Are you not in a warm room, and in society from which you may learn something. But you are a chatterer, and your company is not very agreeable. Believe me, I speak only for your own good. I may tell you unpleasant truths, but that is a proof of my friendship. I advise you, therefore, to lay eggs, and learn to purr as quickly as possible."

"I believe I must go out into the world again," said the duckling.

"Yes, do," said the hen. So the duckling left the cottage, and soon found water on which it could swim and dive, but was avoided by all other animals, because of its ugly appearance. Autumn came, and the leaves in the forest turned to orange and gold. then, as winter approached, the wind caught them as they fell and whirled them in the cold air. The clouds, heavy with hail and snow-flakes, hung low in the sky, and the raven stood on the ferns crying, "Croak, croak." It made one shiver with cold to look at him. All this was very sad for the poor little duckling. One evening, just as the sun set amid radiant clouds, there came a large flock of beautiful birds out of the bushes. The duckling had never seen any like them before. They were swans, and they curved their graceful necks, while their soft plumage shown with dazzling whiteness. They uttered a singular cry, as they spread their glorious wings and flew away from those cold regions to warmer countries across the sea. As they mounted higher and higher in the air, the ugly little duckling felt quite a strange sensation as he watched them. He whirled himself in the water like a wheel, stretched out his neck towards them, and uttered a cry so strange that it frightened himself. Could he ever forget those beautiful, happy birds; and when at last they were out of his sight, he dived under the water, and rose again almost beside himself with excitement. He knew not the names of these birds, nor where they had flown, but he felt towards them as he had never felt for any other bird in the world. He was not envious of these beautiful creatures, but wished to be as lovely as they. Poor ugly creature, how gladly he would have lived even with the ducks had they only given him encouragement. The winter grew colder and colder; he was obliged to swim about on the water to keep it from freezing, but every night the space on which he swam became smaller and smaller. At length it froze so hard that the ice in the water crackled as he moved, and the duckling had to paddle with his legs as well as he could, to keep the space from closing up. He became exhausted at last, and lay still and helpless, frozen fast in the ice. Early in the morning, a peasant, who was passing by, saw what had happened. He broke the ice in pieces with his wooden shoe, and carried the duckling home to his wife. The warmth revived the poor little creature; but when the children wanted to play with him, the duckling thought they would do him some harm; so he started up in terror, fluttered into the milk-pan, and splashed the milk about the room. Then the woman clapped her hands, which frightened him still more. He flew first into the butter-cask, then into the meal-tub, and out again. What a condition he was in! The woman screamed, and struck at him with the tongs; the children laughed and screamed, and tumbled over each other, in their efforts to catch him; but luckily he escaped. The door stood open; the poor creature could just manage to slip out among the bushes, and lie down quite exhausted in the newly fallen snow.

It would be very sad, were I to relate all the misery and privations which the poor little duckling endured during the hard winter; but when it had passed, he found himself lying one morning in a moor, amongst the rushes. He felt the warm sun shining, and heard the lark singing, and saw that all around was beautiful spring. Then the young bird felt that his wings were strong, as he flapped them against his sides, and rose high into the air. They bore him onwards, until he found himself in a large garden, before he well knew how it had happened. The apple-trees were in full blossom, and the fragrant elders bent their long green branches down to the stream which wound round a smooth lawn. Everything looked beautiful, in the freshness of early spring. From a thicket close by came three beautiful white swans, rustling their feathers, and swimming lightly over the smooth water.

The duckling remembered the lovely birds, and felt more strangely unhappy than ever.

"I will fly to those royal birds," he exclaimed, "and they will kill me, because I am so ugly, and dare to approach them; but it does not matter: better be killed by them than pecked by the ducks, beaten by the hens, pushed about by the maiden who feeds the poultry, or starved with hunger in the winter."

Then he flew to the water, and swam towards the beautiful swans. The moment they espied the stranger, they rushed to meet him with outstretched wings.

"Kill me," said the poor bird; and he bent his head down to the surface of the water, and awaited death.

But what did he see in the clear stream below? His own image; no longer a dark, gray bird, ugly and disagreeable to look at, but a graceful and beautiful swan. To be born in a duck's nest, in a farmyard, is of no consequence to a bird, if it is hatched from a swan's egg. He now felt glad at having suffered sorrow and trouble, because it enabled him to enjoy so much better all the pleasure and happiness around him; for the great swans swam round the new-comer, and stroked his neck with their beaks, as a welcome.

Into the garden presently came some little children, and threw bread and cake into the water.

"See," cried the youngest, "there is a new one;" and the rest were delighted, and ran to their father and mother, dancing and clapping their hands, and shouting joyously, "There is another swan come; a new one has arrived."

Then they threw more bread and cake into the water, and said, "The new one is the most beautiful of all; he is so young and pretty." And the old swans bowed their heads before him.

Then he felt quite ashamed, and hid his head under his wing; for he did not know what to do, he was so happy, and yet not at all proud. He had been persecuted and despised for his ugliness, and now he heard them say he was the most beautiful of all the birds. Even the elder-tree bent down its bows into the water before him, and the sun shone warm and bright. Then he rustled his feathers, curved his slender neck, and cried joyfully, from the depths of his heart, "I never dreamed of such happiness as this, while I was an ugly duckling." - -

———◆———

THE EXPLORATIONS OF FISH AND CHIPS

Credit: Margo Fallis

The boat rushed across the loch, it's engine churning the water in its wake. A moss-covered rock jutted out of the water. "There it is," Fish shouted. "I've got the map. The treasure is supposedly buried on the other side of that island. Go around to the back of it." James Edward Cameron Ross pointed to the left.

"You're awfully bossy for a ten year old," his older brother said. "Maybe I should toss you overboard and you can swim with the other fish, Fish." Harry rustled Fish's reddish brown hair.

"Leave him alone, Harry. You're always teasing him. This time he knows what he's talking about," Chips scowled.

"You're lecturing me? A girl named Chips? How did your parents ever come up with that nickname from Fiona Moira Campbell?" Harry steered the boat towards the rocky shore.

"It doesn't matter, does it. Just do as Fish asks," Chips said.

"Yes, Ma'm." Fourteen year old Harry rode the boat onto the pebbles. "There. We're here on Haggis Island. I suppose we're going to see wild haggis running around." The boy roared with laughter.

Ignoring him, Fish said, "I found this map behind an old picture Mum and Dad had in the loft. I think it's real. It says there's a chest of gold buried here."

"Who buried it here? There were no pirates in this area, unless I missed something in my school studies," Harry said.

"Not pirates, Harry; the Spanish Armada. During the war a Scottish ship, the HMS Ormsdon, captured a Spanish ship. They took all the treasure, gold, emeralds, rubies and all that, and put it in their hold. They were on their way back to Edinburgh when a storm came up and carried the ship clear up here. It finally crashed into Haggis Island and sunk. Two men from the coast watched the ship flounder and rowed over to this island. Their names were Angus McGregor and Walter Lamont. They found the wreckage, salvaged all the gold and jewels and then rowed back home. Neither of them wanted anyone else to find it." Fish took a deep breath.

"Why didn't they go back and get it later and when did you hear such story?" Harry glanced at his brother.

"I learned about it in school. They didn't go back to get it because they both went out fishing the next day and their boat sunk. The only reason anyone knows about the gold is because one of the men told his wife. People have been searching for the gold since that day. The map was hidden by Angus McGregor and stayed that way until I found it a few days ago. I've been researching the shipwreck and it's true, Harry. Chips and I want to find it."

"Fish and Chips. What a team! I hope you find it and that I get my share for riding you over here in the dingy." Harry stepped out of the boat. "Come on. Help me tie this up and we'll search for the gold. I hope your map has good directions."

The three of them looked around the ancient volcanic rock.

"There's not much on this island, is there, Fish?" Chips crunched her nose to the side. "Looks rather barren. There's hardly a tree or a bush in sight. I agree with Harry. I hope the map is accurate."

Fish pulled it out of his pocket. "Here we are right here," he pointed, showing the others their location. "It says we have to climb to the highest spot of the island. That's high, don't you think?"

"I hope we don't die trying to get up there. The rock is covered with wet moss and bird poop," Chips said, shaking her head. "Why do we have to climb to the highest point? Surely they didn't bury it up there. Everyone knows you bury treasure in the sand on the beach."

"Not always," Harry added. "The sea erodes the beach. It's been over 400 years since they buried it. The sand surely would have been washed away. Of course, they weren't planning on leaving it in there for that long. Let's just follow the map and see what happens. If nothing else, I'm having a good time watching the two of you make total fools of yourselves."

Fish and Chips ignored him. A trail wound its way up to the top, though narrow and slippery. Flocks of screeching birds flew into the air with each step they took. "I can see our house," Fish said. "I can see your house too, Chips."

"Me too. This loch is much larger than I thought it was," she said.

"Answer me this, Fish. If the ship was carried by the sea up the coast, how on earth did it wreck on this island in the middle of a loch?" Harry put his arms on his hips.

"This is a salt water loch, or at least part of it is," Fish answered.

"Salt water? Don't be daft, lad." Harry sat on the jagged stones. "I know it's tidal. I've just never thought much about it before now."

"A sea river comes into the loch during high tide. It mixes with the fresh water, so by the time it comes here, it's pretty diluted. The ship must have drifted in during high tide." Fish shrugged his shoulders.

"All right, Fish. We're up here. What do we do next?" Chips didn't feel like spending her entire day on top of the rock admiring the scenery.

"What's the rush? What else is there to do? I'm tired of looking for birds in the moor and I'm tired of digging up blocks of peat. At least here we don't have to do chores." Fish glanced at the map. "We have to go down this other side about half way. There's a cave." He showed them the path on the map.

"Let's get going then. It looks like it might rain later. We'd better hurry," Chips said.

They clambered down the trail, careful not to slip. "Is this it? It looks like a cave." Harry stuck his head inside.

"Go in and find out then." Chips leaned her hand on the rim of the cave. "Watch out for haggis. They say wild haggis live in caves."

"Very funny, Chips." Harry ducked his head and went into the cave. Fish and Chips followed. "It's dark. Did one of you bring a torch?"

"I did," Fish said. He pulled one out of his pocket and handed it to his brother. "Here."

Harry turned it on and shone it about the cave. "I can't see any treasure chests in here."

"It's not buried in here. We have to look for a marking. The marking points to a key," Fish said.

"A key? They buried a key to the chest in a cave under a marking? This sounds like it is out of a Robert Louis Stevenson book. I suppose you're not going to tell me we have to make a bargain with a ghost?" Harry swung the beam of the torch along the walls.

"The marking looks like a..." Fish didn't finish.

"A skull and crossbones? Come on, Fish. This is a joke," his brother said.

"No, it's not. It's real. We're not looking for a skull and crossbones. We are looking for a triangle with a circle inside it. I doubt very much if Angus or Walter spent too much time carving something elaborate on the cave wall. Start looking." Fish ran to the back of the cave and ran his hands along it, feeling for an indentation.

"I found it," Chips shouted. "It's a triangle with a circle inside, just like you said." She followed the point of the triangle down to the ground. Brushing the dirt out of the way, she felt a hole. "I think I've got it." She stuck her fingers in and pulled out a long, rusty key.

"It's a key!" Harry took it from Chips, shining the torch on it. "It's rusted and definitely old-fashioned."

Fish ran over to them. "Wow! It is real. Now all we have to do is follow the map to the treasure."

"Does X mark the spot?" Harry burst out laughing. "Sorry, Fish," he said, seeing his brother's scowl.

"Where do we go next, Fish?" Chips took the key and put it in her pocket. "It'll be safe in here."

"We have to go down the trail. There's another cave and it can only be found when the tide is out." Fish stood high above the entrance to the cave and stared down. "The tide is out right now. Come on before it starts coming in again."

"Fish, the sky's getting dark. I don't want to be stranded out here all day and night."

"Don't you trust my boating skills, Chips?" Harry poked her in the ribs.

"Not really. My dad has a hard time with a boat in the stormy waters of this loch. You know about that. Your dad nearly drowned a few years ago, Harry." Chips frowned and glanced at the sky.

"She's right. Let's get on with this." Harry headed down the trail. "We need to get to the bottom." Half an hour later they stood in front of the cave. "The tide is out. Let's go inside. What are we looking for this time?"

"They carved a square with a triangle inside," Fish said.

Harry shook his head. "They weren't very creative, were they."

"Use the torch, Harry and let's find the marking. Once we find it, Fish, what then?" Chips stepped into the cave. Water rushed in, splashing on her legs. "The tide's starting to come in. Well?"

Fish looked at the map. "There's a stone in the shape of a horse. We need it to get into the chest."

"A horse? Why in the world do we need a horse-shaped stone to get into the treasure? Sounds like Angus and Walter were a wee bit off their heads if you ask me." Harry twisted his fingers around in a circle just off his ear. "Madmen."

"Harry, if you're going to be negative, just go sit in the boat and wait. Otherwise be quiet and help look for the square. Use the torch." Chips sighed. "Start looking. I don't like this at all. The tide's coming in and there's a storm on the horizon. Let's just hurry up and do this."

It only took a few minutes to find the marking and the stone. Fish put it in his pocket and they rushed out of the cave just as the waves rolled in. "That was close. We'd have been trapped in there and drowned," Harry said.

"What next, Fish?" Chips felt her pocket to make sure the key was still there.

"Back down to the beach. After we get off the rock, we have to take fifteen steps."

"Fifteen of your size steps, or fifteen of Harry's size steps?" Chips looked down at the map. "It doesn't say. I suppose it would be more Harry's size. Walter and Angus were grown men."

Once they reached the sand, Harry took the steps, stretching his legs as far as he could. "Thirteen, fourteen, fifteen. This is it then?"

"It should be." Fish looked around.

"What's wrong, Fish?" Chips showed concern.

"I forgot to bring a spade. What will we dig it up with?"

"Our bare hands, I suppose." Harry knelt and started moving wet sand to the side. "Well? Are you two going to leave me to do all the work, or are you going to help?"

Fish and Chips knelt and pushed the sand out of the way. They dug until the hole was deep enough for Fish to stand it.

"Where's the treasure chest?" Harry tapped his foot on the sand.

"I'm not digging one more handful, Fish. This has been a complete waste of time." Chips rambled on.

Fish eyed the walls. "I see something. Jump down in here with me."

"No way. One of us has to stay up here. Besides that, the tide is coming in and in a few minutes that hole will be under water." Harry refused to move.

Chips jumped into the hole. "There is something." She and fish dug with their fingers. "It's a chest. It's true. There is a chest."

Harry changed his mind and jumped in. "I'll help you."

Ten minutes later they had the chest in their hands. Harry said, "You two climb out and stand near the hole. You're going to have to help me from up there." He grabbed the sides and struggled to lift it to his knees. "Grab it. It's heavy."

Fish and Chips reached down, grabbed the handles and pulled it out onto the ground.

Harry climbed out and the three of them sat staring at it. The first waves lapped at their feet. "Let's take this to higher ground."

"What about our boat? Did we pull it far enough so that the tide doesn't carry it out?" Chips glanced at Harry.

"Yes, I think so. Let's take the chest back to the boat. We can take it home and open it there." Harry dragged it across the sand. "Are you going to help me with this thing or just stand there all day?"

Chips stood behind the chest and pushed it. "We don't have to climb back the way we came, do we? Can't we walk around the beach?" She looked at the incoming waves. "If we hurry, I'm sure we can make it." Huffing and puffing, they hauled it all the way around the island.

"There's the boat!" Fish left the other two with the chest and ran. "The tide is about to carry it out. Run!"

"Hey! Get back here and help!" Chips felt the first raindrops fall, splattering on her face. She and Harry lugged the chest to the dingy. She looked at the sky. Gray clouds, dark and heavy, unloaded their moisture on the island. "We're doomed. We can't possibly go home in this weather. Harry, we're all going to have to help lift this thing into the boat."

"If we put it in the dingy, then the waves might carry it and the dingy away," Harry said.

"What?" Fish glanced at the waves. "The storm's not that bad."

"We're going to have to take it to the cave," Harry said.

Chips glared at Fish. "Now, pull the boat onto the sand."

The waves grew and the rain came down harder with every passing moment. "All right. Let's get to the cave and wait this storm out. We can open the chest in the cave," Fish said.

"It will be nearly impossible to carry this heavy chest all the way up there. However, I might be motivated if I knew it held rubies and emeralds and gold." Harry snickered.

"You're right. We should open it right here. I'm rather excited, aren't you?" Fish winked at Chips. "We might become the richest people in Scotland in just a few minutes."

Chips reached into her pocket. "Here's the key."

Harry opened the lid. "What? There's another compartment. Give me that horse-shaped stone, Fish." Harry pushed it into a matching shaped hole. The second lid popped open.

"Bottles?" Chips stared at the glass.

Fish lifted one of them up. "It's Spanish wine. That's their treasure? We did all this work for a case of wine?"

Chips laughed. "This is brilliant."

Harry laughed too. "Wine? I suppose to 16th century men this would be a treasure. Say, if this wine is over 400 years old, it must be worth a pretty penny. I say we take it to Hamish McMillan at the Heather and Thistle Inn. He'd probably give us a few quid for it. At least we can have enough money for a fish supper, eh Fish?" Harry nudged his brother.

Fish sighed. "I wanted it to be gold and jewels, not wine."

"Don't fret, Fish. We'll have lots of other adventures. I hear there's a load of Celtic treasure buried in the Garlochie Hills. Maybe we can search for that." Chips patted Fish on the back.

"Enough of this, glum behavior. We'll get paid a pretty penny for this wine." Harry slapped Fish on the shoulder.

They spent the next few hours telling stories of ghosts and robbers and even shared a few haggis tales.

The storm passed and Harry took them and their cache of wine back to shore. Immediately they headed for the Heather and Thistle Inn. Hamish was quite pleased to see the wine, paid them enough to bring long-lasting smiles to their faces. After a fish supper, Fish and Chips and Harry headed home, knowing they'd never forget their day at Haggis Island.

————◆————

THE ADVENTEROUS FISHING TRIP

Credit: Margo Fallis

The sun's golden rays, shimmering in the morning sky, peeked out from behind the lofty peak of Ben Collin. Morning mist blanketed the countryside until the sun's warmth began to burn it off, leaving small patches dotting the landscape. Several ducks flew from the banks of the loch into the golden-lined, pinkish clouds.

As Maggie stirred in her bed, the sun burst through her window. "Time to get up, Maggie," Gran said, pulling the covers away from Maggie's snuggling body. "We're going fishing this morning. Remember?"

Maggie yawned and stretched, and then sat up and rubbed her eyes. "Are you going too, Gran?" she asked.

"Yes, lass. I want to go. Is that all right with you?"

"Oh Gran, of course it's all right," Maggie smiled, reaching her arms up to hug her grandmother.

Maggie climbed out of bed and quickly dressed in her blue and green tartan pants, a white turtleneck with long sleeves and a small cluster of bluebells embroidered on it, and tied her pleated hair with blue ribbons. When she went into the kitchen, her gran and grandpa were sitting at the table. "Come and eat your porridge, hen," Gran said.

"Good morning, Grandpa," Maggie said, smiling. "Isn't it wonderful that Gran is going fishing with us this morning?"

"Aye, lassie, it is. Now, eat your porridge and then we'll be off," he urged.

They finished their breakfast and cleaned up. Gran had packed a picnic lunch for later and had put it in a basket. Grandpa had the fishing tackle box and several poles in his hand. "Let's be off," Gran said.

They walked for a mile or two through the wildflowers towards the river. Maggie stopped to pick a daisy or two and put them behind her ear, in one of her pigtails. As they walked over the hills, Maggie saw a few sheep and cows grazing. Birds flew overhead, and now and then she saw smoke rising from a few of the crofts scattered about. "How much longer, Grandpa?" she asked.

"We're almost there. See those trees up there?" he pointed? Maggie nodded yes. "There is the river."

Maggie ran ahead and stopped when she reached the bank. She looked around for a grassy area. "Over here, Gran. Here's some soft grass we can sit on."

Gran and Grandpa soon arrived. Maggie sat down while Grandpa baited her hook. She watched the river. It was moving quickly, bouncing off rocks in the middle of it, and swirling around tree trunks that stuck out into the water. She looked down. The water was so clear that she could see everything perfectly. "Oh, there's a fish," she squealed excitedly.

Grandpa handed her a pole. She walked to the edge and cast it into the water. She sat down on a rock and waited. Gran joined her a few minutes later with her pole. "I didn't know you like to fish, Gran," Maggie said.

"Aye lass, I've fished since I was a wee lass, like you. My father taught me. Grandpa and I used to bring your mum here to fish when she was wee. She loved fishing," Gran sighed. Then, more cheerfully, she added, "But now we have you to fish with us." She smiled and patted Maggie's hand. A few minutes later Grandpa sat down next to them. The three waited patiently for a nibble on their lines.

"Let's sing a song," Maggie suggested. "Or maybe Grandpa could tell us a story, or a poem."

"Oh, my dear Maggie. I'm not very good at singing, but I can tell you a story," Grandpa said. The time passed quickly as he spoke. He had just finished up when Maggie felt a tug at her line.

"Grandpa, I caught a fish," she laughed. She stood up and pulled the pole towards her.

"Roll in your line, lass. Bring the fish in slowly," Grandpa urged.

Maggie turned the handle on her reel and within a few moments, a good-sized fish came flying out of the water and landed on the grass near her feet. "A fish! It's big."

Grandpa grabbed it, took the hook out of its mouth and showed it to Maggie. "Aye, that's a big fish, Maggie. Good girl." He then put it on top of some ice a container.

About that time Gran caught a fish. "I've got one too," she said, reeling it in. It wasn't as big as Maggie's. She pulled it onto the grass and took the hook out of its mouth. She held it up to her face and made her lips move like the fish's.

"Silly, Gran," Maggie said.

During the next hour they each caught two more fish. Most of them were trout. Grandpa caught a salmon. "We've got plenty of fish; enough to last for a week now." He reached over and picked up the picnic basket. "Who's hungry?" he asked.

Gran raised her hand and so did Maggie. Granpa handed Gran the basket and went to the stream to wash the fishy smell off his hands. Gran pulled out a cloth to put the food on and spread it on the grass. It was pale lavender with thistles embroidered on it. She'd packed sandwiches, potato crisps, pastries, pickled onions, and iced tea for she and Grandpa and Ribena for Maggie. "I love Ribena," Maggie said, picking up her half-filled plastic cup. What's it made of, Gran?"

"Black currants, I think," Gran answered. Maggie took a big sip. Gran unwrapped one of the sandwiches. "Who wants the cheddar and pickle sandwich?" she asked.

"What other kinds are there?" Maggie enquired.

"We've got smoked salmon and cucumber," Gran said. Maggie turned up her nose. "This is for me." She put the sandwich down next to her. "We've got a cheddar, Swiss, and tomato sandwich with spicy mustard," she continued. Grandpa raised his hand and Gran passed it to him.

"I'll take the cheese and pickle, Gran," Maggie said.

They feasted as the water flowed by. A few magpies landed in the grass not far from where they sat, hoping for a crust of bread or fallen crumb. Grandpa shooed them away. "These pastries are delicious," Grandpa said, wiping the custard and chocolate off his mouth. "I'll have another, if there's any left. Maggie, are you gobbling them all up?" he laughed.

Maggie wiped her mouth with her napkin. "No, Grandpa. Don't be silly. I've only had one. It had cream and raspberries and flaky crust with vanilla icing. It was delicious." She reached into the basket and handed him another pastry, just like the one she'd eaten.

When they'd finished, the three of them lay down on the grass. Grandpa dozed off right away. Maggie lifted her head and looked at Gran. The two of them giggled at Grandpa's loud snoring. Gran fell asleep next and Maggie lay there, staring at the puffy white clouds that were floating by. She soon fell asleep.

They woke up after an hour, packed everything up and headed for home. Grandpa carried the bucket full of ice and fish and all the poles. Gran carried the empty picnic basket with the lavender blanket inside. Maggie ran about, carefree. She picked a handful of daisies, bluebells, and heather to put in the vase on the kitchen table when they got home. "That was fun fishing," Maggie said.

"Aye, lass, it was at that," Grandpa said.

She reached up and slipped one hand into her gran's hand, and the other into her grandpas and they walked back to the house together after a wonderful day.

———◆———

HEART TOUCHING INSPIRATIONAL STORY

Credit: Anonymous

A long time ago, there was a huge apple tree. A little boy loved to come and play around it every day. He climbed to the treetop, ate the apples, and took a nap under the shadow.

He loved the tree and the tree loved to play with him. Time went by, the little boy had grown up and he no longer played around the tree every day.

One day, the boy came back to the tree and he looked sad.

"Come and play with me", the tree asked the boy.

I am no longer a kid, I do not play around trees any more" the boy replied.

"I want toys. I need money to buy them."

"Sorry, but I do not have money, but you can pick all my apples and sell them. So, you will have money."

The boy was so excited. He grabbed all the apples on the tree and left happily. The boy never came back after he picked the apples. The tree was sad.

One day, the boy who now turned into a man returned and the tree was excited.

"Come and play with me" the tree said.

"I do not have time to play. I have to work for my family. We need a house for shelter. Can you help me?"

"Sorry, but I do not have any house. But you can chop off my branches to build your house." So the man cut all the branches of the tree and left happily. The tree was glad to see him happy but the man never came back since then. The tree was again lonely and sad.

One hot summer day, the man returned and the tree was delighted.

"Come and play with me!" the tree said.

"I am getting old. I want to go sailing to relax myself. Can you give me a boat?" said the man.

"Use my trunk to build your boat. You can sail far away and be happy."

So the man cut the tree trunk to make a boat. He went sailing and never showed up for a long time.

Finally, the man returned after many years. "Sorry, my boy. But I do not have anything for you anymore. No more apples for you", the tree said. "No problem, I do not have any teeth to bite" the man replied.

"No more trunk for you to climb on." "I am too old for that now" the man said. "I really cannot give you anything, the only thing left is my dying roots," the tree said with tears.

"I do not need much now, just a place to rest. I am tired after all these years," the man replied.

"Good! Old tree roots are the best place to lean on and rest, come sit down with me and rest." The man sat down and the tree was glad and smiled with tears.

This is a story of everyone. The tree is like our parents. When we were young, we loved to play with our

Mum and Dad. When we grow up, we leave them; only come to them when we need something or when we are in trouble. No matter what, parents will always be there and give everything they could just to make you happy.

You may think the boy is cruel to the tree, but that is how all of us treat our parents. We take them for granted; we don't appreciate all they do for us, until it's too late.

————————◆————————

PARABLE OF THE TALENTS FROM SCRIPTURE

Credit: Sharla Guenther

This story is called the Parable of the Talents. A parable is a type of story Jesus would tell so we would learn something from it.

Jesus' stories had more than one meaning. For example, this story is about talents which were a super large amount of money in Bible times. Today a talent might be worth a million dollars!

A talent in this story can also mean our gifts or abilities. Something special and amazing God gives just to you, almost like a super power.

The parable starts like this: A man decided to go on a long trip, so he called his servants and asked them to take care of his house, his stuff and his money.

Keep in mind that the man in this story is like God and the man's servants are God's people (you and me!) The man in this story trusted his servants and believed that they would take care of his special and valuable things.

The man decided to give one servant five talents of money (let's say that it's about five million dollars), to another he gave two talents (or two million) and to the last servant he gave one talent. He gave each servant a large amount he thought they could handle or according to their ability.

Our abilities are our special gifts that God gave to each of us. He made some of us smarter about some things than others. Some of us are good at memorizing, some of us are better at certain sports, and some of us are better at knowing how to help others. Some can solve problems better and some are more generous. Our ability is something special we have that's different than anyone else.

Back to the story, the man left on his trip and the servants each did something with the money that they received.

The man with the five talents went right away and used his money and got five more! The man with the two talents also used his money wisely and gained two more talents.

But the man with one talent took his talent and buried it in the ground to keep the money safe. He didn't even try to do something with it.

He reminds me a bit like a dog that buries a bone. He had lots of time to do something with his money. He could've bought some seeds and planted a garden and made some money but he didn't do anything!

After a nice long trip the master came back and wanted to know what his servants did with his money. The first man with the five talents said, "You trusted me with five talents and I made five more!"

His master smiled and replied, "Great job, good and faithful servant!" You are trustworthy with a few things so I will put you in charge of lots of things. Come celebrate with me!

I think it's interesting that the master says he trusted him with a FEW things. He gave him five million dollars! That's ALOT of things. But to this master it was small compared to what he would give and trust him with now.

Then the man with the two talents came and said, "You trusted me with two talents and I made two more!"

His master smiled and replied, "Great job, good and faithful servant!" You are trustworthy with a few things so I will put you in charge of lots of things. Come celebrate with me!

Then the man who received the one talent came and told his master, "I know you work hard for your money, so I was afraid to lose any of it. I decided to bury it and keep it safe. Here is your one talent back."

The master was not impressed and said, You lazy servant! At the very least you could've taken the money to the bank and you would've at least collected some interest from it."

He immediately took the talent away from the man and gave it to the first man who used his money to make more.

The point Jesus was trying to make is that if you use your special gifts and abilities God will give you more to keep doing these things you are good at. He will trust you with so much more.

If you have a chance to do something for God that he gave you special abilities for and you don't do it, you will lose your special gift.

God considers you very valuable and trusts you to do something for him using your gifts and abilities. If you have a chance to do something and don't because you want to watch tv, play video games or because you just don't want to do anything; God will take that valuable gift and give it someone who is doing something with their gifts.

Maybe you're not sure what your special abilities are yet. Ask your parents or teachers what they think you're gifts are.

Listen and watch when others compliment you or notice something good about what you're doing. To you it might be something small but to God it's a special and very valuable gift that only you can give. If you keep using it God will continue to make it bigger and better.

Also try to encourage and compliment others if you notice something special in them. Your friends, teachers and parents might forget that God put something special in them and you might see it. Tell them that they're good at it and remind them that it's a special ability given to them by God.

————◆————

THE QUEST OF KALADRI

Credit: Samyuktha

Vdharma, the biggest kingdom in Panchamani district, seemed to have been blessed by the Gods for its prosperity, wealth and peace. With such stunning atmosphere, it was no less than heaven on Earth. The only issue which stole the comfortable sleep of the King and the Queen of Vdharma was the lack of an offspring. They have lived a happy married life but even they could no longer ignore the absence of a child in their life. They performed series of yajnas and great ordeals of prayers, and finally the Queen gave birth to girl twins on a dark, stormy night.

Maduri, older by a few minutes, was as fair as snow in January, her skin radiant and glowing all the time, whereas Kaladri was as dark as the night on which she was born. The Queen, the mother of these two beautiful girls, always preferred Maduri. Proud of her fairness and the attractiveness associated with it, unconditional love and affection was showered on her, when her sister, Kaladri cried for just a few drops of it. She was left to the hands of the maids of the house to be raised. They refused to acknowledge her as their own as they believed her darkness-which kept deepening day by day-to be the black sheep of the family who will and is going to ruin their family name and status. They could bear it no longer, and one day their patience reached its limit, and they journeyed to the nearby forest in the stillness of the night only to abandon Kaladri under a tree.

285

A sage, who was making his way back to his hermitage in the early hours of the morning, found her sleeping peacefully wrapped in a blanket and decided his hut would make a better home for her than the shade of the trees. His divine sense informed him that she was the abandoned princess and he decided to raise her like one, providing her all the teachings which would come in handy in the future. A great change was coming and he had to prepare her for it, proving her worthiness along the way. He loved her like his own child. A few years passed and she grew up to be a talented and courageous woman with great skills in Vedas teachings, dancing, music, archery, literature, horse-riding and many more. She was always hungry for knowledge and like a sponge, she absorbed everything the sage taught her. She was humble, noble and considerate; always full of enthusiasm and willingness to help everyone and work for the betterment of humanity. She traveled around the world and visited religious institutions which helped her to broaden her horizons.

Meanwhile in the kingdom, Maduri's upbringing was very different and as a result, she grew up to be the opposite of Kaladri. Over dosage of love and pampering led Maduri to be a mean, proud and condescending woman. She had no interest in taking educational lessons. She was snobbish and arrogant, which worried her father so much so that the kingdom's business started going downhill.

Seeing this as the right time to attack, the neighbouring kingdom, Adharma, started plotting an attack. They strengthened their army and sent spies to find loopholes.

Kaladri returned from her worldwide journey as an apt warrior and a great leader. She was strong, powerful, intelligent and not even once the colour of her skin stood between her and her success. With the blessing of the sage she befriended the neighbouring villages and everyone instantly loved her. She was an icon for young girls; parents allowed their daughters to dream big and spread their wings.

New Year came with the expectations of new beginning, new relationships, new expeditions and progress, but at midnight Vdharma was attacked by Adharma, who having the advantage over Vdharma's lack of preparations, won. The royal family was taken as prisoners. Maduri cursed her parents for the ill fate. The message spread far and wide and reached the ears of Kaladri. The sage could no more hold the secret of Kaladri's origin and informed her as soon as he could. Kaladri thanked him immensely for all the kindness he had shown to her and prepared herself to fight for her homeland and family. With the help of her goodwill, she convinced locals to join her in the fight and together they formed their own army. She planned strategies to free Vdharma. She personally visited villagers and boosted their spirits. She sent a message to the king of Adharma to release her captured family, but the Adharma king only laughed at the naivety of a young girl and opted to fight.

Kaladri and her army fought with great valour and vigour. The battle did not last for long as the king of

Adharma, surprised from her power, surrendered his kingdom to Kaladri and released her family. After learning the truth, the King and the Queen were full of remorse for mistreating their own daughter who had no obligations to save their life and their kingdom, but still did. Kaladri accepted their apology and embraced them with respect and love. The kingdom of Vdharma and Adharma were unified and renamed as the kingdom of Darma. Kaladri was coroneted as the ruler and formed a peaceful society with her utopian form of government where everyone lived happily. Her sister was sent to Gurukul to gain better morals and teachings.

THE LAST RIDE

Credit: Anonymous

I arrived at the address and honked the horn. After waiting a few minutes, I honked again. Since this was going to be my last ride of my shift, I thought about just driving away, but instead I put the car in park and walked up to the door and knocked.

'Just a minute', answered a frail, elderly voice. I could hear something being dragged across the floor. After a long pause, the door opened. A small woman in her 90s stood before me. She was wearing a print dress and a pillbox hat with a veil pinned on it, like somebody out of a 1940s movie. By her side was a small nylon suitcase. The apartment looked as if no one had lived in it for years. All the furniture was covered with sheets. There were no clocks on the walls, no knickknacks or utensils on the counters. In the corner was a cardboard box filled with photos and glassware.

'Would you carry my bag out to the car?' she said. I took the suitcase to the cab, then returned to assist the woman. She took my arm and we walked slowly toward the curb. She kept thanking me for my kindness. 'It's nothing', I told her. 'I just try to treat my passengers the way I would want my mother to be treated.' 'Oh, you're such a good boy', she said.

When we got in the cab, she gave me an address and then asked, 'Could you drive through downtown?' 'It's not the shortest way'', I answered quickly. 'Oh, I don't mind', she said. 'I'm in no hurry. I'm on my way to a hospice.' I looked in the rear-view mirror. Her eyes were glistening. 'I don't have any family left', she continued in a soft voice. 'The doctor says I don't have very long.' I quietly reached over and shut off the meter.

'What route would you like me to take?' I asked. For the next two hours, we drove through the city. She showed me the building where she had once worked as an elevator operator. We drove through the neighborhood where she and her husband had lived when they were newlyweds. She had me pull up in front of a furniture warehouse that had once been a ballroom where she had gone dancing as a girl. Sometimes she'd ask me to slow in front of a particular building or corner and would sit staring into the darkness, saying nothing.

As the first hint of sun was creasing the horizon, she suddenly said, 'I'm tired. Let's go now'. We drove in silence to the address she had given me. It was a low building, like a small convalescent home, with a driveway that passed under a portico. Two orderlies came out to the cab as soon as we pulled up. They were solicitous and intent, watching her every move. They must have been expecting her.

I opened the trunk and took the small suitcase to the door. The woman was already seated in a wheelchair. 'How much do I owe you?' She asked, reaching into her purse. 'Nothing', I said 'You have to make a living', she answered. 'There are other passengers', I responded. Almost without thinking, I bent and gave her a hug. She held onto me tightly. 'You gave an old woman a little moment of joy', she said. 'Thank you.' I squeezed her hand, and then walked into the dim morning light.

Behind me, a door shut. It was the sound of the closing of a life. I didn't pick up any more passengers that shift. I drove aimlessly lost in thought. For the rest of that day, I could hardly talk. What if that woman had gotten an angry driver, or one who was impatient to end his shift? What if I had refused to take the run, or had honked once, then driven away? On a quick review, I don't think that I have done anything more important in my life. We're conditioned to think that our lives revolve around great moments. But great moments often catch us unaware - beautifully wrapped in what others may consider a small one.

Author: New York City taxi driver

————•————

THE TIGER'S WHISKER

Credit: Anonymous

Once upon a time, a young wife named Yun Ok was at her wit's end. Her husband had always been a tender and loving soul mate before he had left for the wars but, ever since he returned home, he was cross, angry, and unpredictable. She was almost afraid to live with her own husband. Only in glancing moments did she catch a shadow of the husband she used to know and love.

When one ailment or another bothered people in her village, they would often rush for a cure to a hermit who lived deep in the mountains. Not Yun Ok. She always prided herself that she could heal her own troubles. But this time was different. She was desperate.

As Yun Ok approached the hermit's hut, she saw the door was open. The old man said without turning around: "I hear you. What's your problem?"

She explained the situation. His back still to her, he said, "Ah yes, it's often that way when soldiers return from the war. What do you expect me to do about it?"

"Make me a potion!" cried the young wife. "Or an amulet, a drink, whatever it takes to get my husband back the way he used to be."

The old man turned around. "Young woman, your request doesn't exactly fall into the same category as a broken bone or ear infection."

"I know", said she.

"It will take three days before I can even look into it. Come back then."

Three days later, Yun Ok returned to the hermit's hut. "Yun Ok", he greeted her with a smile, "I have good news. There is a potion that will restore your husband to the way he used to be, but you should know that it requires an unusual ingredient. You must bring me a whisker from a live tiger."

"What?" she gasped. "Such a thing is impossible!"

"I cannot make the potion without it!" he shouted, startling her. He turned his back. "There is nothing more to say. As you can see, I'm very busy."

That night Yun Ok tossed and turned. How could she get a whisker from a live tiger?

The next day before dawn, she crept out of the house with a bowl of rice covered with meat sauce. She went to a cave on the mountainside where a tiger was known to live. She clicked her tongue very softly as she crept up, her heart pounding, and carefully set the bowl on the grass. Then, trying to make as little noise as she could, she backed away.

The next day before dawn, she took another bowl of rice covered with meat sauce to the cave. She approached the same spot, clicking softly with her tongue. She saw that the bowl was empty, replaced the empty one with a fresh one, and again left, clicking softly and trying not to break twigs or rustle leaves, or do anything else to startle and unsettle the wild beast.

So it went, day after day, for several months. She never saw the tiger (thank goodness for that! she thought) though she knew from footprints on the ground that the tiger - and not a smaller mountain creature - had been eating her food. Then one day as she approached, she noticed the tiger's head poking out of its cave. Glancing downward, she stepped very carefully to the same spot and with as little noise as she could, set down the fresh bowl and, her heart pounding, picked up the one that was empty.

After a few weeks, she noticed the tiger would come out of its cave as it heard her footsteps, though it stayed a distance away (again, thank goodness! she thought, though she knew that someday, in order to get the whisker, she'd have to come closer to it).

Another month went by. Then the tiger would wait by the empty food bowl as it heard her approaching. As she picked up the old bowl and replaced it with a fresh one, she could smell its scent, as it could surely smell hers.

"Actually", she thought, remembering its almost kittenish look as she set down a fresh bowl, "it is a rather friendly creature, when you get to know it." The next time she visited, she glanced up at the tiger briefly and noticed what a lovely downturn of reddish fur it had from over one of its eyebrows to the next. Not a week later, the tiger allowed her to gently rub its head, and it purred and stretched like a house cat.

Then she knew the time had come. The next morning, very early, she brought with her a small knife.

After she set down the fresh bowl and the tiger allowed her to pet its head, she said in a low voice: "Oh, my tiger, may I please have just one of your whiskers?" While petting the tiger with one hand, she held one whisker at its base and, with the other hand, in one quick stroke, she carved the whisker off. She stood up, speaking softly her thanks, and left, for the last time.

The next morning seemed endless. At last her husband left for the rice fields. She ran to the hermit's hut, clutching the precious whisker in her fist. Bursting in, she cried to the hermit: "I have it! I have the tiger's whisker!"

"You don't say?" he said, turning around. "From a live tiger?"

"Yes!" she said.

"Tell me", said the hermit, interested. "How did you do it?"

Yun Ok told the hermit how, for the last six months, she had earned the trust of the creature and it had finally permitted her to cut off one of its whiskers. With pride she handed him the whisker. The hermit examined it, satisfied himself that it was indeed a whisker from a live tiger, then flicked it into the fire where it sizzled and burned in an instant.

"Yun Ok", the hermit said softly, "you no longer need the whisker. Tell me, is a man more vicious than a tiger? If a dangerous wild beast will respond to your gradual and patient care, do you think a man will respond any less willingly?"

Yun Ok stood speechless. Then she turned and stepped down the trail, turning over in her mind images of the tiger and of her husband, back and forth. She knew what she could do.

Source: Korean fable

———————◆———————

EVERYONE CAN PLAY

Credit: Anonymous

At a fundraising dinner for an American school that serves learning disabled children,the father of one of the students delivered a speech that would never be forgotten by all who attended. After extolling the school and its dedicated staff, he offered a question:

"When not interfered with by outside influences, everything nature does is done with perfection. Yet my son, Shay, cannot learn things as other children do. He cannot understand things as other children do. Where is the natural order of things in my son?" The audience was stilled by the query.

The father continued. "I believe,that when a child like Shay, physically and mentally handicapped comes into the world, an opportunity to realize true human nature presents itself, and it comes, in the way other people treat that child."Then he told the following story:

Shay and his father had walked past a park where some boys Shay knew were playing baseball. Shay asked,"Do you think they'll let me play?" Shay's father knew that most of the boys would not want someone like Shay on their team, but the father also understood that if his son were allowed to play, it would give him a much-needed sense of belonging and some confidence to be accepted by others in spite of his handicaps.

Shay's father approached one of the boys on the field and asked if Shay could play, not expecting much. The boy looked around for guidance and said, "We're losing by six runs and the game is in the eighth inning. I guess he can be on our team and we'll try to put him in to bat in the ninth inning."

Shay struggled over to the team's bench put on a team shirt with a broad smile and his Father had a small tear in his eye and warmth in his heart. The boys saw the father's joy at his son being accepted. In the bottom of the eighth inning, Shay's team scored a few runs but was still behind by three. In the top of the ninth inning, Shay put on a glove and played in the right field.

Even though no hits came his way, he was obviously ecstatic just to be in the game and on the field, grinning from ear to ear as his father waved to him from the stands. In the bottom of the ninth inning, Shay's team scored again. Now, with two outs and the bases loaded, the potential winning run was on base and Shay was scheduled to be next at bat.

At this juncture, do they let Shay bat and give away their chance to win the game? Surprisingly, Shay was given the bat. Everyone knew that a hit was all but impossible because Shay didn't even know how to hold the bat properly, much less connect with the ball.

However, as Shay stepped up to the plate, the pitcher, recognizing the other team putting winning aside for this moment in Shay's life, moved in a few steps to lob the ball in softly so Shay could at least be able to make contact. The first pitch came and Shay swung clumsily and missed. The pitcher again took a few steps forward to toss the ball softly towards Shay. As the pitch came in, Shay swung at the ball and hit a slow ground ball right back to the pitcher.

The game would now be over, but the pitcher picked up the soft grounder and could have easily thrown the ball to the first baseman. Shay would have been out and that would have been the end of the game.

Instead, the pitcher threw the ball right over the head of the first baseman, out of reach of all team mates. Everyone from the stands and both teams started yelling, "Shay, run to first! Run to first!" Never in his life had Shay ever ran that far but made it to first base. He scampered down the baseline, wide-eyed and startled.

Everyone yelled, "Run to second, run to second!" Catching his breath, Shay awkwardly ran towards second, gleaming and struggling to make it to second base. By the time Shay rounded towards second base, the right fielder had the ball, the smallest guy on their team, who had a chance to be the hero for his team for the first time. He could have thrown the ball to the second-baseman for the tag, but he understood the pitcher's intentions and he too intentionally threw the ball high and far over the third-baseman's head. Shay ran toward third base deliriously as the runners ahead of him circled the bases toward home.

All were screaming, "Shay, Shay, Shay, all the Way Shay" Shay reached third base, the opposing shortstop ran to help him and turned him in the direction of third base, and shouted, "Run to third! Shay, run to third" As Shay rounded third, the boys from both teams and those watching were on their feet were screaming, "Shay, run home! Shay ran to home, stepped on the plate, and was cheered as the hero who hit the "grand slam" and won the game for his team.

That day, said the father softly with tears now rolling down his face, the boys from both teams helped bring a piece of true love and humanity into this world. Shay didn't make it to another summer and died that winter, having never forgotten being the hero and making his father so happy and coming home and seeing his mother tearfully embrace her little hero of the day!

———————◆———————

STAY ALERT EVERYTIME

Credit: Anonymous

Once upon a time, there was a lion that grew so old that he was unable to kill any prey for his food. So, he said to himself, I must do something to stay my stomach else I will die of starvation.

He kept thinking and thinking and at last an idea clicked him. He decided to lie down in the cave pretending to be ill and then who-so-ever will come to inquire about his health, will become his prey. The old lion put his wicked plan into practice and it started working. Many of his well-wishers got killed. But evil is short lived.

One day, a fox came to visit the ailing lion. As foxes are clever by nature, the fox stood at the mouth of the cave and looked about. His sixth sense worked and he came to know the reality. So, he called out to the lion from outside and said, How are you, sir?

The lion replied, "I am not feeling well at all. But why don't you come inside?"

Then the fox replied, I would love to come in, sir! But on seeing, all footprints going to your cave and none coming out, I would be foolish enough to come in.

Saying so, the fox went to alert the other animals.